FireSeed One

A FireSeed Novel

Catherine Stine

with illustrations by the author

Konjur Road Press
NYC

Map by Taili Wu

Ocean Dominion, Land Dominion and the Hotzone, 2089

Fireseed One

Konjur Road Press
NYC

Summary: Set on the future earth, the son of a famous marine biologist
must travel to a lethal hot zone with his worst enemy, a girl who helped
destroy the world's food source, to search for a mythical hybrid plant that
may not even exist.

Library of Congress Cataloguing-in-Publication Data:
[Fantasy—Fiction, Adventure—Fiction, Dystopian fiction, Thriller—Fiction,
Secrets—Fiction, Future on Earth—Fiction, Eco-Terrorism—Fiction, Pharma
Crops—Fiction, Climate Change—Fiction, Cults—Fiction, Science Fiction]

First Edition

Cover art Copyright © 2011 Jay Montgomery
World map Copyright © 2011 Taili Wu
Inside illustrations Copyright ©2011 Catherine Stine
Book Design 2011© Elizabeth Ennis

ISBN-13: 978-0-9848282-0-3
ISBN-10: 0984828206

For questions about appearances, school discounts and study guides go to:
KonjurRoadPress@gmail.com
www.catherinestine.com
www.catherinestine.blogspot.com

For Shelley Tyre who loved the sea

1.

Sea-uplink: Arctic temp holding steady at seventy-eight degrees. Be on high alert for underpools of Cutter bacteria around Vostok Station. Raging winter currents have uprooted buried lake and seabed dumpsites. Undertravel discouraged until next Monday, March 7th, 2089.

Fish Ministry says, "Stay home and eat leftover bisque!"

I squint into the first faint rays of the sun as I snap on my diving suit. Sweet Ice! It's March in Vostok and the three-month polar night is finally over. Just in time, because I can't stand one more hour of darkness.

Varik, I say to myself, *you've survived.*

Smiling, I picture light licking the late-winter crops of WonderAgar and Flyfish plants, coaxing them back to more fruitful growth.

I walk the short array of planks from my house to the dock of our floating island, and survey my father's sea farm—the one that was supposed to be our father-son business. I inherited it a mere five weeks ago at eighteen. Suddenly it's a son-only business that I hardly know what to do with.

The farm takes my breath away, though. Always has. Dotting the ocean in every direction are the angular silhouettes of our Finnish-blue-kelp prairies, agar factories, and twenty-story skyscrapers of Flyfish. A matrix of floating gems. Each greenhouse structure is framed with the anemone pink of new spring morning. I wish I could stare out at this all morning. But I have some nasty business to attend to.

Shuddering, I think about what I have to do—go underwater.

Immerse myself in the terrifying murk.

The last time I went down was to check the stalled engine under Agar Farm 6, I found my father's body there, his diving suit caught in a clump of invasive vines. The image still makes me gag. I still feel the shock of cradling my father in my arms, and the despair while dragging him up, realizing he'd be gone forever. He was a master diver, so it was hard to imagine the water conquering him. For whatever reason, he'd removed his mitts, and famished viperfish had gouged his hands. Swallowing a lump of bile, I shooed the fish away. They wriggled off a few meters, then paused, observing me, jaws quivering, needle teeth glistening in the beam of my shoulder lamps.

Up above, on the loading dock, I pulled off his helmet. Some of its contacts were loose. Had he tried to remove it? His nose was broken and twisted to one side. His diving helmet was thick but pliable. He was hypertensive, and the possibility that he'd had a heart attack and smashed into a reef made me feel faint. *What a horrible way to go,* I'd thought. In fact, that's indeed what the Fleet determined after later examining the body.

Shaking off the memory, I grab a scorcher cable from the tool shed by the dock and attach it to the clamps on the right leg of my suit. I'll need to burn through weeds to open my father's secret seed vault hidden on the underbelly of our island because he rarely ventured down there.

But someone else might have, because an hour ago, the

computer link to this vault crashed. There were many fail-safes to the link, and it's never before completely shut down. Lately, Vostok Station's had its share of theft and antisocial behavior, from drunken freshmen out on a whirl to clumsy activists calling for an open border to the Hotzone. These naive pundits don't know what havoc they'd wreak if the border were actually opened. There could be dozens more like last week's spraying of three of our farms with the words: *Rich pigs hoard!* Or like last week's refugee from the Hotzone slashing a poor fisherman's throat for a paltry pail of dogfish.

Our vault contains the master seeds and genomes to our entire hybrid sea farm, and the agar seeds for all of Ocean Dominion, so there's no time to waste. Many sectors of Ocean Dominion depend on our produce, as well as cities in Land Dominion, most of which is too polluted and crowded to cultivate. Developing hybrids to withstand these waters was my father's life's work. If something did happen, I'd never forgive myself for not going to check.

A loud splashing tells me Juko is slapping at the water with his prosthetic flipper fins. I'm always happy to see my pet dolphin, but the sound only reminds me I have to go back under; it makes every fine hair on me bristle. I must overcome my new undersea phobia. It's ridiculous, an Ocean Dominion dweller frightened of his own watery plot, a frying storm petrel afraid to fly. I've only done this a million times before.

Juko chops at the breakers as if trying to stun a rabid hatchetfish.

"Easy, boy, you'll break off your peg leg fins." When he was a dolphin calf, Cutter bacteria ate his fins clean off, so I crafted him new ones from agar gel. Juko seems to think they're his own.

The thought often occurs to me that, with all of the swimmers who get seared and rotted limbs from straying into pockets of corrosive waters, I could open a business in agar prosthetics. I'd like to help folks feel whole and live again, the way I helped

Juko. Be a doctor who heals.

But I've been bred to be an ocean farmer.

Juko ignores my warning. He's frantic—for play?

"Boy, I'll be there in a minute. I can't run a marathon in this massive fat suit." I wade into the brackish surf; take a cleansing breath to start my oxygen, slice under. Juko noses me, then continues his thrashing. "Don't rush me, Juko. I'll get over it," I mutter, trying to talk down my panic.

His head thrashing could mean a shark's approaching. I never go in when sharks are around. Or else I take the insulated darter sub that my best friend, Audun Fleury, custom made.

Because, aside from sharks, the vault's way down in the Disphotic Zone where the water pressure can absolutely flatten you. But who knows what, or who, I might find down there. The ability to shoot back up without worrying about staying close to an anchored vehicle is essential, so I'll forgo the darter in favor of the pressurized, self-propelled suit.

I navigate slowly and carefully around Juko as he swims in my wake. His blips are piercing.

"You're blasting holes in my eardrums. What is it? Sure, I'll be careful. Don't follow me. You'll get squashed."

He pauses, snaps his head at me. Juko's no fool. He knows what I'm talking about.

"Good boy." I glance up over my shoulder to see him stationary, and then as my hip rockets power me down, he gets smaller. They say dolphins don't have expressions, but I swear he looks betrayed.

An octopus undulates by. I shift away so he won't ink me. Weeds that have broken away from the underside of the man-made floating islands are pulled along in clumps by the strapping current. Their acidic whisks are known to burn dents in Eupho diving suits, worse in skin, so I steer around them. They've been multiplying. When I surface, I'll have to rev up the island's orbit to lose the stubborn suckers.

I whoosh down past the Euphotic, with its waving patterns of sunlight, into the Disphotic Zone, where the water is dark and thick with a soup-sludge of metals and old dump and free-radical bacteria. The hungry Hyperplankton and BattleAgar my father created, which the farmers pump out each week to gobble up the mess, seem less and less able to do the job. I'll have to power wash my gear when I get back.

If I get back.

My auto hand-brights click on. Dim light bleeds into the black. Although sea temp is slightly cooler down here, warm fog builds inside my suit from my trickling sweat. A phosphorescent eel slithers past my mask. These eels gorge on dump and survive. Yummo.

Finally, at forty-one fathoms under, I round the island bottom. It was built to look like an upside-down reef, but its three twenty-meter angled ridges are overgrown with weeds. The vault is further under it, at a coordinate I scribbled on my glove in permo-pen so as not to forget. It's not like I go down to the vault every day. More like never.

I plunge on, making sure to stay far below the swaying claws of invasive vines. Rather than use the scorcher cable on them, which might swing back and burn my suit, I have to keep stopping to clean the weeds with a vacuum attached to my left leg. They're cling-ons, instinctively spreading their seeds and whisks.

The dark down here creeps me out. Kilometer after kilometer, as I shimmy blindly along the underside of our island, I feel trapped again in polar night. I think wistfully of Audun soaring upwater in his latest, most chill darter. I want to be with him, flirting with girls and riding simulations in the clubs. I'm not up to this task.

Then, I picture my father's strong hands being devoured by ravenous fish, and keep on.

Something glows up ahead. I check my coordinates a second time. *Only fifteen meters from the vault, so why the light?* The only glimmer should be from my hand and shoulder beams. Am I seeing things, suffering from an inner-ear ailment brought on by pressure? Shaking my head, I stare again at the vault. The light glows even brighter. My heart catches in my throat. Sweat pours off me and soaks into the thick insulation of my suit as if I'm in a Hotzone desert. *Keep going,* I tell myself.

I stop, gulp hard. Something, or someone, has already scorched the weeds covering the door. The outer door is cracked open. And light is filtering out.

I shudder so hard I somersault. Let me rocket up to sunlight.

Let the whole system fail. It's not worth my life, not worth some seabed monster devouring me like that whale did Ahab.

In my mind, my father's craggy face appears. *"Varik," he's saying in a cheery voice, as if I'm twelve and we're going for an afternoon dive, "be a good boy and go check the template vault, will you? I'll take you out to Tundra Squidhouse tonight for a steamy bowl of chowder."*

No way can I give up now. I enter the igloo-shaped chamber. A hard wall of water shoves me back toward the outer rim. I snap off all but one beam, and dim that as I struggle against the current and toward the second door that leads to the sealed inner vault. I'm about to try it, when it opens. Jetting behind it, I take cover, my breath coming in ragged surges.

A figure rockets out in a silver diving suit, smaller than me, weighed down by a large case. I reach for my scorch cable, unclamp it, skate slowly forward, praying that the intruder doesn't wheel around. Thrusting out the scorcher, I press the button.

It burns a manray-sized hole in the middle of the guy's suit. Even through the pulpy water I hear a muffled yelp. He loses hold of the case. It overturns, ejecting its contents into the current.

My father's hybrid seed code disks! Their transparent jellyfish shapes with embedded rings of seeds rock down, down. I manage to catch a few and quickly drop them in my latchbag.

Burn it! Do I go for the rest of the disks, or the thief? Disks or thief?

I'm in his sight now. He scowls at me through his mask slit, while his hand reaches for his own scorcher cable. I blast him quickly, just under his neck. It blazes a wide swath, paralyzing him long enough for me to bind his arms with heavy cord attached to my belt. He kicks back at me as I yank it taut.

Pain shoots into my kneecaps. The robber lands another kick, higher. Even though my suit is heavily padded, the air's knocked out of me. Still, I manage to turn and jab him hard in the ribs.

Flicking on my shoulder lights, I focus down past the open vault door to determine where the code disks have gone. Dare I retrieve some while hauling this cretin after me? No. I can only hold so much, plus the cord might slip from my hands in the process. At least the inner-vault door that keeps the water at bay is sealed. The most important seeds are still in there.

And some of the outer-vault seed wheels have safely caught in the door hinges. I can come back for these dozen or so soon, as long as they're stuck here. It's not as if we have no actual plants left, I tell myself. Our fifty farms are intact. There are other farms, too. Still, I almost weep in desperation to see that other disks have charged past the door and are wending down to the seabed. If we lose the backup seeds, we lose variety, the ability to strengthen the weakened genomes.

While I'm craning my neck, the thief rams his helmet into my gut. We wrestle inside a blinding burst of inky bubbles. As I struggle to regain control, images of my father straining against the coiling parasitic plants or some dark figure just like this decides it.

No way can I let this guy free; I'll come back for the disks.

As he thrashes to break away, I yank the binding tighter around his mitts and rocket up. Drag him behind me.

By the time we reach the dock, I'm gasping and Juko's swimming in my wake, nipping at the robber's insulated boots. I throw down my mask and mitts, and haul the guy onto the dock.

While shoving him forward to the house, I quickly rate the security of the various rooms I could jail him in. I want to find out what outfit the intruder works for or whether he's on his own. The Fleet did a shoddy job in searching for my father, so I'm not keen on forking this guy over until I do my own interrogation. Underwater, I hadn't had a second to panic, but now the idea of holding him here makes me shaky with fear. I picture him slipping out of his binding and knifing me while I sleep.

He lands a swift boot in my back. On second thought, no sleep for me tonight.

Pushing the guy in front of me and tightening the cord once more, I worry about how I'll get him to talk, and what I'll have to do to him if he won't. I'm not a muscle-reorg bully type. I've never hit anyone in my life.

We enter my place and head to the den. I pause there as I make the final decision. My father's meditation room, off the den, has one tiny porthole only a water rat could squeeze through. It has dense walls, and a two-way video-page. No precious files in there that would be in jeopardy, so it's the perfect padded cell. The thief suddenly wheels around to land a clumsy punch, but I veer out of harm's way and push him ahead of me through the den into my dad's think tank. Once inside, I struggle to triple-tie the cable binding his hands in front of him to one of the solid columns as he again tries to kick me. I yank off the sludge-dump's mask.

And gasp.

Long, red hair cascades down. Pearly skin, heart-shaped lips pursed. Fry me in the Hotzone if it's not a live girl close to my age. Her sapphire-blue eyes gleam with hate.

I step forward, but not close enough for her to tackle me. "What in hell were you doing down there?" I ask.

Her ensuing hiss sounds like a water snake poised to attack.

I toss her mask on the floor. "I asked you a question." No answer, so I add, "You'll stay tied up like this for weeks then."

She laughs. Kicks the mask I dropped.

I'm sorely tempted to slap her hard across the face. "Who are you?" I shout. "What were you doing in that vault?" I'm thinking she looks oddly familiar, like someone whose image is printed on a cereal box or advert. But I can't place her. Certainly she's no starving refugee or common thief. Her demeanor's way too haughty. She looks well taken care of, as if she's never missed a night of sleep, as if she's recently rubbed lotion on her face and given her hair a comb. "Where are you from?" I ask.

There's a long silence. Her hateful eyes bore into my equally hateful ones. She finally talks. "Get me out of this suit."

"What were you doing with those disk templates? I asked you a goddamn question!"

Silence. My fury's risen so fast I want to beat her to a pulp, which scares me. I must calm down, because I'll need to get information out of her. If she's unconscious that won't be an option.

"Rot in your suit then," I growl, then tromp out, locking the door securely after me. I make sure to position the video-page at her, to view any antics from the safety of the den. Let her stew in there. Get hungry. Thirsty enough to talk.

With every limb trembling, I return to the dock. Juko's still agitated, speeding back and forth, and then breeching.

"You were trying to tell me something all along, weren't you, boy?"

After I struggle out of my suit and put it away in the gear shed by the shore, I sit on the dock and watch Juko swim. The memory of my father coming home for the day shifts into consciousness. The way he shucked off his seaweed-covered high boots on the mat, his heavy gait as he trooped into the den, how he came over and ruffled my hair the same way he'd done since I was a boy. The image of him stroking his beard and then pushing up his spectacles while he read is so ingrained in me. I loved his warm voice that could break into raucous laughter. His steady presence in the kitchen as he fixed dinner, calmed me after Mom was gone, and the way his eyes gleamed when he spoke about his work inspired me. I'll miss our dockside fishfries, our midnight boat rides and debates about destiny versus the random drifting of life. I'll miss our poker games for abalone.

Before I know it, I'm sobbing. How did I ever manage to hold in my grief for five long weeks?

Not long before his death, my father tried to teach me more

about the farm, despite my resistance. He proudly introduced me to the old distributors and some of the new ones. We spent hours in his lab while he described each hybrid plant in development. He showed me how to release the payloads on the fertilizers should the computer links ever go down.

The links . . . ha. I wipe bitter tears on my sleeve.

I'm ashamed to admit that most of my year before Dad's death was spent skimming the surf in my friend Audun's racers, zipping to the clubs in Snowpak City, checking out college girls in their sheer agar-thread smocks on SnowAngel Island. I was hoping to go to college. Maybe even study medicine.

Now it looks like I won't even finish out my senior year.

I can't possibly fill my father's shoes, and it's hard to forgive the Fleet. My father was down there for three days before I found him. The Fleet claimed to have checked that same underroute, but they couldn't have looked too carefully, even if my dad *was* swaddled in weeds. While the farm managers and I were frantically organizing search parties and calling all of my father's colleagues and friends, the Fleet followed fruitless leads. They interrogated a lush from Snowpak who claimed he saw my dad get into a bar brawl, and a nomad in an ancient Finnish houseboat living off noxious starfish that surely had him hallucinating when he bragged about offing the "old blowfish scientist" with a harpoon. (Sad waters when that's one's sole claim to fame.) I didn't, and don't, expect wonders from the troopers. It's a dangerous and thankless job, and it's a widely known secret that most of the sharpest minds work at the populous part of the border at Baronland, where they reap the most perks. Our local force busies themselves with parading around in their shiny Fleeters and whaling down free fishfry at Tundra Squidhouse.

After my father's memorial service was over, and his friends had left me the last of the casseroles they'd so thoughtfully cooked for me, I collapsed in a heap for days. It was all I could do to spread my father's ashes on Vostok Reef as he'd always wished before bidding his spirit a safe sail.

Even now, I can hardly manage the simplest tasks of shipping out orders, determining the proper orbit and speed of the farms and islands, and keeping them producing in a way that, despite my reluctant internship, still confuses me.

"Dear Father," I mutter to myself, as I dangle my boots in the dirty dockside foam. "Show me strength. How can I manage without you?"

"'Get moral support'" comes a voice from deep in my brain-stem.

I lumber toward my domed house to call Audun.

2.

Inside the den, I call my friend and check on the computers. There's still no signal from the vault, but the other monitors are working. I rev up the speed of the islands and farms to shake off the latest mess of underwater invasives.

My father said that many years back, these weeds migrated here from overheated water after the polar ice melted in 2051. Along with the weeds, after each weather calamity, the population shifted northwards. As a result, the northern zones—Ocean Dominion, the former Arctic Circle, and Land Dominion, the band of countries inhabiting the next latitude down—became hugely congested.

That's when Land D stepped in to build the Beltway border wall to stop the horde. Everything south of that latitude was coined the Hotzone. Dad said that Ocean D cultivated the weeds to create an additional underwater barricade, but now they're out of control like the other strange bacteria that swarmed here too. Their underborder has morphed into a monster forest that

must be continually cropped with cables. Plus, all farms must be kept in orbit or sink from the choking overgrowth.

Yet the forest does its job. It discourages even the most intrepid of marine explorers, even those from our testy ally, Land Dominion. The snobby diving clubs from Land D are obnoxious enough when they crowd our reefs and restaurants, but the illegal climate refugees from the Hotzone who sneak past the Beltway border walls frighten both dominions.

Refs are often armed. They will stop at nothing to keep from being flown back. What do they want from us? They have decent construction jobs. Okay, so it's broiling down there and cooler up here in Ocean Dominion. But certainly they've adapted to the heat. With their criminal ways, let the refugees stay in their own zone.

Sinking into a chair to wait for Audun, I feel the island jerk forward and pick up speed. A few moments later, the moving band of light on the wall from the News Stream blasts out a report. Even though I also hear its intermittent blasts in my head from the chip installed in my brain when I was a kid, I rarely listen closely. It's been in so long, I've learned how to mentally phase out its silly gossip shows and other drivel. But now? There might be some news about a refugee or some freak on the loose.

Or something about the girl I locked in my father's zendo meditation room. Who knows, she could be a refugee herself.

Eruptions from the Hotzone!
According to Sub-Beltway AutoBots, temps climbed to a mammoth one hundred sixty degrees from the coasts of Nevada to the sands of Ohio, fatally scorching two nomadic families camping in the Virginian Desert.

Land Dominion Uplink: On Sunday, Bots stationed at Toronto Lat 4,869 shot down a pair of climate refs using a stolen flycar to cross the forbidden zone north of the Beltway border. Ten BotLinks guarding that sector were found to have damaged circuitry. Land Dominion Troopers suspect hackery.

Today's uplink brought to you by GenoSalmon —For a safe, skyfarmed taste long after Dominion waters have soured.

Nothing specific about the girl. I sigh and wait. After about twenty minutes, Audun nears my island dock. I know this because the skipping of his darter across the breakers hums like a humpback on steroids. From the den porthole, I watch my friend secure his vehicle with an electric sinker. Then he bends over the dock to pop Juko a Sardino. He always brings biscuits for Juko.

Never one to ring the bell, Audun marches through my front door the same way he's done since we met in school when we were seven. His dad deals AmphiAutos in Snowpak City. Back then, my dad got to know Mr. Fleury when asking his advice on who sold the most durable AmphiTractors.

Audun couldn't be more different than me, in my faded waders and agar-stained workshirts. He's a total style whore. Today, his tinted blue hair is done in the trendy Inuit way—long on the sides, with a fat braid streaking back over the top. As long as I've known Audun, he's forever fixated on some new article of clothing, while I wear a shirt until the buttons pop off or boots until seawater leaches into the soles. When Audun was seven it was a neon wetsuit for trash diving. These days, it's handmade Inuit lug-boots his crush Brigitte made. She's a designer at a high-end shoe shop on SnowAngel. Audun loiters there a lot, waiting for a chance to chat Brigitte up. Did I mention he's a social pack hound, while I prefer to observe the scene from some quiet corner? That's another way we're polar opps. It takes me many midnight suns to chat up even the shyest Eskimo queen.

"Hey, Seadrifter." Audun claps me hard on the shoulder. Varik means 'seadrifter' in Icelandic, and after Dad let that slip, Audun's never let me forget it.

"Hey, Audun. Thanks for coming over so fast, there's something I—"

"Let me guess." Audun starts pacing from the kitchen counter to the den porthole, where the sun casts wave patterns on the yellow-tinted agar pane. He never sits still. He's had synaptic reorg for ADD, but clearly, not enough. "You've broken into your father's old brandy cabinet," he declares, "and we're going to get toasted before SnowAngel Island."

"Nope. Let me tell—"

"Wait, I know." He paces the other way. "You're finally ready to help me open a race-darter outlet in Vostok Station. I'm too stupid for anything else. Might as well make some big cash Ds."

I groan. "Who said you're too stupid for anything else?" Audun's insecurity is sad. "Listen, I . . ."

"My *dad* says I'm stupid. You know that." Audun launches into a perfect imitation of his father's typical gravely tirade. "You can't be a News Stream host, son. People on the News Stream have to know a thing or two. Like current affairs and *politics*." It's because of his dad's dirty manipulation to keep Audun feeling small and close to home that he doesn't even consider anything but helping to expand his father's business. We're both tied to our fathers' trades but at least my father never felt the need to put me down.

"Look, I feel for you," I say, "but I've got a huge problem here."

"Lay it on me; I'm all blowholes and earflaps, or however that Ancient-Mariner line goes." Audun sits on a stool at the kitchen table and toys with his shark-tooth earring.

I sit beside him. Whisper urgently, "There's a girl in my father's zendo."

Before I can explain, Audun's up, and scrambling into his spray jacket. "You've captured a SnowAngel? How'd you talk her over here?" He jabs me in the side. "You must've told her you inherited an entire sea farm and promised one day it would all be hers. Fry me! You're good. I'll go get Brigitte and we'll get this party started. Put on some polar Nordic tunes and break out the best of . . ." He clears his throat "Dr. Teitur's bubbly . . . oops. Rest his—"

"Can't you ever shut up?" I pound the counter with my fist.

Audun slumps back down, looking thoroughly disappointed. "Sorry about the dad crack."

"Yeah, whatever." I motion for him to follow me to the desk in the den, flick on the video part of the page, and peek in. "C'mere. Have a look."

The girl's leaning against the post with her legs splayed in front of her. She could be asleep because her head's lolling forward, cascading red curls over the chest of her bulky diving suit.

"My lord, Drifter," Audun exclaims, craning his neck for a better view. "She's the Mona Lisa on fire. You frying tied her up? Is she from the Hotzone?"

As if all girls from the Zone have fiery red hair. "What makes you think that? I have no idea."

I've never once flown below the Beltway latitude; there's a danger of heatstroke. No one from the North goes there. Why would they? No one in his right mind would live there—only the nomadic climate refs and the luckier ones stringing the southern side of the border, who build housing for our northern neighbors in Land Dominion.

Blowing through his teeth, Audun presses in for a second look. "So, you've gone crazy since your dad's, um, been gone. You've taken to stealing women and jailing them?"

As if the girl could hear me through the thick agar walls, I whisper, "She's a *thief*." I quickly fill him in on the situation.

Audun's eyes shimmer as black as underwater peat bogs. "No shit, Seadrifter? That's serious stuff." He takes another long look and launches into questions. "Why would she want to steal from the vault? We have plenty of trees and plants around here. And how the heck did she get in? Doesn't . . . um, *didn't* your father have, like, multiple locks on that thing? Where's she from?"

"You asked me that. No clue." I take another peek. She's yawning, a delicate hand with a turquoise ring hovering over her mouth. Even though her hands are tied above her wrists, she's managed to pull off her bulky diving mitts. Remarkable. I can hardly fasten all the layers on the cumbersome things with two free hands.

"You mean you didn't *talk* to her?" Audun shakes his head disdainfully as if I'm a vacuous cleaning bot.

"I tried. She wouldn't."

"Let me have a go at it." Audun puffs out his chest as if he's screwing up the courage and marches toward the zendo.

I unlock its door and switch on the lights.

The girl's already on her feet.

"Untie me!" she demands as the Stream belts out one of its perpetually annoying slogans.

Uplink Motto says Tighten the Beltway!

Tight borders make Relaxed Neighbors.

"Not relaxed today," I mutter back to it. "Got bad neighbors."

Audun stomps past me, pulls up a chair, and sits inches from the girl. "Why were you on my friend's property?" he asks her.

She makes that hissing noise again. Unsettling. She *is* quite the poisonous snake. "Get me out of this suit," she roars, "and I'll talk."

If we give her what she wants on this, maybe she'll be more compliant. I'm not into torturing her to get her to talk. Not sure I'd know how. What if she *is* from the Hotzone? I've heard rumors that Zone tribes learn warrior ways. She obviously knows some fierce fighting techniques; my muscles still ache from the fight she gave me underwater. And I wonder again why she looks familiar.

I motion to Audun. We return to the den and confer.

"We can't afford to screw this up," I say. "We can't have her escape, or worse."

He taps his fingers against his jaw. "Do you have more stuff to tie her with so she can't run?"

I gather supplies. Back in the zendo, we end up knotting heavy fish cord around her ankles, while she lobs insults and demands at us. "Selfish pigs! You'll pay for this. Get me out of this suit. I'm suffocating, you big, fat hoarders."

I'm not fat and neither is Audun. I guess she's referring to the stash of goods in the vault. The goods *she* selfishly stole!

I'm not playing her game by returning the insults. Finally, she shuts up and stands there unmoving while I carefully remove her suit by unbuckling the waist clasps, and the side ones used to quickly disengage from invasives or prey. The clasps are incredibly handy for maneuvering around bound limbs. With a mix of curiosity and fear, I peel off the pieces—two front halves and back halves—like four quarters of an orange. I do this very slowly, because for all I know she has an incendiary device in there. Climate refs have been known to blow up BorderBots, our digital border guards. They've also bombed troopers trying to herd them into overcrowded ocean parks.

But this girl carries no bomb. She's simply wearing clothes— snug blue pants and a top. Different than the smocks the girls wear around here. More like the poured-in pantsuits of Ocean Dominion girls. While Audun keeps hold of her ankle binding, she shuffles over to a chair I've arranged for her and sits down. She gives us a long, blank stare and then busies herself snicker- ing over the two zen koans on my father's wall.

The giver should be thankful

Your head becomes very heavy if you carry a stone in your mind

"He ought to be more mindful of his own goddamn slogans," she mutters.

"Who ought to?" I ask.

She scowls at me in response.

"Does she look familiar to you?" I whisper to Audun. "I've seen her somewhere. On an advert or at Tundra Squidhouse or..."

"Yeah, actually." Audun tugs on his braid. "Hard to place, though," he whispers back.

She has muscled shoulders and hips like the huntress Diana, from that ancient Greek myth. And she's almost as tall as I am- must be about 5'10". Audun and I are both gaping at her. He's probably thinking what I'm thinking. The girl would a formi- dable wrestling opponent. Even against a guy. I look over at him as he chews on his knuckle.

"I know where I've seen you!" Audun shouts at the girl.

"Where?" I whip around in surprise.

"On the Stream." Audun steps over to her. "You're the daughter of the biggest realtor in Land Dominion. Your father owns three-quarters of Land D, and now he's building a huge condoplex on the south side of the border—*in the Hotzone!*"

The girl doesn't confirm this, but glances over at the videopage and narrows her eyes as if she assumes it's recording.

"I guess paying attention to the Stream has its benefits," I say to Audun.

"Right, it's coming back to me." Audun has started madly pacing. It's always helped his thought process. "Three years ago, the biggest News Stream, corruption exposed," he says. "Builder was bilking homebuyers big-time and was put on trial. Not a lot of hard-core evidence because the guy gourmet-cooked his online data and then let loose a hungry virus to chomp it down. The guy should've gotten a year, but he got three. His daughter testified against him." Audun widens his eyes at the girl.

This girl!

Strange: a daughter testifying against her own blood. I look at her for clues, but she's not offering any. Her gaze emits defiance. She grips the sides of the chair and plants her feet apart. I can't even imagine testifying against my father.

"Tell me your name," I demand. Loud silence punctuated by the onset of the Stream's classical segment. "We'll call you Thief then." I yank on her agar ankle binding. More than scaring me, she disgusts me.

"Meg," she spits out.

"That's whale crap." Audun has his HipPod out, and he's scrolling down it. "I just looked you up. Your name's Marisa Baron."

3.

After another bout of fruitless interrogation, in which Marisa Baron plays deaf and seriously dumb by simply grunting rather than talking, Audun glances at his HipPod and announces he's late for work. I go out to the den with him, after adding another set of binds to Marisa's hands and ankles and locking the door to keep her jailed. I'm thinking of making a super-quick run to get those remaining disks. Just as Audun's about to zip off, I get a call from my farm manager, Serge. He sounds harried.

"Mr. Varik, the help is here waiting for their pay," he says sternly. "You forgot to bring signed stipends, sir. Also you must review and approve our new client from Svalbardia. We are very late on this."

Fry me, I forgot again. With all of the recent larceny and terrorism in Ocean D, the Fleet has stepped up security. Now owners must hand-sign their payouts. What a major pain. I can't keep all of my farm duties straight. And now, preoccupied with this thief in the zendo, I've blown it by forgetting my appointment with Serge. I picture the hardworking farmhands in the galley, grumbling that because of their negligent boss they won't be able to buy dinner.

"Can it wait until the morning, Serge?" I ask him.

"Nyet," he says firmly in his residual Russian. "The help is upset. They need to stock their larders, too. If you don't want to do this part, then we must make other arrangements—"

"All right. I'll be over." I don't mention Marisa. I'll make it quick; get back to this hostage. After I hang up, Audun asks me what the problem is. I explain.

"Don't sweat it, Drifter," he answers. "How long could a round trip to Flyfish 4 take—

an hour or so? That wench in your father's zendo is tied up so tight she won't budge."

I'd like to forget this whole day, start over with no Marisa. I'd like to avoid the mess of trying to fix the computer, recover the rest of the hybrid disks, and never bother figuring out how to make this impossible girl talk. "You don't think going out right now would be completely irresponsible?"

Audun slaps me on the back. "Go. Take care of your business. I'll be right back at you tomorrow morning. You know me, I hate to miss the fun," he says sarcastically.

"Fun, ha-ha." I'm already grabbing my spray jacket before I think to switch off the video part of the page. The mic's already turned off, but Marisa's probably been watching Audun and me from the zendo. It won't do to have her see me go out.

Audun and I walk down the path to the dock. He climbs in his darter and revs up. Juko and I watch him go.

When he's out of sight, I decide to take my father's old Sail Tern for a change. There's something to be said for old-fashioned boats you have to help steer.

The wind's just right. It whips up frothy peaks to keep me going at a rapid clip, but not enough to make the Tern pitch. The sun pulses hard against the dome-capped sky. Each strobe shifts the tint of the waves—teal, ultramarine, brown, and then back to teal. Just one day of sun so far, but thankfully there's a MagiCool antiradiation dome in the sky over the whole of Vostok Station, constraining its fury.

On the first reef out, about two kilometers from home, I veer around the channel buoy adverts. Their orange crawls read *Drink Cups of Kelpie-Coffee*, or *Toss a Few Hijiki Steaks on the Grill*, and voices from their sensors clamor to buy their products. Hijiki manufacturers have gotten especially desperate. Those frying adverts are everywhere. They only make me more determined to stick to cheapo Noodle Bowls or fresh-picked Flyfish from our own factory.

Further out, way past the second reef, three darters and an AmphiTractor hauling agar bales on a flatbed barge pass in quick succession. Agar is our most essential crop. It's derived from red algae, though now we have green and yellow and WonderAgar, to name a few. You can do almost anything with agar—eat it, build with it, mold houses, boats, floating islands and blend it with fabrics to make clothing.

On the tractor is our farmhand, Pyotor from Agar Farm 6. I can tell him by his ruddy cheeks, his sailor's cap and fluffy white hair. We signal to each other.

Three knots on, I sink anchor at Flyfish 4 and walk along the rows of hydro-exchangers to the factory.

The workers pour out of the galley with disgruntled faces and say hello before congregating on the loading dock so I can go in and sign their stipends. The irritation on their faces fills me with guilt. They've always been cordial to me, even when I was a tiny menace, racing down the halls and tripping over the feeder wires.

Some of these same farmers helped me on that awful day last month. They were the ones who called the Fleet. They helped me remove my father's suit and wrap his body in a blanket. Eel-thin Serge, who is number one in command at Flyfish 4 and many other departments, slipped me an earring he found on Agar 6's loading dock.

"You may want this," he said as we examined it together. The earring has a square, flat piece dangling from it. On it is a raised image of a three-pronged flame. It looked vaguely familiar but I couldn't place it. My gut reaction told me to keep it from the incompetent Fleet.

I push those thoughts away; too many at once and I freeze up.

As I sign stipends, Serge discusses the new client. In his hand is a packet of geno-breed glyph codes, which he taps against his thigh. It's probably a set of slight changes to the Flyfish—to make them ever more fertile or mineral-rich. "They want to start at fifty barrels of Flyfish, and three hundred bales of WonderA-gar," he reports.

"Okay, sounds reasonable," I say distractedly. "Do we have that kind of agar in stock?"

Serge laughs gruffly. "You should know by now that we don't need to back-stock much agar, as it grows quite fast, sir."

I nod. Serge would never speak this way to my father. But then, my father kept his facts and figures straight about the sea farm. I'm at one with the ocean; I love living on the farm among the plants themselves, but I'm aware that my disinterest in the day-to-day business routine exasperates Serge no end. Again, I think of telling him about this female thug, Marisa, but something tells me to wait. Maybe it's my own need to prove that I can, indeed, handle things. That Serge would cast doubt on that. I need to get more out of her before I open the interrogation out to others. *If* I open it out.

Even to Serge.

I hand him back the signed stipends, which he pockets. "How are the numbers to Land Dominion?" I ask him, trying to feign interest. "Are we up to date with the shipments?"

His long face brightens. "One hundred barrels of Flyfish to

Restavik, three hundred to Baronland."

"Good. Hey, I think I'll pick up a fish or two for supper, while I'm here."

Serge points upwards. "Many fat ones are ready on Second Tier." His sudden smile shows off the teeth my father bought him after he lost his front ones in a boating accident.

"Thanks for the tip." I step onto the airlift, gazing up at the profusion of purple vines as I rise.

Walking down a row on Tier 2, the doughy odor of feed envelops me. These fish plants were an early cross-species triumph for my father: a clever hybrid of rust-free tundra grapevines, Russian perch, and WonderAgar. No more need for fish to spawn in polluted waters. Just grow them up on clean vines.

At intervals of thirty centimeters each, vines shoot up the poles. Fish on the vines jerk this way and that; their mouths flap to catch the amniotic mist. Abruptly I think of Marisa Baron. Treacherous klepto. I suppose I'll have to feed her. I twist off two and toss them in a sack I've brought.

On the way back to my place I stop briefly at Agar Farm 6. Might as well pop in there, too, for the weekly inspection and then hurry back home, so I won't have to come back for a bit. Pyotor's come and gone again with the barge, having deposited hundreds of agar bales in the horizontal silo off the main hall. The other workers are on break, playing poker in the galley. I check the tiers alone; take in huge breaths of sweet, oniony aroma. I'm at home here the way a puppy is, rolling in spring grass. These factory fields remind me of the faded images my dad hung in his lab of a certain Iowa ranch. That ranch belonged to my great-grandfather. He farmed corn for ethanol there before the land became a barren dirt flat and everyone with the wherewithal migrated north.

In a far corner of Tier 1, the raunchy, overripe scent of boiling turnips makes my nose prickle. Starting down a side row, I

notice the odor growing stronger. I stoop down and examine a four-by-four-square-meter section of agar. Its sprigs are darker green than they should be, and curling in on themselves. I pull off a few and pocket them, make a mental note to ask Pyotor about this. Perhaps the feeder's worn out, and overshooting fertilizer. It's probably just a fertilizer burn. I brush my hands on my pants and head back to the Tern.

After the ride to my island dock, Juko meets me and swims abreast of the boat as I drop sail and drift in. He raps his fins against the breakers, but not as frantically as when I went down this morning. Does he sense the world is a different place for me today?

"What now, bud? Haven't you had enough disaster for one day? I know I have."

I moor the Tern to the dock. Juko tries to paddle right up on the sand like some prehistoric amphibian. He throws me a mournful look.

"Keep your sonar out for weirdoes," I say, and turn reluctantly up the path, feeling almost as if I'm a prisoner myself, walking a creaky pirate plank to my doom.

What will I do with Marisa now? It was a complete relief to get away from her. I hate to admit, the girl frightens me. Who is she, really, and what does she want with me? How in Dominion's name did she learn the coordinates of my father's undervault, and then get the codes to gain entry? That vault's encrypted with non-crack KodeWayre, and so is my dad's info system that was hacked.

I should have talked Audun into skipping work. His father has a hearty sales force. He could have spared his son for one night.

"Grow some balls, Varik," I mutter to myself as I open the door, and walk purposefully to the kitchen. Kitchen bots made to look like blue crabs scuttle over. They help scale the fish and season them for baking. After that, I set the fish in the griller. Then I backtrack to the den and peek in the video-page.

No one. No one, anywhere in the zendo!

I take a second look. "Hell!" I spit, "Why did I go out? What a dumb move." I can't exactly blame it on Audun telling me not to sweat it—I can only blame myself.

Grabbing a harpoon from the wall mount, I try to calm my fear that the worst of this is coming over the next crashing wave.

With my free hand I unlock the zendo door and inch it open. Inside, something soft and heavy falls over my head. I hear a pop. Something else hits my chest, which jerks me back. It burns like fire.

My legs buckle and I pitch over.

4.

I startle, try to leap up, but my hands are stuck. They are tied to the chair back behind me.

"Payback time," says Marisa, who's in front of me now. My harpoon's in her hands, and she's pacing, like Audun. How did she ever get out of all those tight knots? How do I get out of mine? My wrists burn from trying to stretch out the cord, and my chest is stinging so bad that my eyes water.

"What did you hit me with, freak?"

"I used your own stunner," she answers gaily. "In your father's desk drawer." Marisa puts the harpoon down behind a chair she's positioned near me, and picks up the stunner, leaning against the wall. She turns it slowly, admiringly. "Nice weapon, handy for all kinds of underpests. Like me." She laughs.

Infuriating. How did she know the stunner was in my *dad's* desk?

"What do you want from me?" I ask.

"I should ask you the same."

"You were the one who trespassed."

"Oh, that." Her lips curl into an exaggerated pout.

"Why did you want those code disks? What were you going to do with them?"

"What if I just wanted to watch them drop to the seabed? Performance art."

"We happen to supply all the food for your whole frying country with those," I remind her. "Would you and your fellow citizens like to starve?"

"I didn't say it *was* performance art, I said what *if*." Marisa affects an offended voice, as if I'm the thief and she's the innocent victim.

"Quit playing games. Tell me why you came. Are you trying to start a competitive farm business? Don't you have enough cash from your dad's sleazy development business to start one without stealing our seeds?"

Marisa puts the stunner, unfortunately, out of my reach. Then she slides her chair in front of me, and sits. "Ha. You don't understand the outside world, do you? You're living in this paradise."

"And you call your Baronland a patch of desert? It has some of the last green forests around. My friend says you're the richest girl in Land Dom—"

She snorts. "Well, he's wrong."

"He says your father builds condos all over the place, that he owns most of Land Dominion."

"You think you know me, but you have no idea who I am."

"Your name's Baron. You're on the Stream. Your father's case—"

She slaps her hands on the armrests. "That joke of a trial? What do you know about it?"

"My friend said you testified against your father."

She sniggers. "Big Melvyn Baron, king of all real estate in Land D—and now? I exposed his little plan to squash the refugees in the Hotzone even further south so he could build condos on their best parcel. Ha! He and his skeezy spokesman Freddie Vane have to actually pay the workers now. Though not much. The refs still work way too long in that killer sun."

So Melvyn's a megalomaniac. And Melvyn's not above exploiting his employees. I feel a wash of satisfaction to have gotten a nugget out of her. And here, I'm the one tied up! But why bother building a luxury condoplex *south* of the border? Why would anyone from the northern dominions want to live down there? And why would this rich girl want to break into my father's vault?

"Your father's holdings *are* impressive," I say, to provoke her into revealing something more that would help me connect the dots. "I heard you got perks to testify against him."

"Where'd you hear that?" she asks sharply. "From that same lame friend? Can't you think for yourself?"

I shrug. "I've got better things to do than concentrate on the Stream all day."

"See? You're ignorant. Willfully so, which is reprehensible. Okay, so you hate mainStream, but haven't you at least checked out the altStream for the facts? Or have you been living in a sub fifty fathoms down?" She squints at me as if doubting the slight decency she sees in my otherwise revolting soul.

I won't disappoint. "Who cares about Zone criminals?" I say. "I don't. Let them bake."

She shakes her head disdainfully. "What did the refugees ever do to you?"

"Not to me, to my mother."

"Oh, right." She laughs rudely. "I find it highly unlikely any refugee had the bucks to buy a fancy electro-shielded darter that would make it over the border to mess with your unimportant mother. That border's fortified with so much juice that any ref would be toast before he could think about it. Besides, if a ref was lucky enough to get across, he'd keep a low profile so he could actually *stay* up north."

"You must not listen to the Stream either, because that's not how it happened. My mother was an important lawyer; and I never said the ref came up north."

"Sure, smartass." She leans forward and rests her arms on her thighs. "You're telling me she went down to the *Hotzone?*"

"That's exactly what I'm telling you. My mother was a public defender for the refs before . . ." I try working my throbbing hands out of the binding but it's useless. "Untie me."

"I don't recall you offering *me* that courtesy."

"How *did* you get out of those ropes, anyway?"

She smiles—dimples, and scorching eyes that reveal a spitfire inside her. Some other guy might be charmed. "Ever hear of the Baronland Diving Club?" she asks me.

"We hate those idiots. They're loud, and snobby, they buy up all of our primo sea gear and clog up all the pubs."

"Well, that so-called idiot club taught me how to master the art of nautical knots. Houdini 101." Marisa flings up her hands. "I was an ace student, better than all you *ocean* dwellers." She's beyond arrogant. No wonder Land D people have a reputation for being snobs. Marisa gets up, grips my shoulders, and shakes me. "Anyway, don't change the subject!"

"Why the sudden interest in my mother?" This girl will be sorry she did this to me. Not sure how I'll pay her back, but I will.

"Out with it." She grabs my shoulders and digs her nails in hard.

I pull away as best I can with my hands tied. At least my tale will make her feel guilty. "My mother heard that an escaped refugee was being tortured in your neck of the woods. Before the guy escaped north to Ocean Dominion he was probably slaving away for your father." Glaring at Marisa, I hint that she's a perfect mirror of her asinine dad. "My mother had a big heart. She took the refugee on as a *pro bono* client. The guy needed material for his case. He worked for the ZWC, a bunch of loser activists supposedly campaigning for better rights. More like murderers and eco-terrorists," I say. "He talked my mom into flying him down to his home in the Kansas desert to get some papers."

Marisa flinches. She shifts back in her chair and pulls her hair behind her in a move that seems designed to distract from her sudden unease. Everyone knows the sand and dirt flats in Kansas are lethal. From what I read, even desert mice steer clear.

"His family *lived* there?" she asks.

"In an old tornado shelter. They foraged underground for tunnel lizards and . . ." I stop because the memory of my father telling me this still makes me shudder with powerless rage. I'm still that six-year-old desperately longing for my mama.

"So, what happened?" Marisa nudges me.

"Forget it. I don't know why I told you that much."

She digs her fingernails harder into my shoulders. "I said tell me."

"Why? Why should I?"

She hovers so close her breath is hot on my face. "Because I asked you a question."

Her manic face offers no clues as to why she's putting me through this. Suddenly weary, I slump in the chair and drop my head forward. "You don't get it," I mumble, as much to myself as her. "The bastard took my mother into the desert to some god-forsaken ridge where he robbed her and stole her flycar. Then . . . left her to cook out there. As if she was a husk of an animal he liked to eat. It took five weeks to find the body."

For a long few moments we're both silent, and then I slowly raise my head, realizing this happened to my dad, too, only underwater. "Rotting and half-eaten before being found. Story of my parents' life," I add bitterly.

Marisa looks truly stunned. Her blue eyes shift from sharp slits to searching a distant, threatening terrain in her mind. She fiddles with a wrinkle on her pant leg. "Lousy break. But . . . the refugees . . . they're not all bad."

"How would you know, and why would you care?"

"Because I'm human. Because I'm here for the refs—the good ones."

"Refugees, ha!" I shout. "Let the temperature there rise to two hundred fifty degrees. Let them fry. They're not even animals. They're worse than sharkshit, not even fit for—"

"Shut up, jerk!" Marisa slaps me; then again, brutally. "Shut up."

I can feel blood springing from my nose. This seems to bring her to her senses. She stands there looking shocked by her own handiwork.

Catching drips of my blood with her sleeve cuff, she says, "You don't know what you're talking about."

"Untie me, then. Get me out of here." Blood is trickling into my mouth. I'm feeling woozy.

She steps back. "Look," she whispers, "It's bigger than me; bigger than little you and your entitled friends. It's about how people are starving. How you need to share. They're mad, and desperate. Believe me, Varik. We all know you. We'll get you if you don't let them have some of those seeds." Hearing her say my name sends icy jets through me. "Varik." She's repeating it, and I'm trying to stay alert, but I'm seeing windy paths in front of my eyes. What does she mean by *get* me? She's already *gotten* me tied in this chair. Is she planning to kill me next?

"You don't know me any more than I know you," I muster. "Who's *we*? Who's *them*?" I strain to hear her answer, but she's not giving me one.

My eyes flutter open. The look on her face switches from uneasy to smug, as if, deep down, she's not all that comfortable to be here torturing me, but she feels justified nonetheless. Or is it me—am I going crazy? I'm in one of those Kafka novels I was obsessed with, where there's no way out, just further stumbling into the rotten core of the labyrinth.

Plinky afternoon children's fare bursts from the Stream into my head. It sounds so wrong. It scares me. The Stream normally attunes itself to each person's profile. All of this chaos must have knocked it off its game. I can tell she hears it, too, because she's rubbing her ear as if a fly got into it.

Wally Porpoise here, calling all children to the Energy Fair on Tundra Island, Saturday March 28th. Ride the virtual elephants! Take the plunge into the Wacky Waterfall! Meet all of your favorite animals from Wally's Water Village!

"Okay, what do you have to say about the inequality of the food situation?"

My nose is burning. I close my eyes and tilt my head back to make sure my blood congeals.

"Huh? I asked you a question!" The girl persists.

Need a minute to figure out a plan. The Stream babbles on, distracting me.

Brought to you by Kelpie Cones, makers of the yummiest, greenest soft serve around!

It launches into Wally's interactive theme song, which I know by heart from when I was little. A chorus of sugar-buzzed kids sings it.

We are the Wally Porpoise Bunch!
We're going to sing a salty tale for you.
We are the Wally Porpoise Bunch.
We want to hear you sing one, too.

I squint just wide enough to catch Marisa in the chair in front of me, rolling her eyes at the song. Behind her right shoulder, there's a blurry movement on the video-page over the back cabinet.

The image sharpens. It's Audun! He's back early. His face is strained with worry. Staring at my blood-smeared face, he presses a finger to his mouth to shush me.

Just as quickly, he's gone. I take another momentary peek at Marisa. She doesn't seem to have noticed me squinting over her at the video-page, but she's facing the zendo door, so if Audun comes in he won't have a chance to sneak up on her. Need to think quickly.

I groan loudly. "Get me something for my face?"

"What?" Marisa's still there in a daze. Wally's song does that to you.

"A cloth for my face. In that black cabinet behind you."

She rises, walks toward it. Rummaging in my dad's chest of drawers, she says, "It's just a bunch of meditation books."

Audun charges in. Marisa whips around and opens her mouth to yell. Before she does, Audun holds the stunner at arm's length and zaps her.

She stumbles back a few steps and then slips to the floor in a heap, breaking her fall with her hands. While she writhes, Audun crouches down and struggles to steady her head on his lap. He turns her head to the side, and injects an InvisiTag into the nape of her neck, just under the hairline. Brilliant move. Painless procedure, and she won't know its location, since she's incoherent. We'll have total control over her. We use InvisiTags to track large fish. It's a virtual line you can send current through at any time. They're similar to electric dog leashes. *Zip-zap* to potential escapees. Not terrifically cruel, though. It offers the leashed about fifty meters of "freedom," with no actual burn when zapped.

Ha! I can definitely visualize Marisa as a monstrous poison rotfish.

Audun runs over with a fish knife. Cuts me loose.

"Thanks, man. I thought you had to work."

He snaps the knife closed and pockets it. Hands me a napkin

to wipe my face. "I was at my dad's store for a couple of hours when I decided you need help, since she's such a handful," he says. "So, I told him I was feeling sick, and took off." Audun's still in his straight showroom clothes: black blazer, with the blue dye rinsed out of his long, auburn hair.

"Thanks. A handful, yeah," I grumble, rubbing my sore wrists.

Marisa flops in intermittent waves on the floor. No damage done to the brain or body, but it takes a few full minutes to come to. I've seen it happen. Once my dad had to stun a temp farm-hand who broke into our boathouse and tried to make off with the Tern. The guy did a jig on the floor and couldn't remember where he was when the Fleet came to arrest him.

Audun smiles at me. "We could toss her out to sea; let the sharks take care of her."

It's sadistically fascinating to watch her twitch. "No, I need her. She has information. She seems to . . . *know* stuff."

"What stuff?"

"She says this whole mess with the vault is bigger than her, as if she was only second in command. She knows stuff about the climate refs, about the Hotzone. She said that people are out to get me."

Audun snorts. "Like *her*."

"That's why she'll either stay locked up in there, or go with me wherever I'm going. I'm not letting her out of my sight again to do more damage."

Audun gives me a long look. His dark eyes emanate concern. "Hammerhead, you believe her?"

"I'm going to find out." I shrug. "Look, she didn't kill me when she had the chance, so maybe she needs information from me, too."

"Doesn't mean she won't try."

Audun's words make me shudder.

Marisa gradually comes to. Still flat on her back, she looks around, and over at Audun, as if she's trying to remember where she's seen him. When she spots me, she scrambles to her feet in a clumsy attempt to bolt. Before she can, Audun zaps her with InvisiTag current. Marisa's arms shoot out from her sides in spazzy movements as she trips over her feet in her effort to get to the chair. She crashes onto it. Her head is lolling and she mumbles to herself.

"Followed orders. A good soldier in the sortie—it didn't exactly go . . . no. No! Can't talk about it. Dangerous." She sounds like a half-tanked junkie. A thin line of drool runs over her bottom lip. "Get those disks . . . undercover. Tell you. Before . . . checks up on . . ." she trails off. Her eyes are orbiting wheels of fear, as if some guy already has us surrounded.

Did the electric jolt act as some kind of truth serum? She didn't sound paranoid before, but she sure does now. I get this feeling, as if my skin's been turned the wrong way round and my organs are spilling out for everyone to gape at. Claustrophobia. When I feel trapped it happens. Wiping my clammy palms on my pants, I glance over at the tiny zendo porthole to the side of the lacquered cabinet. The curtain's open. I imagine someone in the scrub brush shadowing the porthole, spying in on us. Why didn't I think to close it? I usually leave the curtains open, but I shouldn't. Not anymore. That person Marisa's mumbling about may even be tracking our conversations right now. It's a real stretch, but my gut doesn't feel right. There have been way too many weird incidents in Vostok these days. In one swift motion I slap the curtain shut and retreat to the center of the room.

"The disks!" I say. "I've got to go down for them."

"We need . . . they need . . . not safe," mumbles Marisa, in and out of consciousness. "For the mission. They're waiting . . . Yellow Axe."

"This babe is certifiably insane," Audun says under his breath. "What a Stream story this could make. I wish I could write the lead report on this. If only I had the chops. Everyone would follow it."

"Pretty darn screwy." I look at her, still jerking about every so often. "Almost sounds like she's in a trance."

"Hey, she's rich and sheltered, maybe not too smart. Aren't those girls ripe for manipulation? Some guy could have mesmerized her into doing this. Like, you know, that cult guy Lionfish?"

I consider this. Lionfish forced his devotees to jump naked from a cliff onto jagged rocks. He convinced them (and himself) that they were supernatural Flyfish who would soar over the rocks and into the ocean to devour all the Cutters, free-radical bacteria, and invasive vines.

Audun shakes his head. "It's sad. Think of all those beautiful young girls who lost their lives." Holding his arms out in front of him, he takes stiff steps as if he's sleepwalking.

"You never know. . . . But the fact remains: she broke in."

"And jeopardized the seed bank. That's hard-core." Audun looks down at her as she stops thrashing and is finally still. "Yellow Axe?" he mulls, "sounds like an Indian chief."

"Yellow Axe," I echo. I have a vague memory of my history teacher mentioning it as a forest in Land Dominion that was still undeveloped. Something about long-dead natives carving dens in behemoth tree trunks there.

But really, what more would anyone want from me now that Marisa has raided the vault and my father's gone? I glance over at her. If she's running a fear game on me, why does she look so haunted? Maybe she's a spy, working for the Fleet on some obscure case against my father. I mean, he was working on some high-level marine hybrids.

He was the scientist, not me.

The Stream belches more of its dismal barrage into my head and out onto the monitor out in the den. It goes off and on, and it's usually personalized, but again, I can tell that Marisa and Audun hear it, too. Have we shifted into some parallel track? If so, why? We look sideways at each other with stiff poker faces.

Border Patrol: At dawn, BorderBots shot down a Fleet flyer over the border at Puffin Marina. Intel said the flyer had been hijacked. In fact, it contained members of the terrorist group ZWC. No one knows how the ZWC could have obtained a Fleetcar down in the Hotzone, nor what they were planning to do with it up in Ocean Dominion. Ocean Dominion's Fleet is quick to place the responsibility on authorities in Land Dominion for lax border control. Land Dominion places the accountability on the Fleet in Ocean Dominion for not keeping closer track of their vehicles. Both agree that a shoring up of the border is essential to warm this impending cold war.

Buy AuroraLux laser shuffle for your island. Make your patch of sky a mini Aurora Borealis!

5.

I take few minutes to clean up from my nosebleed. While I do this, Audun paces and Marisa sits across the room, looking alternately dour and outraged. If she had any doubts about the ethics of her actions while she was zapped, they are gone now. Audun and I decide to haul my dad's scouting sub out of storage. We need to recover as many code disks on the seabed as we can. It's a multi-fisted vehicle for locating, nabbing, and transporting dump. On its robotic grabby hands are sensors to scout for metal, synthetic, and organic material—dead *or* alive. When I was a kid, my father and I used it for treasure hunts. One time we found a birdcage full of nesting eels. Another time, near Tundra Island, we hauled up a rusty motorboat from 2021 with one of the last gas outboards.

Audun and I grease the grabby hands and clear them of cobwebs, while Marisa sits on the dock and watches Juko nose his playball. Her moods change confusingly fast. After she found out where we were going she got this earnest expression on her face and asked me if she could go along. Con if I ever saw one. "Why?" I asked her. "To steal more?" I declared that I wasn't about to leave her behind in the zendo. I've bound up her hands with stronger cord, and I'll be keeping a trigger finger on the InvisiTag.

It takes real muscle to lower the scout sub into the water. One of us has to hold the device steady with all of its protruding arms while the other guy pushes it to the dock. We'll need it, though. No getting out of the ship to scout in the sunless Aphotic Zone, because if the acid muck doesn't suck our bones dry, the water pressure will pulverize them.

We suit up and climb in. The sub holds two people in padded suits, three if you squeeze in. It's shaped like a closed-in Ferris-wheel pod. Marisa scrunches up in the tiny backseat and Audun gets in the front, pulling his long legs tight against him.

When I fasten the InvisiTag controller to my suit and tie Marisa's hand binds to the side door, she grumbles to herself in the back. "You don't need to tie me up and zap me. I'm not going to freaking kill you. In fact, if you let me go with a bag of seed disks, I'll be gone."

I ignore her. Pointing to switches that flip from the heat of my fingers, I fire the air rockets.

With a pressurized thrum and a spectacular explosion of bubbles, we're down. Bubbles give way to a golden green, and then to a murky olive-brown shot through with rising and falling weeds.

When we reach the Disphotic Zone, roughly halfway to Aphotic, we round the ridge to my father's vault, and skim at a fast clip along its underside. I'll need to assess the damage and re-secure the seed vault before we explore the ocean floor for lost disks.

Already, invasive vines are coiling around both inner and outer doorframes and snaking up into the pentagonal outer room. In the space of a minute they grow slithering branches as long as my thumb. When I first went down earlier this morning, I was too busy struggling with Marisa to shut the second door. I should have made time. The poisonous water could corrode pockets of the inner-sanctum agar wall if given enough time.

We anchor to the vault, exit the sub, and glide into the outer vault, the size of someone's living room without the easy chairs. It's studded with locked cabinets of processed agar that hold all disks not stored in the inner vault. When I first came down this morning and encountered Marisa, all were locked, as was the inner sanctum, where the most precious seeds are stored. Now all the cabinet doors dangle at crazy angles, as if someone has literally ripped them in haste to get to the goods inside.

"What in hell is this?" I scowl at Marisa.

"A mess!" says Audun, already working to pick up disks.

"This wasn't how—" she mumbles in her helmet mic.

"Who broke into the inner vault?" I grab Marisa by her padded shoulders and shake her. "Who? What were you were babbling about before? Answer me!"

"Babbling?" Her brows knit. Clearly, she doesn't recall giving away any secrets. "It wasn't supposed to happen like this," she says under her breath. "But it's your fault, for hoarding the seeds. For being so stingy."

"Bullshit. How was it supposed to happen?"

"A handful of disks from the *outer* vault."

"You call this a *little* breach—a *handful?*" I want to kill her. Right here, right now. Yank off her mask and watch her drown. But I can't. I've got to coax the truth out of her.

Later.

Right now, I need to save any disks in the inner vault that I much too carelessly assumed were safe before. I tie her wrist cords to a vault pole and spin around to survey the damage.

The indestructible inner vault door has been *removed*. Only a brilliant criminal mind could have figured out how to breach the matrix of coded locks. Why didn't the inner-vault alarm go off? You can't even laser-torch through that level of fixed agar. The sight makes me seasick. Sure, there are other sea *farms*, with plants that we could take seeds from. But ours was the only seed *bank* in Ocean Dominion. This inner sanctum held every kind left in the world—even that last weakened Hotzone corn, wheat, and soy, from before the deadly Zone wars, from before the construction of the Beltway border when my grandfather first moved north and began to farm this ocean. I scramble in. The vault's almost empty. The full awareness of what's been stolen turns my legs into runny strands of seaweed.

The WonderAgar. The BattleAgar. The agar. Where are those disks? I hate to think what would happen if we don't find those. Everything's based on agar: our food, shelter, transportation systems, our meds and clothes. And what about the seeds for sea apples, sea cabbage, sea grapes, Flyfish, ten strains of hijiki, Finnish kelp? To say nothing of non-edible bushes and trees and flowers!

All of the master agar seeds are stored in those center disk rims, and on the outer rim of the wheels are their genocodes. My father and I were holding all of the world's future food in case of worldwide blight, or war. All of the information to refresh weakened plant DNA was here. That vault is all of nature, especially if Ocean D ever goes the way of the Hotzone to become one vast, lifeless desert.

I can't tell a soul about this. Not yet. Hopefully there's still a solution around the corner. And we do have plants left. If need be, we can scavenge plenty of seeds from them. If I talk to anyone, it will be the farmers' league. Unfortunately, I can't rely on the government. It consists of a corrupt few fat sovereign whales who would only botch up any investigation. And that'd be after they'd greased their pockets with any cash they could suck out of the tragedy. After all, they are the same incompetents who hire the border guards.

I grab whatever I can and stuff it into my latchbag. A dozen or so remaining disks have floated to the floor. Others, saved by the current that has rolled them perpendicular to their mounts, are stuck in the shelf lips. I fight to uncoil the invasives winding around them. This is as easy as freeing a dying fish from the arms of a ravenous octopus.

Over by the pole, Marisa strains to escape her binding. "I'll collect some," she claims.

"Like hell you will," I huff through my helmet speaker.

"Look, I came to make a statement, not to destroy you."

"Drifter, don't trust her," warns Audun, stuffing another disc in his latchbag. "I know a lyin' snake when I hear one."

I power over and tighten the bindings she's loosened.

"I *should* destroy you," Marisa roars, "I mean, shit! You don't believe me even when I'm trying to tell a truth."

Audun snorts. "Why believe a hardened criminal?"

"Or a pathological liar?" I add.

"Why listen to spoiled brats?' she mimics. "I took those things to grow starter crops down in the Hotzone, not decimate the world's food source." With one bound hand she unhooks the whisks of an invasive cinching her waist. With her other hand she lobs a freed disk at me. It's hard to square this image of her as helpful disk-gatherer with the other of her as crack thief.

"You should be ashamed of yourselves not to share more of your harvest with the starving," she reprimands.

"What about you? It's not as if you have no resources in your own frying dominion," I say.

She cocks her head toward the outer door. "Shh. Hurry. Someone may still be—"

My back prickles as I glance nervously behind me. But all I see is Audun, packing a few more seed disks in his bag. By the time the vault is cleared, we've gathered about seventy seed disks, a tiny fraction of the vast geno-bank.

We've collected no agar disks, though. They're the most important disks of all. Not good. In fact, this is disastrous. Just as we're about to head back to the ship, and down to the seabed, Audun waves me excitedly over to the still-frozen and water-logged bank of monitors.

"Drifter, look!"

On one of the screens is a blurred profile of a guy in a helmet—it's as if he was quickly swimming away from the camera when the video caught him. I missed this earlier when fighting with Marisa distracted me. The guy has a narrow face, a jutting brow, and shaggy black hair sloping over an ear.

I loosen Marisa from the pole and yank her over to the monitor. "Is this why you wanted to rush us out of here? Is this guy a colleague of yours?" I shout at her through my helmet mic. This must be the "bigger than me" element she's referring to. Another furious impulse to strangle her overwhelms me, and I have to punch the monitor table to quell it. Her partner in crime executed this absolute pillage of all that my father stood for! I could rip off her helmet and crack her scrawny neck. I could—

"Someone else must've come in here after me," she says in a tone suggesting that she didn't want this information to leak in this way, yet all the same, she's vindicated.

"Who is he?" I hold up the zapper on the InvisiTag to show I mean business.

She shrugs. "I heard a rumor that . . ."

"That what?" I'll zap her. I will. My finger grazes the trigger.

Audun glides over. "What's going on?" he asks.

"I'd like to know, too," I answer cryptically. "Give us a few minutes, okay?"

He glides away and busies himself with picking up disks. No doubt he's eavesdropping.

"Look, people are angry with your father," Marisa says finally. "People never forgave him for stopping short of . . . Can't we talk later? I told you, it's not safe here."

"No. Now. Why were people angry at my father?"

"He decided not to help the refugees in the Hotzone."

"What? My father was all about helping people with his hybrids. But he had no direct business with the refs, other than shipping out agar to Land Dominion, who then shipped the refs their quotas."

Marisa comes close to me, helmet to helmet. "Fireseed One," she whispers so low I barely hear her. "I'm talking about Fireseed One." Her eyes are blazing from her mask slit.

"Why is it that every time you claim to be explaining things you totally confuse me?"

Her low hiss rings in my helmet. "Fireseed One was your father's pet project."

"You're ridiculous. I've never heard of that." *Fireseed.* I roll the word on my tongue, trying to jog my memory. I'll never forget the excitement of my dad's first animal-plant hybrid, the Flyfish, or his project for Tundra that involved molding playgrounds from his first crop of WonderAgar. Or the invention he dubbed BattleAgar—that's the freewheeling bacterial hybrid that wolfs down the lethal Cutters.

But, Fireseed One? No. Marisa is intentionally misleading me. I glare at her.

Audun floats over. "Drifter," he says. "Are you, like, in some sim trance? Let's get a move on."

With a pained glance back at the hazy image of the guy onscreen, I say, "We need to talk later. Right now I've got to get those disks that fell even further." I secure what's left of my father's inner vault, bind the door closed with cord, and power my way to the scouter sub, all while keeping a firm grip on Marisa's binding.

The Aphotic Zone is a massively *thicker* black than the muddy ink of the Euphotic Zone. Down here is a semi-solid sludge you could slice. It's a dark fiend that strains to digest you in its greasy soup. Even wrapped in my fat suit *and* the insulated sub, its pres-

sure prevents me from getting a decent breath. It smashes my nose into my face, my calves against their shinbones. I quiver like a fish in a knot of stalking sharks.

I flick on the high lasers. This causes a herd of eyeless fish to scatter. Sections of mucky ocean floor are illuminated. It's like that stuff that squishes between your toes at the bottom of a pond, but I sense this mush is kilometers thick. Poking from it are cans and corroded darter parts, fish corpses, limbs of blond coral, and the skeleton of a Eupho boot.

Skimming the roof of our ship, pale jellyfish with periscope eyes perched on their gluey torsos swim every which way. Their tongue-like eyes lick the view pane hungrily. One of the creatures suctions on and spreads its jiggly rump over the pane. I try to swish it off with the wiper, but it simply wobbles over a bit and attaches itself lower down.

Craning to see around the blob-on, I steer over gunk hills and through gelatinous eddies. Another jellyfish gloms onto the pane. With two there, it's a real challenge to see out, so I try to pick the second one off with a grabby arm. The arm juts out. Just before it's about to nab a blob-on by its leering eye-frond, the grabby arm spazzes as if we've zapped it with the InvisiTag. With a dull thud, it collapses against the ship. Perhaps a blob creature has jammed its sensors.

I try plucking one off with a second grabby arm. This works, but soon a third blob has spread its bulk over the pane.

After almost an hour of this annoyance, the ocean floor finally produces pay dirt. Like discovering pearls in barnacled muscles, at least forty more code disks peek up from the sludge.

Audun and I cheer. I can't help reverting to my six-year-old self. We've excavated exquisite pirate treasure.

6.

Back at my place, we struggle out of our bearish suits. Audun helps us hose down the disks and return them to the latchbags. We haul the bags up to my father's office solarium on the third tier and I line them up in order of genophile. Turns out we've retrieved mainly early, and less successful, crop disks that were mostly shelved in the less crucial outer vault. We see disks of nu-corn, marine potato, aqua soy, and three varieties of marine celery.

Some more important phylos are hopefully saved: the disks for Flyfish and Kettlefish.

But every disk is corroded. Between the invasives' parasitic whisks and the exposure to Cutters' toxins, all of the outer rims that store the actual code resemble the gouged chewbones of dogs. I worry that the seeds encased in the wheel will be unfruitful. The seal may have minute leaks. The only way to find out will be to plant the seeds.

"I have to admit, your father's office is amazing," Marisa

exclaims, surveying the solarium in a semi-circular motion. I've tied her into a chair that I've rolled into the center of my father's Inuit hemp rug so I can keep a sharp eye on her.

Normally I don't notice the office in detail—it's just a part of who my father was. But I imagine what Marisa sees, viewing it for the first time. The main porthole, which opens out an entire wall, overlooks the agar and Flyfish fields. They glimmer like hazy diamonds and emeralds on the brownish water. You can even see the sturdy beige domes of Tundra Island, and farther, to the west, the Cloudland Islands. Of course, this view changes every few weeks, due to the orbit of the islands. Next week, we could just as easily see SnowAngel Island, and our crops of sea apples. But Marisa doesn't know this, coming from a landlocked Dominion that doesn't have to deal much with undersea invasive vines. I always find it incredible to think that once, long ago, this ocean was sealed in ice.

"Curious artwork." With her bound hands, Marisa gestures to a cluster of framed works above his desk. There's a painting my mother's friend did of our family when I was five. My dad and I are holding up a cluster of dripping Flyfish; my mom, with her dark features and long arms that used to fold me into hugs, is presenting a basket of sea grapes. We're leaning on each other with carefree grins. Then, to its left, hangs a painting of a stormy sea. That came from a Swedish gallery before I was born. Curious how after the Zone Wars some of the old names of states and countries, like Sweden, stuck, while others got new names, like Cloudland.

Anyway, the art masterpiece sits in the center.

It's the WonderAgar code, spelled out three times, in three ascending lines like the ancient Rosetta Stone. The bottom line is in the early-21st-century DNA alphabet; the middle is mid-century barcode. The top line is WonderAgar spelled in light glyphs. The glyphs are a laser lexis my dad invented when I was a baby. Their floaty pastel curves give the piece a sense of weightlessness.

"Yeah, it's polar," I agree. Warm memories rush in. I remember sitting at my father's feet, mixing a batch of agar in one of his lab beakers the way other kids mix papier mâche. My aim was to mold my agar into a bird's wing to replace the one a pet canary lost when he was unlucky enough to scald his wing on my dad's desk lamp. I was going to fix this bird. I was going to fix Audun's gimpy kitten too.

No doubt I was moved by all the horrible stories on the Stream about the refs. Stories about how the sun was burning them alive. One day—I must have been about twelve at the time, because it was years after Mom was gone, and I remember my cheeks coated with red pimples—I announced to my father that I was going to fix the human race (and maybe my pimples, too) like he had fixed our food source. Like his hybrids that reflected UV rays instead of absorbing them so plants didn't burn up, so we could all keep eating and not die.

He had taught me the genocodes at home. After school I'd sit by his side with the laser pen, practicing the rainbow glyphs, memorizing them by rote. He taught me the classics, too, like *Moby Dick* and *Head Tide*, a classic about a philosophical sailor from this century. He prepared me for scholarship in the manner of a Renaissance tutor. Not trusting the Vostok Station public schools to cap off his son's education, I had many classes at home as well. I'm afraid I didn't inherit his brain for abstract math, though. It was always a struggle.

Still, I was my father's son, a descendant of the impressive Teitur family, whose accomplishments were farming for ethanol, and creating new food sources. Therefore I, too, should be a healer of the planet. I'd secretly decided to invent a type of extra skin for people whose own had been roasted in the Hotzone. It was to be in the form of an injection that I'd actually managed to write the light code to.

My father would be so proud.

The day I revealed my concoction, his patient grin shifted into a terrifying snarl. "Fix Juko, son, fix Audun's pet cat!" he shouted. "But don't even think about fixing anyone in that hell-hole. Never mention it again!"

He might as well have stabbed me, the cut felt so bloody. I left my injectables for extra-tough skin on his desk and ran downstairs in terror. Soon after, he filled in the details of my mother's cruel death. Before that I thought she'd been flying solo when her flycar expired in the desert.

At least I fixed Juko's flipper fins; molding agar with embedded sensors wasn't nearly as hard as writing glyph codes, and my father didn't resent me helping Juko. I glance over at his old desk. It's a confusion of papers, paperweights, dried leaves, a jungle of pencils. If I'm being totally honest, in his last years he was bitter, barking at the farmers, sprouting an alarming Poseidon beard that caught bits of fishfry.

He was a celebrated, if curmudgeonly, marine biologist. But I will only be a farmer. I'm afraid I don't have the time or the chops to be a doctor. Anything grander is an illusion.

Irritably, I page Audun to escort Marisa downstairs while he cooks dinner. His dad taught him gourmet cooking, and Marisa could be put to better use as Audun's sous-chef. *Ha, she'll have to work with her hands bound. We'll see how far her Houdini 101 gets her with that.*

No way will I let her see where I stash this last precious disk treasure.

As she waits for Audun, I focus on the disks. Her silent presence on my left side is simultaneously hostile and pleading. I catch myself sneaking peeks at her blue boots, a smudge of seabed mud on one from where she scraped it against her suit. It will eat into the boot; I think of brushing it off.

"Don't make me go downstairs," she says softly. "Let me see your father's system; I'm pretty good at curing computer viruses. Maybe I can unfreeze the system. This way I can show you the files."

Femme fatale. I've heard of those. Is she luring me in for the attack with her soft voice? "What's to say you won't totally kill it?"

"Well, some virus has already done that," she reasons. "I'll look for the Fireseed file. The best way to explain it is to show you the video of your father." She leans in. "Maybe you'll join our cause. It's more worthy than any other Ocean Dominion charity."

"Charity!" I burst out. "Fat chance. Your cause, your evil frying *cause* destroyed what my father spent his whole life working on."

"Only *part* of what he spent his life working on," she insists.

Fireseed, huh. It's a conjured-up name. She'll hack the system worse. Or steal the disks while I'm ogling a bogus Fireseed weblog.

Marisa Baron came to torture me. That's it.

"I won't mess it up. Promise."

I look up. Big mistake. She catches my gaze and holds it with her cunning eyes. It's the way they bore into me, or her violet-scented jacket, or her amoral influence that weakens my resolve. But more, it's my need to unfreeze the monitor and the mystery at all costs.

I press the page. "Audun. Forget it. We'll be down in a few."

"You sure? Page me if you, uh, need help."

"Will do."

I roll Marisa, in the chair, over to the desk, and coil a cord around her neck. The other end I wind around a pole. Any fast moves and she won't be breathing.

Then I raise my dad's antique rolltop that he inherited from his father's grandfather, turn on the monitor, and slide over another chair.

"My hands?" She holds out her bound hands.

Reluctantly, I cut the binding with my father's scissors.

Marisa sits next to me and begins running her fingers just above the lightboard.

Curiosity's gotten the better of me. The word *Fireseed* has already bored its slimy imprint into my gray matter.

In bleeps and a flashing color storm, the monitor springs to life. My heart does a faint pirouette. She just might fix my dad's system. A yellow line begins to spiral out from the center.

"It's on," she says. "It's working!"

"Just wait."

The spiral enlarges to cover the entire screen, and now a red line spirals counterclockwise, around the yellow one. Raucous laughter erupts from the image, and a crusty red face with pointy ears appears inside the spirals. "A zee for your eff, baby!" it says and launches into its terrifying cackle.

"Z for F," I repeat. "Some dumb alphabet game. Have you seen this virus before?" I look sideways at Marisa for any evidence that she recognizes this nonsense. Her face is unmoved. Except for her soft cursing.

"What the heck," she mumbles a few times while fingering the lightboard. The face keeps chuckling. Its pointy ears wag back and forth as it repeats its devilish jingle. "We're screwed," says Marisa. "I've never seen anything like this."

"I told you," I say simply, and then wonder for the millionth time if she's conning me. She and her cronies could have easily planted this hideous carnival face.

"This is beyond annoying," she snaps with no trace of guilt or remorse—only intense frustration. Either she's a stellar actress or she knows zip about this spam.

"I need a tek wizard who I can trust to figure it out," I say.

"What about Audun?"

I have to laugh at that. "He couldn't fix a computer if someone promised him a Bering Sea cruise with twenty hot Angels."

Marisa bites down on a cuticle. "Are there any professional fixers around?"

"No. Um." Then I think of Shin. Shin Kaskade.

Unlike me, who can hardly stand the Stream implant we get installed at age three to stay abreast of the news and to upload lessons, Shin was always in full photonic bling mode. In science class he designed pens that sensed the right answer on tests. He also devised hats that alerted guys when their exes were headed their way down the school hallway. Seniors paid big Ds for them. Audun totally wore his to shreds. Not me. I had one serious crush in ninth grade, and then a lesser one during sophomore year with a cute history buff—lasting four skimpy months before the girl's family relocated to one of the Cloudland Islands. I'd only just worked up the nerve to kiss her.

The slightest quiver of optimism passes through me. "Wait! I used to know someone good with systems."

"Used to?" Marisa chomps on another fingernail.

"I lost track of him. The guy was in my class in middle school. Used to hack school sites, and send phony love confessions from one teacher to another. He flipped out my math professor. Made him think he got the gym teacher preggers." We share a hesitant laugh over that. "Audun would know if anyone would. His Hip-Pod reads like the Dominion phonebook."

I page him in the kitchen. "Yeah, Drifter, I'm in touch," Audun remarks. "You should see the Shin now. He grew his hair out and he has, like, this huge hair nest and all these trendy embeds." Audun should talk; he changes hair color like the tides.

"I don't really care about his hair nest. Where can we *find* him?"

"He fixes the systems at L'Ongitude. He's also, like, their DJ."

"You mean that bar near the college on SnowAngel Island?"

"Right, that one."

"Can we call him?"

"He doesn't usually check his video-page in the club; too busy in there. Let's sail over. Make it a night. Drifter, I *know* you need a break from all the heaviness," Audun adds.

"Kind of," I admit. "But we can't take a lot of time."

"It'll be good for you to hang out."

"I need to speak to him. But I can't hang out."

"One drink. What's the harm? By the way, dinner's served." Audun clicks off.

Marisa shifts in her chair. "I'll stay here," she says stubbornly.

"Absolutely not!"

"Tie me up with your best rope. I'd rather not go out to the club, I—"

"Prisoners don't vote." I hold up the InvisiLink toggle and stroke it with my thumb. "You broke into my father's vault, remember?"

She gives me a black stare. It's settled. I'm so out of here. Dragging Marisa through the hordes will be small punishment for her ruining my peace.

Downstairs, while Marisa picks at her rice and Audun

describes in ridiculous detail how to sauté fruit into a glaze, I dive into his skytrout and spiced sea apples with a vigor I thought I'd lost. He may not have the intellectual chops to write news stories, but he could definitely be a master chef.

Eruptions from the Hotzone! Midwest Ana winds blew roofs off the abandoned megapolis that was once Chicago, and up into the construction zone of Baronland South, a condoplex city being built by Melvyn Baron. Baron's spokesperson, Freddie Vane, said the damage was extensive, that the skywalk would have to be rebuilt. He lamented that Baron Inc. would have to offer stipends to entice rioting refs back to work. Freddie Vane added with a wink, "It's only a matter of time before they get hungry. It's not like they have a union."

This uplink was brought to you by Magyk Mansions, a Baron Inc. planned city in Restavik 2 to rival the utopian City of Oz.

People in the same locations often get different Stream inputs. But as I look around I can tell we all heard the same one. Are we already synched in some hellish union? I check for Marisa's reaction to this mention of her dad.

She sniggers. "Stunning, isn't it? Melvyn Baron gets to whine and advertise all in one breath." She stabs a sea apple and pops it in her mouth.

Audun and I exchange bemused glances.

I leap to my feet. "Let the bot clean up. Time to go."

7.

We anchor at SnowAngel Island, trek toward the center of town, and pile into L'Ongitude. It used to be a whale-blubber processing plant. Now it's a club full of striking, well-heeled young people gyrating to Nu-Arctic beats. We flash the fake IDs that Audun lent us. Good light show. Snowflake and icicle shapes in silvery colors whirl across the walls and across peoples' bodies. Swallowing a lump of envy, I glance at the couples, lucky enough to already be in college, who will soon be unfolding the fronds of their dream careers.

As I watch them, I suddenly get this awful vision of the world, in, say, three or four years. A world where we never found those agar seed disks and the food bank has dried up. It's a world where these healthy, lively party-hounds are haggard and hungry, and no longer dancing. Where they're on their bony hands and knees in their backyards, scratching for mushrooms and sinewy worms. I grab anxiously at a pile of pink-and-yellow agar-pastries that a L'Ongitude waitress is carrying, and stuff one in.

Shaking off the vision as I chew, I glance over at Marisa. She's arching her brows at a girl's skimpy garb. The girl ignores Marisa but her dance partner gives Marisa an appreciative once-over. Even though Marisa's hair is hastily pinned up with strands that blew out from the wind, she stands out in this crowd because of her unusual Land-style suit—its long pants hugging her legs. Most girls on SnowAngel dress in short frocks with hike shorts.

Little does this guy ogling Marisa know that I hold her captive with an invisible fish-tracker; that without that she'd escape in a hot minute. The irony of it makes me cringe. I don't need to fish with virtual line to snag a girl, and she's certainly not my girlfriend. Marisa's keeping step with me, and after that first bold stare at the dancers, she bows her head when someone looks her way. Anxiety is practically sweating off her. Why does she hate crowds so much? Is she in hiding? If so, why?

"Brigitte coming?" I ask Audun to distract myself from the weirdness of the captive-captor relationship, and my impatience.

"She's running late," he remarks, throwing off his spray jacket and flinging it rakishly over a shoulder. Only Audun would find time during a crisis to slip into a faux starfish-skin vest, color his hair purple and braid it with rare woodcarvings from Restavik. I have to admit, he'd make a polar Stream model. "Looks like an ice theme tonight," he adds.

I snort. "Ironic. Never laid eyes on the stuff in my lifetime. Plus, it's barely March and already up to 95 degrees. They're already swimming on the SnowAngel beaches."

"You're spoiled rotten, boys," Marisa says. "In Land Dominion, it's already 110 degrees or more. And, in the Hotzone, well, it's killing people at about 160 degrees." Audun and I uneasy exchange glances.

I need to find Shin. We can't afford to laze around here. Audun claims that at this early hour he'll be hugging the bar, so we head over. On the way, we pass couples lounging in an

ice-brick igloo and others skiing down an enclosed simulated ski run. Looks like fun, but I'm here on business. We approach the throng surrounding the bar built to resemble a gargantuan ice shard.

Audun points Shin out to me, and asks if there's anything else he can do to help. When I tell him not right now, he looks visibly relieved. We arrange to meet over by the ski simulation when we're done with Shin. Audun floats off to flirt while he can. Marisa trails behind me.

I recognize the middle-school tek geek under my former classmate's present chic. DJ Shin Kaskade, with a frizzed-up hair pouf and manly guyliner, is showing the guy on the next stool the latest holo game. It involves guessing how many angels are dancing on the tip of an ice needle. The needle is glowing just beyond the tip of Shin's nose, and what must be dozens of holo angels are on it, shimmering and batting their tiny wings. At a blistering speed, the needle bobs and weaves. *Dizzy-making,*

I think, as I tap Shin on the shoulder. He turns and graces me with a Zen-master nod. I can't help but gape. Shin's embedded neck-system dragon is shooting tiny jets of steam. It's a living, breathing tattoo. A star-shaped sys on his lower arm twinkles. He's got another one—a winking third eye—emblazoned on his forehead.

We exchange heys and ask each other how it's been since school. I tell him about my father's passing and about inheriting the farm.

"Sorry to hear of your father. But how rocking ice to own a farm," he remarks. He explains that his time is split between DJing and zipping all over Ocean Dominion, or "OD" as he calls it, on sys-tek calls. So, he could've made a house call after all.

I fish my dad's portable system from my spray jacket, flip it open, and show Shin the freaky red-and-yellow spiral virus that's been burning rubber on it since Dad's vault-link went down. "I can't get rid of this pattern," I tell Shin. "First the system was frozen. Now I can't even shut this thing off and reboot." The craggy face erupts with its cackle and alphabet jingle. "You ever see this insane spammer guy?" I ask him.

Shin takes it from me and starts fingering it the way a meth-freak would play a synthesizer. He squints at it, then does more fast-finger pokes. After that, he takes a triangular device from his jacket and zigs that over the screen. Shaking his head sadly, he says, "Some high-level dudes junked this. They hacked through the Throttler, the TsunamiWayre, the FyreMoat, even the Krypton. Dude, four levels. Dunno about the spam devil, but this red-and-yellow spiral, dude, we call it the death ray. Need I say more?"

I scratch my head. Sys-tek, whether it's the Stream in my head or an old-fashioned screen on a desk, it's all Pig Latin in Persian. "Bottom line," I ask, "can you get it up and running?"

"Yeah. For 1,000 Dominion, dude; special fire sale today."

I balk. For a 1,000 Ds I could take a luxury safari through

Siberia. My fingers curl around my credit card. Since my father's death, I've been charging up a storm on it. Seems he gave away much of his savings on marine-life charities. Very soon I'll have to budget myself or sell off half the sea farm. But Ds don't count when the world's food supply is at stake.

"Go ahead, fix it," I hear myself say. My father would tell me to fix it, and figure out why it went down, at any cost.

There are many sys-spazzes like me. That's why Shin, at nineteen, is surely as flush as Melvyn Baron.

While Shin does his unintelligible magic with the voodoo triangle and then whispers into a mic in the dragon embed, which sends out hissing red steam, I glance back at Marisa.

She's gone. Dammit! She seemed so leery of the crowds that I was confident she'd shadow me all night. Overconfident, obviously. Why did I allow myself to be distracted? No doubt she's talking someone into giving her a ride back to Baronland; some ace fisherman who can crack the code to turn off the invisible line that Audun put in her neck after she attacked me.

Come to think of it, I could always shoot charge through the InvisiLink and see who in the crowd hits the dance floor in a spasm. But that would start a mad commotion, which I have no appetite for. She couldn't have gone far. The fish line is only fifty meters long. I strain my eyes in the dark of the club to spot a redhead with an arrogant attitude.

Then I see Marisa to my left, deep in conversation with the heavyweight bartender. She's leaning in eagerly, elbows on the bar. So much for her horror of crowds!

She's probably telling the guy I've imprisoned her. Out of context, he'll deem it a medieval abuse. In a minute this steroid bartoy will be calling in the big guns.

Hollow with dread, I tell Shin I'll be back and then I snake through the crowd toward Marisa. Are her minions here? Is the bartender with the ratty ponytail one of them? Getting more paranoid by the minute, I'm convinced that Bartender Dude is a member of a Zone terrorist group and he's going to follow me out behind L'Ongitude as per Marisa's explicit instructions, and pop a smoky shot in my back.

By the time I storm over to her, I'm short of breath. I grab hold of her arm. "Time to go," I snarl, as if I'm her drunken jealous boyfriend.

"Hands off the lady," the bartender orders. This prompts some of the crowd to stop their chatter and blatantly eavesdrop. "Are you the one who put a fish-tracker on her? Where is it?"

My teeth start throbbing to the incessant tribal Nu beat. "Marisa, let's go," I say in a firm but slightly more mellow tone. I slide my hand down to hers and pull. She glares at me and yanks her hand away.

"I asked you a question, A-hole," grunts the bartender.

My blood pressure is shooting through the roof. The only thing left is to zap her with current, which will make a spectacle and land me a night in Fleet hell.

"Is this the guy? You all right, missy?" the bartender asks in a good-cop voice.

My thumb's on the InvisiLink trigger. Marisa sees this. "Hanging in there," she says. Abruptly, she brushes past me and takes off in Shin's direction.

I feel as if I already had the heart attack and I'm lying on the stretcher, my retinas burning with snowflake patterns. I dash off after her.

"Look, jerk, I'm not your prize whale," she hisses. "You want to see that video of your dad? The only way this is going to work is if you take the stupid fish line off me."

"I can't do that."

"Why not?" She glares at me. "That bartender could have you arrested."

"I could have *you* arrested!"

It's a standoff while we glare at each other, me wondering why I don't just jab her with my fish knife for all the damage she's inflicted, her probably wondering how she can off me and get the rest of those disks. But there's Fireseed, and the mystery video. I need Marisa to find out what those are.

Her face breaks out into a sudden, shocking grin as she holds out a handful of peanuts. "I got us a snack while I was waiting."

I grab some as a watery tension in my chest eddies into my legs morphing them into heavy, wet plaster. On the way back to Shin, I surreptitiously throw my share of the nuts on the floor. For all I know, she laced them with poison.

"Did your friend get that thing fixed?" Marisa asks.

"He's trying. If anyone can, he can."

"Good, I'll prove that Fireseed was real—that you should change your stingy ways. Open up your farm. Open up Ocean Dominion. Or else."

First the witchy smile, and then the threats. I sigh, from tension and sheer exhaustion.

"Dude," says Shin, when we reach his end of the bar, "who's the lady in waiting?" He nods to Marisa.

"Oh, ah. Someone from Land Dominion."

"They make them pretty in LD. Too bad LD and OD are in pseudo cold war. Hard to mingle."

"Uh, yeah. Did you fix my dad's sys?" I ask him as I tamp down my growing impatience.

"Shin makes it spanking brand new. Shin fixes anything, dude." He logs onto a game site to prove it works. "Payment time. On the hand, dude," he adds, holding up the star-embed arm.

"Huh?"

"Dude, the embed scans credit cards."

I take out my card. It feels silly, even slightly pornographic, sliding my card along Shin's embed slit, and then punching in my bank number and the payment—1,000 D—on his tiny star keypad.

But it works. The embed shoots off an elf-sized firework

display as a sexy female voice wafting from his arm thanks me for my payment.

A small crowd has gathered to gape at the star embed. Most personal banking is done on HipPods, so this is definitely new and different.

I want out of this blubber factory so I can log on to my dad's system in private. I thank Shin and he hands me his business card.

"Text me if you have more problems," he says. I nod, pocketing the card and my dad's portable system.

Marisa and I veer around the dancers toward the sim-park where we agreed to meet up with Audun. She doesn't put up a fight. If anything, she's back to her previous state of bowing her head like some Puritan and keeping close to my side.

Her flip-flopping anxiety is rubbing off. That college student whose shoulder grazes mine seems to have shifty assassin eyes. The pretty barmaid in the fuzzy white frock who bumps me with her tray might have planted a mic bug. I brush myself off.

We find Audun waiting by an icy-looking dome the size of my three-ship garage. As usual, he's pacing. "Did you guys find Shin?"

"It's taken care of." I shoot out a long burst of air. "How about we get back."

"We just got here, Drifter," Audun remarks. "You said you were stir-crazy. Take one sim-ride first." He hands me a drink.

"Nah, let's split." Someone in the jostling crowd presses rudely on my back. I jerk forward, spilling the drink I'm trying to steady. It splashes onto Marisa's jacket and the cup clunks on the floor. "Watch it, bud!" I shout over my shoulder, before bending down to pick up the cup.

Audun points to the white pod door with the porthole. "Just one quick sim. The waitress in there will get us another drink."

"*Gonzo Pod.*" Marisa reads the sign on the pod door. "What's that?"

The music tromps out a frenzied beat as the throng behind me surges forward, almost knocking me over. One of them calls out Marisa's name. A girl squeals. Then a bunch of girls start yelling "Marisa! Omigod. Follow her!" Their hands are grabbing our backs.

"Shit! Let's dodge the crowd," I shout. "Into the sim, fast!"

We race in, slam the door, and arrange ourselves around the circular table, trying to catch our breaths. The waitress in the fuzzy white outfit minces in with a tray loaded with a variety of alcohol-laced smoothies. I choose a Glacier, Audun a Polar Cap, Marisa a Snowflake. The waitress leaves, closing the pod door behind her. Good. We'll wait out the mob scene for a minute.

Normally I drink nothing stronger than sea-grape soda, and I can't afford to get wasted now. A few gulps won't hurt, though.

Should've run into the ski sim, anything but this boring pod, I think, when the place comes alive. Virtual polar bears spring from the floor and circle us, growling and rising on their haunches. They tower over us, waving their huge paws in the air. They're so real they're solid. Each detail is convincing: from the slavering tongue that lolls over the lower jaw of one, to the muddy thatch of fur that lines the neck of the smaller bear. Even their rank odor of fish entrails and halitosis is real. I find myself jerking back before taking cautious swipes at them to make absolutely sure they're fake. Seals emerge next, big burping whiskery things. They slap their tails against the slick floor.

"I get it! It's *all* gonzo," Audun exclaims.

"Excuse me?" Marisa yells over the loud sploshing.

"Extinct. Gone. Gonzo. None of these creatures *exist* anymore."

Marisa goes, "Ohhh! Gonzo, I get it."

Next we're whisked away on a virtual dogsled, zooming past fjords and glaciers and caribou, as the sky turns crimson. Real ice must've been so amazing. Distressing that all this is gone from the land. The wind whips up a blizzard of snow. Cold flakes melt on my tongue. Not used to such cold, I wrap my spray jacket tight. It's exhilarating, though. We blow clouds of frozen air at each other.

I almost forget the dire circumstances of Marisa's being here, and that I hate her, and my push to get back, and how terrifying it is that most of the seed disks are gone—until the sled slows and the apparitions fade and I hear a different clamoring at the pod door.

The porthole has become a gibberish of lipsticked mouths and pink cheeks. Someone opens the door a crack and peers in. *Whale crap!* We should've locked it.

"Oooh! Is that Marisa Baron?" asks a girl with her hand on the doorknob.

"OMG, That's her! I saw her on the Stream during that trial."

"She wore an amazingly chill outfit every day."

A flock of girls are now blocking the entranceway. They stand behind the slightly open door, carrying on as if Marisa's a distant, untouchable Stream Star like Cherry Froth. Cherry Froth has played the diva sleuth in a dozen thrillers. Tough girls rock ice. I admit it; I've had many a wet dream about Cherry, imagining us naked and lusting after each other while boating on a tranquil sea. But Marisa?

"What *is* all this fuss?" I ask her. "Was it just your appearance at your father's trial that made you famous? Or what?"

Marisa shrugs. She's staring at her drink, not at all chill with this groupie adoration.

"What's Marisa Baron doing in SnowAngel?" someone asks.

"Is she going to college here? There was nothing on the Stream about it."

"I thought she was broke," says another girl. "Didn't she, like, lose her inheritance?"

Like a kitchen bot, Marisa is stirring her drink in steady orbits. *Did* she lose her inheritance? No wonder she's furious with her dad. Why doesn't she show any emotion?

"Who cares about the inheritance!" someone else says. "She's a star. Let's get her autograph."

Long-legged girls in high boots storm in and surround our table. With moony expressions, they ask Marisa if she's the real Ms. Baron and if she lives here or if she's just visiting. Marisa doesn't answer. But she gamely signs inside the "O" part of the "L'O" printed on the bar napkins people thrust at her.

Audun struts to the door. "Patience, lovelies." He extends an arm to slow the estrogen stampede. "This *is* the real Ms. Baron," he promises, "but please, one at a time." He winks at the cutest girl.

They all giggle. One of them asks Audun if he's Marisa's manager. His knowing shrug hints that it's a distinct possibility. Normally I'd try and get in on the action in my own coy way, but tonight all I can think of is getting home and logging on.

Brigitte shows up dressed in a striped frock and patent yellow boots. She gives Audun a peck on the cheek and then looks questioningly at the other girls.

Audun says to her, "Have a seat with Varik. Doing a bit of crowd control here." He goes back to his shameless flirting.

"Cut it out, Audun!" I hiss. "Your girlfriend's here. I'm going in a sec. . . . You coming?"

Meanwhile, Marisa waves her hands in protest. "No more autographs!"

The crowd groans.

"One more?" A blonde girl shoves a napkin in Marisa's face.

"Look," I shout at the girl, "we're trying to get out of here!" She glowers at me on her way out.

I'm about to jump up, when the waitress serves Brigitte her drink. "Give me a minute, Varik," she says. "I'm really thirsty." I offer her an exasperated smile and nod.

Brigitte stirs her drink with a snowflake spoon. "Tell me, Marisa, what brings you to SnowAngel Island?"

"To Ocean Dominion, really," Marisa corrects her. "I've read about Varik's father, and I'm interested in sea farms. In fact, I did a research paper on them for school." She flashes me a "Be in on this with me" look.

I miss my father terribly, in my muscles, my bones. How dare she use sea-farm research as an alibi for her travesty!

Brigitte continues without acknowledging Marisa's reply. "You can't blame people for being curious. With your testimony against your father, it's amazing he got out of jail at all. It was cascading all over the Stream."

Marisa doesn't look like a tedious kitchen bot anymore. She looks drawn and sad. Too frying bad.

I corner Audun, flirting with yet another prospective Marisa groupie. "I'm leaving. *Now*," I say. He agrees to go, after stealthily pocketing the girl's video-page number. Incorrigible flirt. Even with the danger that Vostok Station is in, that we are all in. We weave through the crush of gawkers as fast as we can.

Outside, Brigitte and Audun ride in the back of my darter, since he left his at my dock. I drive with Marisa up front, my hand on that InvisiTag. Brigitte's finally given up trying to get information out of Marisa, and switched the subject to hand-made boots. "My family owns a shoe shop on SnowAngel. I'm the designer. Hey, I'll design you a pair of faux sharkskin boots. Orange to match your hair."

"Sounds pretty," Marisa agrees in a strained voice.

"And with your fame as a rebel against the system," Brigitte continues, "you'll be a polar spokesmodel for our store. The store caters to lefty college kids and—"

"I've got other things on my mind than being a rebel," Marisa snaps.

She sure seems rebellious to me. I'm reminded that a true rebel might have good reason to keep a low profile. Sweat erupts on my back as I glance in my rearview for unfamiliar ships on the inky horizon. There are a few, in the distance. I should let the whole matter—and Marisa—drop to sea. I can't afford another disaster. But I need more on Fireseed. More on that guy in the frozen video screen—more on the thing that's "bigger than her."

"A spokesmodel makes big Ds, though," Brigitte reasons. "Imagine yourself dressed to kill in a flashy poster. We'd plaster the city with them. Every Angel would be wearing your brand. Cherry Froth was our last spokesmodel, and *everyone* bought her boots."

Can't Brigitte ever shut up? She's as bad as Audun when he's on a rip.

Brigitte barrels on. "The Froth boot had shiny cherries around the top, and gauzy pink pom-poms and—"

Marisa's not saying a word. She looks miserable. Why?

All conversation ceases at the sound of waterborne shouts, and swells so violent they threaten to capsize our darter. We lurch from side to side. Thunderous wakes slap against the darter. A ship veering that close to another is totally against nautical protocol. I glance again in the rearview. Two large boats are swiftly coming abreast of mine. It's not my imagination.

I accelerate to max speed. We swerve dangerously close to a channel marker.

"Hurry!" Marisa slumps in her seat, unpins her hair, and shakes it over her face.

Doesn't she know that only makes her hair broadcast like a red lighthouse? Whatever, it's not my job to reassure her. "Do you know who they are?" I ask her.

"No idea." She sounds defensive.

"They're Stream ships," says Audun, with a bit of awe in his voice. "Reporters."

As we near my island, I look on with horror. Darters and Stream ships surround the place. Their laser beams shoot every which way in a mad scramble to feed the first story. I wonder whether the story is about Marisa or about my dad or some altogether new calamity. I even wonder if my house is burning down. So many fiery lights illuminate the island it resembles a meteorite shower.

"Is this about Marisa?" Brigitte asks. No one answers her, least of all Marisa, who has pretty much curled into a fetal position in her seat.

One of the boats is zipping out to meet us. Printed on its side, the Stream's lightning-bolt logo fans out into a golden waterfall.

Marisa peeks out from behind her fortress of hair. "This is bad," she mutters. If she's so committed to the refugee cause, why she wouldn't welcome this opportunity to brag about her quests? Baffling, really.

"Afraid it's the Streamerazzi," Audun says grimly. "Someone at the club must've leaked the story about Marisa being there. You guys better brace yourselves for your fifteen minutes of fame." His voice oozes cynicism.

"No!" Marisa wails. "No publicity. No posters. None of it."

But it's way late for that.

A Stream ship has pulled abreast of us. Its roof glides open. A reporter emerges on its rising platform and aims a video at us, or more accurately at Marisa. My dad once told me that their photon-videos can even laser through a wall to pirate your image if you're standing too close to it. That's why he lined our house and our AmphiShips with optical block textiles. But I guess that doesn't include the portholes. I picture this chase playing on every screen from the outer banks of Vostok Station to the southern peninsula of Baronland. Maybe all the way to the Hotzone, if by some quirk of fate they ever got Stream tek back after the floods and Midwest Anas. I picture Melvyn Baron, feet propped on his desk in Baronland, cigar and cocktail in hand as he spots his daughter on the news, and wonder what he would think. Would he choke on his drink? He knows my dad for sure, since our farms produce Land D's food. But will he recognize me from the recent press about my father's death?

I cringe. Any trackers with nefarious pursuits will know our location now.

Steering around the news ship, I try to determine an approach to the dock where we won't be pounced on. This will be tough, since the trespassers are already swarming ashore my island like a multitude of sand lice.

"How frying ironic. Normally I'd kill to get noticed by the Streamerazzi," Audun says wistfully.

I wheel around in my seat and stare him down. "Audun, did you . . . tip off the Stream? Is this your way of breaking into reporting? If so, it's so . . ." The word *stupid* is on the tip of my tongue but I manage to hold back, as that's his father's favorite label for him, and I know how devastating it's been.

"That's an insult, Drifter. No way I'd expose your private hell like that." Audun brushes windblown hair off of his forehead. "Think of it, though—don't you want *help* in solving the mystery of why this slimy creature was rummaging through your father's stuff? The last time I checked you were bloodied up by this S & M vixen."

Marisa mumbles under her hair, *"I'm* the one on a leash."

"No, Audun!" I roar. "If you want to weasel into the Stream as a reporter, lead them on a wild-goose chase and get them off our tail. How 'bout that?"

"Not a bad idea," Audun remarks. "I'll see what I can do."

I swerve to the back of my island, aim for a cove between the news ships, and sink anchor by a line of shoreline bushes behind my place. As we race onto land and through the shrubbery, Streamerazzi swarm us, each one shooting a video.

"Tell us, Marisa," one asks. "What perks did you get for testifying against your father?" "Did you flee after he got out of jail or before?" asks a lady with a long mic who's jogging by Marisa's side. She sticks the mic in Marisa's face like a mosquito probing for blood.

"What do you know about the ZWC?" asks a guy Stream-erazzo. "Are you working for the ZWC?" Marisa streaks ahead without a word.

The Zone Warrior Collective?

Marisa's one of the ZWC? Great frying ice. What have I gotten into now? I'm filled with a sudden rush of fury. Rumors were that my mother's client had worked for the ZWC. The ZWC has no conscience. For a free meal they would steal a poor nomad's rowboat and kill him for fun. The ZWC was behind the pointless bombing of a Fleet ship last year. Every month there's another frightening episode. They are the masterminds behind numerous BorderBot hacks that shut down sections long enough for god knows how many crazy refs from the Hotzone to evaporate into the anonymous noise of the north border cities. No doubt, many are living avatar existences in Ocean Dominion. For all I know, my corny high-school English teacher or Ned, the chummy waiter at Squidhouse is an escaped refugee armed to the gills. Just the thought of it makes my insides curdle.

"Tell us, Marisa Baron, what are you *really* doing in Ocean Dominion?" asks a bald Streamerazzo with a catfish-whiskered chin. He puffs loudly in his attempt to keep pace with us. "What can you tell us about the death of Dr. Teitur?" This guy jabs Marisa with the mic to try to get her to face him. She whips around and slaps him.

My father's death, my mind repeats numbly as my chest aches with his memory.

My father's death.

We race on. Audun and Brigitte and Marisa crash around me through the underbrush.

"Varik Teitur, why are you harboring this notorious member of the ZWC?" asks a guy, so close that he's just tread on my heel. I trip and plunge into a muddy bank. He has the nerve to lean over and repeat his question.

"Stick that question where the sun don't shine!" Audun

yells, and reaches out a hand to help me. We hurry to catch up with Marisa and Brigitte. Seeing the back of my house through the hedge provides me one last burst of energy. Ignoring the reporter, who's still barking out questions, we surge ahead. I flash my key card over my back door, and we all scramble in, collectively panting for breath. I'm barely able to slam and lock the door before more Streamerazzi pound on it, demanding an interview.

I bind Marisa's hands again, and pull all the blinds down—as if that will do squat against the laser videos. Gasping, I collapse on one of the couches in the den and yank Marisa down. Audun and Brigitte, both staring stone-faced at Marisa, plunk down on the facing couch. No more dithering about tangerine-hued Marisa boots.

My pulse bangs in my head. "Is it true that you belong to the ZWC? Is it?" I ask her. Our eyes lock in a battle of wills.

"Yes," she says.

"You're out of your mind! What would the daughter of a rich real-estate baron want with a terrorist group? You make no sense. I should throw you out to the Stream as a sacrifice."

"You understand nothing," she insists.

"Explain then!" Up in her face, I slap the side of my hand against my palm. "Explain in plain English!"

"It's not safe. Let's talk upstairs."

"*Not safe, not safe, not safe,*" I mock her excitable voice. I feel like Shin's dragon embed—breathing fire. "Did that ZWC have anything to do with my father's death?"

"No way," she proclaims, unblinking. "We're not about killing."

"Where do those Zone freaks live? I'll crush them. Where's their goddamn lair?"

"That's not such a good idea," Marisa mutters.

I hold up the InvisiLink toggle. "I'm going. Where is it? In the fryin' Hotzone? That's it."

She glowers at me, but doesn't answer. Expressions from hate to deep thought, to uncertainty, to disgust pass over her face, as if she's utterly flummoxed—floundering in the gray areas for once, instead of the stark black and whites.

I turn to Audun. "Can you customize my darter? Add layers of heat-reflecting insulation? Enough to fly it in extremely high temps?"

"Whoa, whoa. I'm not going to any Hotzone with the likes of you," Marisa mutters.

"I told you before," I hiss, "prisoners don't vote."

Audun taps his fist on the sofa arm. "It would take a while. I suppose I could build it in my dad's shop."

There's a tense hush, when everyone is furiously thinking.

"That won't do," Marisa's voice, so unexpected and firm from the silence, startles me. "You'd need to build it here. Smuggle in the parts. Nothing more can leak out. Understand? Nothing! If you want to confront the ZWC, you need to listen to *why* they do what they do. *I* haven't convinced you. Maybe *they* can."

Audun leans against Brigitte as if Marisa's knocked the wind out of him. I know it has me. I get up, grip Marisa by her shoulders and level a stern gaze on her. "Tell me *exactly* where the ZWC hang out."

"Yellow Axe," she says, so low I can hardly hear her.

So she wasn't just babbling nonsense when we stunned her. "Isn't that some wilderness in western Land Dominion?" She nods. "How did they get up there from the Hotzone?"

She gently pulls away from me. The corners of her mouth are taut. "Let's go up to your dad's solarium."

"I'm not interested in you reciting the ZWC Manifesto one-on-one. Talk here, in front of Audun and Brigitte."

"Think safety first. Think hidden mics. Think Fireseed?" she whispers, nodding to the den walls.

Audun and Brigitte make puzzled faces at Marisa.

"Please. Just you," Marisa insists. "Upstairs?"

The computer. Shin fixed it! With this new, horrid ZWC twist, I'd completely forgotten. Audun gives me a conspiratorial look, as if to say if I indulge this whacked-out girl I'll get access to way more important info.

"Drifter, don't worry about us," Audun says with a dismissive flap of his hand. "Brigitte and I, we'll make ourselves comfy. Hold down the fort and all." He slips an arm around Brigitte. "Right, baby?"

"Mmm." She snuggles closer to him.

Straining to contain my rage and confusion, and holding the InvisiLink high so Marisa can see it, I head up with her to third tier, to my father's solarium.

8.

"Do they have my seed disks out there in Yellow Axe?" I ask Marisa as soon as I close the solarium door."

"Shh. Dunno. They might." She runs around, closing all of the blinds.

"What are you doing with those creeps?"

"They're not creeps."

"Tell me!" I start to press the InvisiTag toggle.

"Look, I wanted to do something for the refugees. Always have. I hated my dad for how he exploited his refugee workers. I was in a club one night, and this guy came in. He was talking about activist stuff. About refugee rights, about how he was going to make the Hotzone into a viable place to live. Grow shade trees, more shelters. Your father was wrong for turning against them—and hoarding all the best food."

"They have food down in the Zone. We send it to them from Ocean Dominion drop-off centers. They have construction jobs, too."

"No, not nearly enough—of either." Marisa's eyes are steely. "This guy, at least he was trying to develop a strategy to deal with the starving people, like setting up distribution centers for when the crops started growing—"

"The crops, huh? Crops from our seeds that you guys stole." I scowl at her. "You bought this guy's thieving plan *way* too easily." I don't tell her this, but I do have a passing doubt about why my father assumed that all refs were bad just because of a few crazed nutjobs. He was smart enough to know that hunger must make a person desperate. But I'm not about to admit this to Marisa. Instead, I say, "Okay, okay, you want to prove something to me? Show me that video. But first, let me see what my father had on the computer before the link went down." I blindfold her for this.

Pushing away a tangle of his papers and books, I log onto my father's system. When I'm sure that the kaleidoscope devil face is gone, I settle into the chair and explore the latest files on his monitor. There's his article for *Marine Insider* on the need to strengthen WonderAgar in response to increased cyanogenesis and acid toxicity of Cutters, and a hard copy of a lecture he was set to deliver to the Dominion Institute of Marine Biology on "DNA Plant Glyph Technology." His intellect alternately amazed and intimidated me. He has an impressive online address book that rivals Audun's—mostly colleagues from his work, and friends. I scroll through it. No suspicious names, except for the fact, Marisa notes, that her dad's number is listed with an X on the memo section.

"Any reason why your father's personal number would be on my father's address list?" I ask Marisa. Land and Ocean Dominion are rivals for power. We've been on the verge of a cold war with them for as long as I can remember. Though we do supply them with food, and they protect us with their Beltway border.

Marisa frowns. "Who knows? My, um . . . father never spoke of your dad."

I glide the cursor over other files, pausing at my father's online chess. He often played when he had researcher's block, as he called it. He claimed that puzzling out moves for pawns and knights helped him strategize the reorg of plant DNA.

I should have taken up chess too. It might've given me the smarts to perfect that code for extra-strength skin. Skiin, I called it because it had two ii glyphs.

Yeah, SKIIN.

When I first came up to my dad's office after he died, I was shocked to see that he still had my first mixture of it in the back of his lab fridge. After all of these years, and his roaring protest, it truly shocked me. What was he saving it for?

"Nothing out of the ordinary here," I say. "So, show me that *amazing* Fireseed site." I rip off her blindfold.

As she shifts over to the computer lightboard, and I unbind her wrists, my skepticism leeches out like arsenic from under-mud. After a show of finger acrobatics, a series of passwords, and a blur of sites, few of which I manage to jot down—ZonePo, Weeds, Zbank2074—Marisa punches up a grainy video. I remind myself that I've got Shin to run me back through the list of sites should I need them.

The video shows a blacked-out silhouette of a man—the kind that whistleblowers use when they need to hide their identity. He's facing forward so I can't see a profile, but the wide, rough-edged shape is probably a beard. My nerves come alive. Dad had a beard.

Shadow Man begins to speak. It's apparent his voice was run through an audio scrambler. "Research has shown," he mumbles, as if through the eye of a hurricane, "that one can make spectacular shifts in the molecular toolbox with a single radical gene, as in—" The audio bristles with static. I lean closer to it and make out "—Some of the CO_2 clouds . . . " before the sound fizzles. Then it snaps back into clarity: "Fireseed One will be the hope of the world, bred to withstand otherwise-lethal levels of CO_2

and live without water. It will breathe new life into blight-ridden plants. It will introduce new DNA to our now limited geno-system. Although Fireseed One will be bred to withstand—" At this point both the video and the audio blink out.

Ice pushes through my veins. Not only did my dad have a beard, he was also obsessed with toxic levels of airborne CO_2.

Marisa tries to punch up the video again, to no avail. "Feed's gone down." She curses loudly. "That happens in the Hotzone, where they shot it. Feeds are makeshift there. They go in and out. Mostly out." Turning to face me she says, "Believe me now?" Bluish tinge from the monitor lends her cheekbones a skeletal glow.

"Not necessarily. That guy could've been anyone," I lie. "Where'd you get that footage?"

"That was broadcast on Zone Video. Back in 2074."

"Zone Video!" I shout in disbelief. "But . . . the people in the Hotzone don't have videos. All Zone news comes from Dominion flyovers. It's still complete chaos down there: famine, nomads wandering from place to place with their ratty back-packs. So, no, I don't believe you. You got the footage from up here! You doctored it up somehow! What? Did that ugly terror-ist dude with the square earring force my father to spout those lies at gunpoint?" I'm shouting this. It would be truly remarkable if such a plant existed, but I would've known about Fireseed. And it's a cruel joke to toy with the idea that my father ever hung out down in the Hotzone, doing experiments. I stare at Marisa. "My father said the Zone was about anarchy, robbing, murder. He said the refs were bloodthirsty thieves. Everyone says—"

"No," she says with an edge of firm resolve. "Your father, the government News Stream, they feed us all a line of crap. To keep people feeling that it's okay to have the big border wall up. To make us all feel better for doing nothing to help."

"Sounds ludicrous."

"Hardly. It keeps people from getting too curious about

what's going on down there, and all the unlucky people down there from running north. Even during the worst years, pockets of organized tribes survived. Banded together." Marisa parses her words slowly, as if she knows I won't be able to digest it otherwise.

"How would you know, if you're from Land D?"

"I've met the refugees who work for my dad. I'm not quite as sheltered and stupid as you assume."

I prop my weary head on my hands. A picture of my father cursing the refs fills my senses. How hateful his voice was, how wild his eyes looked. "So, according to your fairytale, what was my father doing?"

"Trying to save the world," she says matter-of-factly. "He was planning to cultivate Fireseed One. Make it a food source, a way to make oxygen and cool off the land, revitalize the geno-codes."

For a second, this image fills me with a perverse sort of pride. But it doesn't jibe with the picture I have of him. Okay, he was already feeding the world in the sense that the refs got a share through the stuff he sent to Land D. But the refs weren't too high on his priority list. At least after my mother died. "Cultivate this, um, Fireseed, where?"

"Ah! That's the big mystery. No one's ever found out exactly where. Or if he even got around to planting any. But we know it was going to be on his land, in the Hotzone."

"Now I *know* you're out of your mind. My father never owned land down there."

"Yes, he did—much of the southwest, in what was the USA. Dead land, my father calls it. 'Good for nothin' but dying in,' he says." Marisa chuckles dryly. "Not even the megalomaniacal Melvyn Baron wanted to develop a frontier condo on that parcel." She pauses. "He probably regrets it now."

A shiver runs through me—and a creeping doubt of all that my father ever told me, and didn't. "Why would he want that kind of land when he had all the green islands he wanted up here?"

"Not sure; maybe he needed dead land for his research. But the point is he aborted Fireseed." She slashes the air for effect. "Your father trashed the whole project, brutally abandoned the refs. And there was no one else brilliant enough to continue his work."

"He may have hated what that refugee did to my mother, but he wasn't a cruel man. When did he supposedly scrap the project?"

"At some point in the 70s."

I was born in 2071. I was three in '74. My mother died when I was six, in '77. So, Marisa's telling me that my father had a secret project for a good ten years that involved travel into a highly treacherous zone, and I never found out? At some point wouldn't my dad have told me? Let it slip somehow? This is so over the top, so sci-fi, that all I can do is gape at Marisa.

"Your father still owns that land, so . . . I guess it's yours now." Marisa's quiet for a long moment, which makes the low whir of the computer sys sound like a roaring tide.

This is overwhelming. I crash back against my chair and rake a hand through my hair, feel the grime of the day coat my fingers. "So, where's the evidence on his sys? There's nothing on it," I say peevishly.

I bind her wrists again, and walk over to the large porthole. Gazing out, I see the sun is setting behind Cloudland in a microwave shimmer of steamy pink fog. Darters, from up here the size of toddlers' wagons, carve intersecting white marks on the surface of the sea as they zip forward to their destinations. Directly below, the flags and mobile systems of the Stream ships poke up through the scrub trees of my front cove.

The Stream. Still camped here. Wind sends up leaves that scrape against the agar pane.

I sigh and return to my dad's desk, where Marisa's head is in her hands. Her hair spills over her pale arms. This saddens me, as if her energy is spilling out, too. I'm surprised to think of her as human, as tired, as vulnerable.

She lifts her head. In one eye, a bloodshot vein branches out to the edge of her lid.

"If what you're saying is true, I guess I need to find the files."

"It's true, Varik. Does your dad have any old work files in storage? Say, from the 70s?"

I have no idea, and there's no reason to trust Marisa with his files. My mind wanders back to Shadow Man speaking of toxic CO_2 levels. Some raw instinct tells me there's enough of a chance it might be my father to at least see where Marisa's leading with this. Besides, most of his articles are in the public domain. It never occurred to me to hack in, though I would have eventually gotten to it, if only to answer farming questions that came up. But I don't tell her that.

"Of course he saved old stuff," I answer irritably, pulling open drawers to seek for any crystals holding holofiles. One drawer is full of them, each marble-sized, each in its clear case. I access one after the other, and parse the documents in them. There are farm invoices, crop reports, client lists, and business letters. There are scientific papers, too, but nothing on the Hotzone, or Fireseed, or even on WonderAgar.

Where else would he hide important files? Where?

After four hours, two black coffees, and great aggravation, Marisa and I sit there alternately glaring at each other and diving back into files we've already sorted through.

I'm beyond tired, and Marisa's nodding off in her chair so we creep downstairs. Audun and Brigitte are asleep on the sofa, tangled up in my dad's old Hudson Bay blanket. Marisa stumbles into the zendo, where I set her up with my dad's meditation mat. There's the tiniest inkling of trust in me, but until I get more answers I'm not willing to take any leap of faith.

"Just answer me one thing," I say as she takes off her boots and sits down on the mat.

"Shoot."

"Why would you want to pal around with a ZWC guy you met at some club, even if he did have a plan? You could have developed a better plan that didn't involve messing people up. You seem smarter than that."

She sighs, swishing her hair behind her as she thrusts her long legs under the blanket. "Did you ever see your father as a god?"

I think of when I was a boy, watching my dad tend to the tiny new hybrids in his lab, how he dribbled water on them just so. Made them spring up like magic. I think of him putting the finishing touches on that agar playground. "Sure, I guess I did, but what does this have to do with the ZWC?"

"I don't know about you, Varik, but it was painful to wake up one day and see my father completely differently. Hear that 'perfect god' order some cowering ref to work overtime even though the guy was covered with burns; listen to him fire people while they begged him not to." She looks up at me to see if I'm tracking this. I nod slowly, averting my gaze to the floor to avoid staring at her under that blanket. "I always wanted to do something to help," she says. "When I was little I'd sneak the workers cups of water. Got in bad trouble for it. When I was older, I'd sneak them food, even clothes, hats to cover their heads from the sun." She snorts. "That went down well with Melvyn. . . . I guess I needed to find another hero."

I think of my own boyhood impulses to do something for the refs, to make new skin for them. Impulses that shriveled after my father yelled at me for it—impulses that totally died after hearing that a refugee basically murdered my mother.

Marisa's voice turns sharp. "And when I saw my father's true colors, it made me want to help the refs in a way that he'd absolutely *hate*."

I think of my father's favorite koan:

Your head becomes very heavy if you carry a stone in your mind

And I think of my father cursing the refs. Even now when I think of it, it's shocking and out of character. Who has a bigger stone in their head—Marisa, my father, or . . . me? I'm confused, really confused, because he was a good man. "Doing something dangerous just to hurt someone is impulsive stupidity, Marisa. I can't relate to that."

"It wasn't *just* to hurt him. And it wasn't out of stupidity. That's where we disconnect." Marisa sounds so lost, so bitter, so small. I picture her as a child with cropped red hair, scuffed knees, trying to catch up to that oversized image I have of Melvyn Baron from the Stream as he walks away from her. I can't recall exactly what he looks like except for a limpid version of that same red hair. But I do recall the smirk.

No, Marisa and I are not the same. I could never hate my father enough to do something destructive, even partly out of fury. Could I?

"Good-night," I say crisply. Then I exit the room and double-lock it without looking back.

Stumbling up to my room on tier two, I crash and drift into fitful visions of a L'Ongitude waitress in her trademark white tutu serving me a poisonous Snowflake cocktail. I'm woozy from the drink.

The setting shifts to a close-up of Marisa. Midwest Ana winds are cycling her hair into a funnel. Shadow Man is standing next to her, whispering in her ear. The dark outline of his beard is stark against the pale sky. It feels like my father, but I'm still not sure. The scene pans out. He and Marisa are standing in a wasteland of parched red plants. Where am I in this?

I am invisible, far removed. Dread is the operative word.

Shin has the dubious honor of being the last freak to strut across my interior stage. He is talking to his dragon embed as it spits out purple smoke.

"Play the game, dude," he insists.

9.

I wake to the sound of Audun's flowery falsetto and the walnut scent of good Cloudland coffee. Leaping out of bed, I run through the craziness of yesterday. My clothes are still damp from spray, and muddy from falling when that Streamerazzo tripped me.

Fry me! The Streamerazzi. I glance out my bedroom porthole to see that they're still holding quite the vigil. Their ships are clogging up all of my docks. What *is* the detailed story about Marisa and the ZWC, and why is it worth their time? I'm tempted to go out and ask. Marisa was so adamant about us steering clear of the reporters. She's not my lord and master, though. If I quiz a reporter off-camera, he may reveal his theory on why she joined the ZWC. I'll certainly get another perspective on Marisa. She only doles out a drop at a time. The catch is he'd ask *me* personal questions that would cascade all over the Stream.

My mind goes round and round about this. Bottom line: pretty soon I'll need to get groceries, or run out in the blustery wind to make farm rounds. I'll decide later.

It's while I'm changing my clothes that I come upon Shin Kaskade's card in my pocket.

"Play the game," I repeat, as per his instructions. "Play it."

Marisa's either safely tucked away in the zendo, or Audun and Brigitte have unhatched her for the express purpose of talking her ear off. Either way, I have some time.

I text Shin.

Hey Shin, Varik here frm last nite. One more question, please. Where would someone hide a top-secret file from hackers?

After a few minutes of mad Audun-style pacing, my HipPod glows in my hand. I click it open.

Most obvious place. In front of ur eyes dude. Last free advice. I do text tek & housecalls for Ds.

Peace, Space Strawberry,
Shin

"In front of your eyes, in front—" I mumble a few times, trying to jumpstart my problem-solving abilities. The Stream blasts its morning message in my head, competing for my attention.

Sea Uplink: Midwest Ana winds, usually confined to the Hotzone, are disrupting tides as far north as Ocean Dominion. The resulting abnormal current is confusing the natural orbit of islands and farms. Tiny Island near SnowAngel was overcome by invasives, killing one inhabitant, and sucking the island undersea. Another island in the Svalbardia group strayed all the way to inner Cloudland and had to be hauled back by five Fleeter tugs. To avoid these disasters, immediately increase your island's gravity and speed.

Brought to you by Svalbardia spray jackets, the garment that protects against squall or sun, and rocks ice while doing it.

Bad weather's coming on fast. Reaching up to a wall panel above my desk in my room, I increase the speed of my island, and our farms. Only in rapid acceleration do I feel the orbit. It jolts the entire house (and gives me a mild whiplash). At my desk, I pick up books and pens, fallen in the lurch, when my HipPod rings. I click on.

"Mr. Teitur, are you there?" It's Serge. I know his droll, guttural voice by heart. He must be flustered because he ends on a high, almost frantic note, unusual for him.

My first impulse is to call upstairs for my father before I realize Serge hasn't asked for *Professor* Teitur, and that my father will never again answer a HipPod. "Hey. It's Varik."

"Serge, at Agar 6, sir. Something's happened to the fields."

My insides drop, recalling the overripe turnip odor seeping from the plants. "What is it? What's happening?"

"They're all black."

"Black?"

"The leaves are shriveled up. I've never seen a blight like it, sir."

I want to tell him to calm down, and remind him that WonderAgar is a Hercules. That it will miraculously bounce back. That nothing can vanquish it.

But he already knows that, which means he's gravely concerned, which flips me out. Planting my feet firmly on either side of the chair legs, I feign calm as I think through the possibilities. "Were the plants fed an excess of fertilizer?" I ask him. "Are there any holes in the fertilizer lines that microbes could enter?"

"I've checked everything. No extra fertilizer. No problems in the feed lines. You should take a look. Honestly, sir."

"Be right over." I sign off. *It can't be that bad,* I think, but my mood tells me different. What do I know about agar, really? Nothing that Serge doesn't already know, and Serge is stumped. If the production fell off in any serious way, there would be nothing to compensate it. *Nothing.* No other crop comes close. Nervously, I throw on my boots and run down to the zendo to check on Marisa. She's up against the inside pane, studying me intently. I unlock the door, and walk in, one careful step at a time, as I hold up the fish toggle.

"What's up?" she asks. "Is it about your farm?" She's in one of Brigitte's short smocks. So quickly she makes herself at home.

"Why are you asking if it's about the farm?" Does she have uncanny intuition, or is it something more sinister? My old dread has returned.

She flips her hair over her shoulder. "Oh, I don't know."

"And you won't," I insist. I lock her back in. Giving Audun the InvisiTag controller, I add express instructions to watch Marisa closely. Her question was way too pointed. My budding trust from last night has rapidly wilted.

I hear her calling from the zendo not to go out; that the Streamerazzi will eat me alive. She warns me not to talk. I slam the door behind me.

At the dock, Juko's not there to greet me. A vicious wind slams against me, and spits sand and sea spray in my eyes as I call for him. I worry that these Midwest Ana winds have swept Juko away, or that the tumult of the Streamerazzi have scared him to rougher waters. My only consolation is the pleasure I get in seeing their boats crash against each other on the white-capped swells.

It's drizzling, and the sun has retreated behind its dome. The sky has turned eerily chartreuse, signaling that a torrent could unload at any moment.

As I pull anchor, a reporter ambushes me. "Varik Teitur, why are you giving sanctuary to a member of the ZWC?"

"What makes you think she's a member of the ZWC?" I ask, playing dumb.

"I would answer that if you grant me an interview with her. 2,000 Ds for an exclusive interview." His rubbery lips curl into a devilish grin to match his Faustian offer.

"Go interview Cherry fryin' Froth!" I yell over my shoulder as I leap into my darter and shut the hatch. I do some fast demo-derby maneuvers à la Audun to create a wake that bashes against one of the news ships attempting to follow me. Then I sink the darter sub-style and do a reverse spin around the island, creating a battalion of bubbles in the process. I tell myself a large ship weighted with Stream gear is unlikely to catch up.

After a twenty-minute ride at max speed limit, and two more sets of underwater spin acrobatics to confuse another persistent news stalker, I reach Agar 6 and sink anchor.

Serge races over. Some of the hired help is milling around. They mumble to each other and stare at me with kindhearted smiles, as if to offer me unspoken sympathy for an unspeakable terror I'm about to witness.

Serge and I shoot up the air ride. Stepping off, I turn toward the fields.

An inferno of burnt crop.

From the crumbled row by my boots all the way to the back windows about a kilometer away, charcoal black leaves curl in on themselves like a trillion rotting corpses. I swallow back bile and a gurgling, raw terror.

This is no simple fertilizer burn.

Breathless, I kneel down, cup one of the plants, and examine it to see if the root is still viable, if by some miracle, the blackened part can be plucked off. Nodules ring the stem like a band of toxic warts. I pull up gently on it. The agar plant pops right out. Its roots have disintegrated. The sight is as horrific as a freshly amputated leg.

"Serge?" I swallow hard again. My mouth has gone dry and my tongue seems huge. "Have we ever had any problem like this?"

"Never, sir. We've had the white blight, and then the rusty mold that almost got the crop five years ago, but we've strengthened the agar genetically since then."

"The point is it survived," I say, as much to convince myself as Serge. "The point is, WonderAgar is the hardiest hybrid we've ever developed."

"Praviuh," he says, "how true. A magnificent super-crop."

Serge speaks reverently, as if he's the preacher at a funeral read-ing the eulogy. "At first I thought this blight was an airborne version of Cutters," he adds.

"And?"

"It wasn't. I ran all kinds of tests on it, sir. For Cutters, for strains of just about all the blights."

Fury rises in me. How dare he not tell me the second he saw it? He might run the farm, but he works for me. "Why didn't you tell me sooner? When did you run the tests?"

"I only noticed it this morning—three or four rows. I ran the tests before I called you. It spread like wildfire."

"From four rows this morning to this in hours? Impossible." I silently curse myself for not reporting what I saw the other day. Was it really yesterday? The hours and days are a blur.

Raking his close-cropped hair, Serge says, "Could be an alien microbe from the Hotzone, from Midwest Ana winds blowing everything off-kilter. Perhaps many monstrosities grow in the extreme heat down there." He bows his head at the nearest row.

The bitterness in my throat spreads through me as I stare out at the ruined field. My father spent his life cultivating this agar, coaxing it into each improved version, staying up all night in his lab nursing each new breed of seedling. I'm glad of only one thing: that he is not here to witness this.

"What about the next tier down, Serge?" I ask, with the slightest flicker of optimism.

"Dead."

"The floor above? All twenty floors?"

"The same. Even if we found one healthy plant, most likely it has been infected as well. The only hope might be to hybridize it with a super-plant from an entirely different region."

"A super-plant," I repeat with a spark, thinking of Fireseed. According to Marisa, no one's ever found it in the Hotzone, or anywhere else. So the likelihood that it ever made it off the drawing board is slim. "Have you ever heard of a plant called Fireseed?" I ask Serge.

He rubs his chin as his hooded eyes study me. "I don't believe so. It is . . . ?"

"Oh, a plant that my father may have developed." My voice trembles nervously. "Just wondering." My father shared most of his successful hybrid news with Serge, so the fact that Serge hasn't heard of it doesn't bode well. There's a weighted pause, where we both seem hollow, uncertain as to how to proceed.

I think of telling him about Marisa—the break-in. But I worry that he'll call in the government, who will then find out about this crop disaster, and create total panic without having a clue as to how to fix things. No, on second thought, I don't think Serge would involve the government. He's a deeply private man, and very skeptical about the authorities. After all, he slipped me that earring he found on my father's body. And never brought the government in for an investigation. But things are too over-whelming. It's not the right time. Yet.

"What about our other agar farms?" I ask him.

"The same." Serge's voice is a hushed cry. "The farmers from 1 through 5 called me before you arrived."

Cold panic grabs me, spreads into my chest. I study my trem-bling hands for evidence of disease. A bug that could kill off a super crop might infect humans. "What about Perseus Agar Farm in Cloudland?" I ask as I brush my hands off on my jeans. Serge shakes his head. "Or Arctic Wonder near Land Dominion? What about Atlas Agar in Tundra?"

"They've all contacted me via the private agar line. Every last one." He can't meet my eyes now. "We must keep this quiet," he says. "Or people will riot."

A new black plague.

"Tell them all to look again, Serge. There must be a healthy patch, just one patch."

He doesn't bother to answer as I race down the aisles, kneeling at intervals to inspect leaves, pulling up plants to check for intact roots, searching for a faint thread of green under a black leaf. I race through the entire building this way.

He may have missed something. I may still find one viable plant. Just one.

Serge offers to accompany me to our other farms. I feel like I'm riding to my father's wake all over again. If he weren't already gone, the sight of this would kill him. If he were here perhaps he could have figured this out. I feel so lonely without him. It's all on me now.

"Have you seen any suspicious activity?" I ask Serge as my darter plunges us into the raging surf.

"What kind, sir?"

"Unusual boats docking near the farms. Strangers coming aboard?"

"No, sir." He holds his lean body taut against the violent rocking.

"Have you hired any new staff?"

"Not for many months." He wipes the fogged up porthole with the heel of his big hand. "I did see some odd seabirds in the sky."

"What do you mean?"

"A species not native to the area, sir." He shakes his head. "Clumsy things. They look like a cross between a vulture and a cat." He gauges the size by holding out his arms. "As big as an eighteen-pound albatross."

"Some bird," I remark. A bird doesn't qualify as a danger . . . unless it carries disease. "Is that where the blight came from?"

"This is no avian blight, sir."

Reflexively, I look up at the sky, at the rain pummeling down. No birds casting their fate on this angry wind.

Finally, we anchor at Agar 2. Waves, clanking the darter against the dock, threaten to crack it wide open. I climb out, stumble to the railing along the feed pipes, and grab on to avoid being whisked off and out to sea in what is surely a fatal under-tow. Serge follows with surer feet.

I trudge across tiers 1 through 20 with increasing terror that borders on hysteria. How did my father ever manage to handle all the stress? Nothing, nothing here at all but charred plants with that nauseating rotten turnip odor.

Then, miracle of ice, in tier 19 of Agar 3, under a curled black ruin, I uncover two seemingly unaffected, spindly but *liv-ing*, emerald-green gems! I shout for Serge, who hurries over with a portable, sterile incubator. Donning gloves, I dig around the seedlings, careful to separate any infected plant material from this chaste section of dirt.

The hired help, lined up in the hallway as we approach, cheer loudly when we carry the treasure to the loading dock. I see from their faces that a few have been weeping.

With each step, I fear the tornado-level winds will steal the thing from my hands. I manage to strap it safely into the back seat of my darter.

This agar must be kept alive! I hope Serge is wrong about the healthy plants being already infected, particularly since we never found those agar code disks. For a prayer of survival, we must re-cultivate. The entire world is based on agar. It's as essential as the wheat or oil of the old days. We dress in agar textiles; we use the agar that's been gene-spliced with hardeners to make darters, mold islands, entire cities. We cure people with agar-based medi-cines. We need it to feed the gaping mouths of the world.

Oh. Lord. I can't stop shaking, and it's not from the storm.

I drop off Serge with a promise to keep him up to date on the health of the plants. He gives me tips on watering and feeding, and offers to check in on them, which I gladly accept. Then I return to my island with the darter idling on its slowest speed. Accelerating too fast or a gust of infected wind through a tiny hole in the incubator could wipe out the most valuable cargo I've ever carried.

10.

It's a challenge smuggling the incubator past the Streamerazzi. I call Audun ahead to meet me at the back dock with an armful of spray jackets. He carefully covers the plants. He's brought Brigitte with him, too. She runs a brave distraction, flirting with the shrouded reporters in the driving rain. When they ask her about Marisa, she insists she has no idea what they're talking about. Some of the Streamerazzi have given up and sailed off, others are camped out in their galleys, obviously waiting for a turn in the weather. I see one guy vomiting off the deck, his boat dipping and keeling in the storm.

With measured steps, I carry the plant box upstairs. On the way up, I can hear Marisa screeching through the zendo door. "Tell me what's going on. Why are you acting this way? Let me out!"

"Absolutely not!" I yell back.

I set up the plants behind my father's old desk, on a table that receives good indirect light and far from the portal where the stream's photon-videos can steal its image. As I sprinkle water over them, I check every branch for blight.

No hint of coiled leaves. "Sweet ice, protect them," I mutter, as if that will make them magically heal and grow.

On the other side of the door, there's more commotion. Audun orders Marisa to stuff it and calm down; that if she doesn't, the Stream will record her whole rant. She keeps on yelling but at a lower volume. He pages me and offers to make us all an omelet with fresh hijiki. My stomach is churning violently but I say yes. Pretty soon we'll be rationing food, I think, and Audun's feasts will be a thing of the past.

With Shin's words again circulating through my mind, I flick on my father's system.

"Right in your face, dude. Right in your face, dude, right . . ."

What's right in my face? I've rifled through the desk drawers and papers. Could it be the monitor itself? The thought of dismantling it is daunting. I've gone through all of his online files.

In front of my face—the files! I glide my cursor over the articles, the online phonebook, and the chess game.

Couldn't be that stupid game, it's too *obvious*. Wait.

I click on the chess icon, review my father's game history. Mostly he played with Serge, or Ned from Tundra Squidhouse, or with his friends from the Marine Institute. He thumped Serge in February 2089, tromped Ned in January, and smashed a colleague back in December 2088.

My dad was an ace player. Seems he won about 98% of the time. If only I were that good with mathematical strategy, I could write ingenious hybrid glyphs, too.

Scrolling through literally hundreds of games, I select a game with Serge from 2080 and examine the moves. Nothing of note there, so I click into another with Pyotor. Pretty mundane. I must admit, chess always bored me. Why did the smart fox keep so many games? Why not delete them? They go all the way back to . . . the 70s. Stop.

There's one against a Professor Flower. Idiotic name. Dad didn't know any Professor Flower, did he? Quickly I run through his address book. No Professor Flower under P or F or even M for Marine Institute.

I close that file and click into my dad's game with Professor Flower; examine the moves. Queen takes pawn, king takes queen, knight takes . . . Is it my imagination, or is the top of the knight's mane molded into an F-shape? On impulse, I click on the white knight. While I ponder this, the monitor glimmers and then flashes into another screen. "Project F" it says. Jolting forward in my chair, I click on the F. Across the screen float the words *Fireseed One*.

Precious frying ice, right in my face! In my excitement, beads of sweat break out on my upper lip. Brushing them away, I click on the icon. Marisa's words ring in my ear: 'Fireseed One, Fireseed One!'

A graphic animation of a flower blossoms and spreads out to fill the screen, brilliant red with petals that sharpen to points. The center pistil resembles a face with meaty cheeks and two smudgy button eyes. It's not a face, though. It only seems that way because the plant is moving, its petals stretching and curling as if it's flexing its muscles. It's half-human, I swear. But I remind myself it's only an animator's version, not a live plant.

Scrolling down, my breath catches in a loud gasp. It's a hybrid form cert; I've seen hundreds of them. But this is no run-of-the-mill report:

Fireseed One: First live lab hybrid: 2069

Unique features: Transgenic plant with reduced stromatic closure response can survive without H_2O; repels toxic levels of solar radiation, CO_2 and other extreme environmental dangers; genetically designed to outcross and interbreed with other flora to create super-beings. Could potentially save any compromised plant from extinction by interbreeding. Contains an extraordinary array of classified DNA.

Comparatives: One other, much weaker, comparative hybrid, the Rezurrekt fern, perished during cultivation in Hotzone fields.

Project Location for Fireseed: deleted

Purpose: To save the refs and possibly the planet from extinction. To xanASH

XXXXXXXXXXXXXEFFFRYINGGCDBJKNHO: L:IHKYFHJTJB>KHKLL>*^-56132123+23bguyfuy opytrrffghhg.

Project terminated: 2077.

Memo: Goddamn the refs and their entire universe.

Holy frying ice. My father deleted the location for his key project. And spewed angry babble all over the cert. Or . . . is it another secret code? My mind spins on.

So there *was* a live Fireseed plant, at least in the lab! A weaker comparable, the Resurrekt fern, didn't survive the Hotzone. But did Fireseed? Did he ever actually cultivate it down there? What if it's *still* growing there? What if it's simply that no one's found it? The Hotzone is a huge piece of land. If I could somehow obtain a Fireseed and breed it with the surviving agar plants . . . A complete long shot, impossible, really. I mean, Serge hasn't even heard about it.

My attention goes back to that cert form babble, which might hold more information. Furiously, I text Shin Kaskade its crazy set of alpha-numericals my father typed, and wait, tapping my fingers impatiently on the desk to the rapid-fire beat of my pulse. After five minutes, my HipPod glows.

Varik: That is some junky junk spawn. Mean nothing. Some dude ran fingers at random over keyboard. No more free advice, dude. Please send me ur credit card # asap. Charge U 100 D. Peace, Space Strawberry,

Shin

No more hidden meanings in irrational sputter. How will I explain all of these "Shin" expenses? Wait. I report only to myself anymore. The truth is worth almost any price. I text

Shin my credit-card info, all the while staring at Fireseed One's project-termination date.

2077 was the year Mom was left to die in the desert, her green flycar with the white stripe stolen. No wonder my dad grew to hate the refs. My dad and mom were best friends. He ran everything by her. He was so lost after she was gone. I remember him in his den chair as he stared out at nothing, staying in his bathrobe half the day, neglecting his work for a year. At the time his moping was almost embarrassing. Now, I feel a pang of sympathy for him, and an overwhelming urge to hug him.

Too late.

I slump over the keyboard. All along Marisa was trying to convince me my dad had stalled on a secret project. After all of my deep conversations with him, it stings that he never shared this with me. The father I thought I knew is slipping from me. The woman I thought was trying to trick me, even kill me, isn't the person I suspected either. My intuition is faulty.

Oh, sweet, melting, sullied ice. Marisa was one hundred percent on point.

But . . . did she have anything to do with this new agar inferno?

Looking fitfully over my shoulder at the seedlings, I choke on a hard knot of air. There's a black patch on one of them. I whirl around, ready to whip off the incubator top and tear off the sick leaf.

But it's not blackened. I see now. It's only a shadow from a storm cloud passing over the pane.

I hurdle downstairs, unlock my father's zendo, and stare at Marisa, who's finally run out of steam for yelling. She's crouched on the futon. When she sees me she leaps up.

"What is it?" she asks breathlessly. "Why have you kept me locked in here all day?"

"It's gone, it's all gone," I mutter.

"What's gone?"

"You know," I snap. "Don't tell me you don't." I'm seething and reeling and ready to pass out—all at once.

"But I *don't* know. I have no idea."

I grab her shoulders and shake her, hard. "The agar. It's dead! In every fryin' farm in Ocean Dominion. All dead." I don't mention the two live seedlings. Why would I? "Your precious ZWC did that, too."

"What? No! No way!"

She shakes me off, but I grab her again. "Stop lying!" I yell. "Stop playing sick mind games. Stop it! We're going to die now. We'll all starve, not just the refugees." I start to laugh hysterically. "Funny fryin' joke you ZWC freaks played on us. Hilarious!" Tears blot my vision, and it's all I can do to keep myself from bashing her head against the stone floor.

"I swear, we had no plan like that!" she shouts. "You have to believe me. That wasn't part of the mission. No way, Varik."

I swipe a hand across my face to clear away the sweat and tears, and glare at her. Her blue eyes are open so wide they're surrounded by white. Her skin looks waxy—dead. Her mouth quivers. I sense she's as terrified as I feel.

I can't track all this. I need my father. If he were here, none of this would have happened. But he's not, and I'm left to my own devices. "Why? Why should I believe you?"

"Don't believe me. Believe what you want. But Bryan wouldn't do that. He's not that stupid. He knows that your agar feeds the Hotzone too, however stingy the rations. He's not crazy. He would never, ever, ever kill it all."

Bryan. So, that's the devil the vault monitor captured on its waterlogged screen. *Bryan,* the name makes me gag with rage. "Dear God, I hope you're right," I whisper. "I guess we'll find out soon enough."

For once, Marisa is speechless.

11.

It's a few days after the Fireseed discovery, and Marisa and I leave tomorrow. We're still not sure how to distract the Streamerazzi. But we'll have to, or risk undertravel and having to painstakingly hack our way through the invasive border. Or Marisa could grant the Stream vampires the racy interview they want to get them off our backs. Make us a few thousand Ds for our trip.

Fry me in the Hotzone, I can't believe I'm considering telling her to do an interview.

It's night. The sun has gone black behind its dome, and lights from the Stream ships blink on beyond the salt-drenched scrub trees. Marisa and I are in the kitchen eating uninspired leftover cod and a small ration of agar soup for dinner. Audun, who's been given all the lock codes to my house and has been crashing here, is late returning from his job.

I've been painstakingly teaching him the care and feeding of agar seedlings, for he'll be in charge of them after I leave. He's customized my darter at a frantic pace, adding heat sensors, sealant tape around the ports, and extra coolant modules. Each time he made a delivery, he marched past whichever Streamerazzo was on duty and loudly announced he was bringing in darter parts. The reporters would laugh and laugh.

Right in your fat faces, dummies!

Marisa and I haven't said much over dinner. She's wringing her napkin after every bite; I'm wolfing food down and tasting nothing. Clearly we're both worrying about the trip ahead. There are tons of questions I want to ask her, but these few days have been so full of last-minute planning that we haven't had another real conversation. Also I've been reluctant to get into much until she's in that darter with me and we're en route. Because getting those agar disks back is my number-one priority. I wonder if her criminal clan will negotiate with me over the stolen disks, or kill me because I know too much about their sorry operation. I consider arming myself. If they had anything to do with poisoning the agar, do they have an antidote?

"Tell me who I'll meet," I say as we eat, taking care to be casual, as if I'm simply asking the name of Marisa's classmate or friend. I know how quickly she'll clam up if something hits her wrong.

For a long minute, Marisa sorts cod bones into a thorny pile. "Bryan wrote the ZWC manifesto 'Sorties for Survival,'" she says finally. "He's the mission guru."

"Missions like 'Stealing the World's Food Supplies 101,'" I say.

Marisa refuses to meet my gaze, but goes on after a loaded silence. "Nevada Pilgrim is a freelance postal runner down in the Zone. Now that the sectors are better organized, but still so far apart, they're desperate for long-distance runners. Bryan pegged the runners to be the produce distributers," she adds under her breath. "Nevada has this fierce vehicle she made from dead copters and a home reactor's radiation shield. She's a nurse, too," Marisa mentions as an afterthought.

"A nurse might come in handy if Bryan tries to sprinkle poison in our oatmeal." I'm thinking of what might have happened to those agar plants. "Do they use toxins in their *activism?*"

"I told you, no. Look. People are suffering. You have no idea. Think about how people felt to have a huge border wall go up so they were trapped in the Hotzone and couldn't go north." Marisa throws me a scornful look.

"Walls built by your Dominion," I remind her.

"And approved by *your* Dominion," she reminds me. "If you're going to be an ass, I refuse to show you where they live."

"Why are you showing me at all?"

She kicks the floor, making dull tapping noises. "Do I have a choice?" She snorts. "If you talk to them, maybe you'll get it. Maybe you'll even help us look for Fireseed."

"Huh. I doubt I'll get their brand of activism."

"Tornado," Marisa continues, as if she hasn't heard me, "is the newest embed. He's the secretary. Keeps logs and stuff." She shrouds the pile of fishbones with her crumpled napkin. "He gives me the creeps sometimes."

"How so?" I get up and sit on the couch in the den. Marisa joins me, on the far end.

"He slicks his hair back with disgusting licorice oil and he's always sneaking looks at me. I don't know why Bryan hired him. Sometimes I would catch the guy following me."

"Fatal attraction," I snap, running my hand along the Invis-iTag toggle.

"What else needs to be done before we leave?" she asks in a businesslike tone.

"We're just waiting on a good moment. Um, I'm worried about Juko."

"Why?" She plops back down on the couch, a little closer.

"He's still missing. Hasn't come back since that last storm."

"Dolphins use sonar. You could try to call him. Do you have a sonar-type radio?"

"Actually, yeah, I used the boat's signal to call for him on today's run to Agar 6. The only thing it attracted was one of those ugly cat-vultures Serge described." Seemed like a bad omen, but to say so might jinx our trip.

Marisa leans in. "The bird. What did it look like again?"

"It was barrel-chested with big, brown flapping wings. It circled my boat as if I had minnows for it." The worry in Marisa's face unsettles me. "What?" I ask her. "Have you seen them, too?"

Just then, the Stream blasts an interview in my head.

Judging by her swift transformation from haunted to surprised amusement, Marisa hears it too.

We both scream, "Audun!"

—the latest on the "Snorkling for Gems" show. Audun Fleury interviewed suspected ZWC terrorist Marisa Baron this morning at the home of the late geno-farmer, Professor Teitur. In Fleury's words:

My girlfriend, Brigitte, and my friend, Varik, the Prof's son, you know . . . we're involved in talks with Ms. Baron about her becoming Angel Boot's new spokesmodel and designer.

"Since when?" I ask Marisa.

"Since never!" she retorts.

Where is Ms. Baron now?

Marisa flew to outer Cloudland yesterday. She thinks the tangerine cloudscapes will totally inform her new boot line.

Marisa makes a confused face. Audun signs off and the Streamerazzo continues:

Why talks would be conducted at the late Professor Teitur's home is cause for speculation, including the possibility that Teitur's son, new owner of the vast sea farm, is romancing the heiress-turned-terrorist. Mr. Fleury insists

Ms. Baron's activist days are behind her as she looks forward to this exciting new chapter of her life. Ms. Baron did not return calls for verification of the story.

Brought to you by Cloudland airbeds, soft as sea mist on a spring breeze.

Marisa sniggers. "I wouldn't answer their calls if they paid me a trillion Ds." She glances my way, a trace of a lopsided smile on her face.

Is she as appalled as I am over that mention of me romancing her?

We go into cleaning mode. Marisa, hopeless with the kitchen bots, fills the dishwasher herself. Good job, considering the bound wrists.

Sly old Audun finally got interviewed! Maybe he has what it takes to weasel into his own news show after all, especially if he hires a writer. He just might prove his dad wrong.

Marisa comes over, drying her hands on a dishtowel. "Did you hear that part where Audun said I was in Cloudland?"

"Yeah, that's weird." As I pop Audun's portion of dinner in the fridge, the full scope of his genius tactic dawns on me. Crossing the room in just a few steps, I peer under the blinds and bust out laughing. "He's sent the Stream on a wild-goose chase!"

"Wow. That means . . ."

"Exactly! Let's head out. Now."

Marisa shrieks and then starts zooming around, picking up clothes that Brigitte has given her and stuffing them into her pack.

I pen Audun a note to please let Serge in to check in on the plants, and to care for the agar seedlings precisely as I taught him should Serge be detained, and then I jog upstairs to fetch some basic trek essentials. When I'm done packing in my room, I run up to my father's solarium to check on the agar plants. Amazingly, there's a new leaf on one. The other plant seems a bit puckered, so

I mist some distilled water over it as Serge suggested.

I paw through Dad's lab fridge for an old item: my formula for Skiin in two injectable sharps. I never did a trial run, so who knows if it works. We just might need these in the Hotzone if the sun starts to burn us beyond recognition.

As an afterthought, I log onto dad's chess site, and choose the so-called Dr. Flower's other knight—the black one. I gasp when this opens into another Fireseed page—an even more important one! It's dated a few years earlier than the last, and it proves that Fireseed was more than just a brilliant idea on Dad's drawing board. My heart is pounding out of my pores.

Fireseed One

On-Site Report: 2074

I sowed crop between the cup and flower mimetolith, offering some protection from sandstorms. In two days, ten plants reached a height of five feet before self-combusting. This was my first viable crop!

Results: Fireseed grows at an incredibly fast rate. Crossbreeding is simply a matter of pressing two pollinating plants together, and Fireseed is perennially pollinating. Fireseed is a firestarter. Must find out what activated this.

Remnants: charred stalk nubs, 3" to 6" in height.

Question: Will they regenerate, as trees do after fire?

Next objective: Create a stronger strain in the lab, resistant to self-combustion.

So Fireseed grew in the Hotzone! Between two mimetoliths, whatever they are. It grew as fast as a beanstalk in a fairytale, and then burnt itself up. The story's gotten very weird. Are there more clues in Dr. Flower's other chess pieces? Clicking into every other piece, I find nothing more. But this cert gives me something—a direction, a place, a flicker of hope.

"Thanks, Dad," I whisper to myself. Thanks."

I won't tell Marisa. This part, I'll keep to myself.

12.

We've been gliding above a hypnotic beige cloudscape for hours. Darters do fly, but they're tortoises out of water. To fill the silence, Marisa and I have stopped exchanging hostilities and drifted into a comparison of our lives. I suppose that's what happens when you're locked in a cell with your archenemy.

"I went to Vostok Station's public school," I tell her, "but my father homeschooled me, too. How about you?"

"I went to Melvyn Baron's alma mater, an exclusive private school," Marisa says in a mocking voice. "It was cliquey and pricy. With huge sports fields and stuff. I played soccer, became the captain of the team." It's odd to imagine Ms. Activist Marisa in cleats and kneepads doing fancy footwork, not so hard to picture her ordering her team around. "You?" she asks.

"No organized sports. I was pretty bookish," I admit. "But I liked sailing and scavenging. Did a lot of that with my dad."

"Mine was too busy, so he bought me expensive baubles." Marisa folds her arms across her chest as if she's cold. "I got a red flycar with gold trim for my sixteenth birthday. Crashed it a few weeks later," she says matter-of-factly. She goes on after seeing how disturbed I must look. "Being rich always bothered me. I didn't like where the money came from. . . . What kind of friends did you hang out with?"

"The brainy geeks at school, except for Audun." I laugh uneasily. "And some of my dad's friends' kids from the Marine Institute. How about you?"

"Soccer jocks. After that, the bad kids, the rebels. We used to sneak into clubs, stay out way past curfew." She asks in a low voice. "Did you date?"

"Not a lot," I say, doubting it's any of her business. "I had one girlfriend who I was just starting to get heavy with when she had to move away. You?"

"I had my share." She laughs too hard. As if it was work, as if she didn't really like the work.

"We're different," I say. We go back to being silent after that.

Eventually, the slow pace of the flycar tires Marisa. After giving me the coordinates, she falls asleep. With each burp of turbulence her hair slides over her shoulders, and she sags in her seat. She seems so alone, so lonely. When we were talking earlier, I almost told her about trying to make that Skiin for the refugees, but I'm glad I held off. I don't want her to know how I feel inside, that I'm as lonely as she seems. Every so often the smoggy cloudscape opens out below me to reveal our progress. I look down as much to distract myself as to marvel at the view.

We're flying over the westernmost Grey Fjords, a series of oblong islands with deep valleys that mark the end of Ocean D and the entry into Land D. Seeing my beloved oceanland slip beneath and then behind the darter fills me with unexpected panic. Our islands that always seemed impenetrable look so vulnerable from up here, such easy fodder for eco-terrorists. I can't imagine what the border wall down south near Yellow Axe will be like. It's hard to picture an impenetrable wall so tall and heavily guarded that one can't fly over it without being vaporized. I'm so used to freely soaring over islands and farms, like a seabird, immune to borders.

I worry about how long I'll be gone, and whether Audun— and Serge, who I finally told—will be able to keep the two plants alive in my absence. What if the ZWC doesn't have the agar code disks? What if Fireseed One was never more than a one-shot miracle in the desert?

Perfection is rare. So are miracles. Since my miraculous find, no other agar farmer has found another viable plant. And I dare not tell them about the ones clinging tenuously to life in my father's office for fear of offering false hope.

When our food source dwindles to nothing, people will likely riot. They'll probably also loot the factories and take out their hunger and fear on Serge and Pyotor and the workers. Not a pretty picture at all. Thinking this, I feel an unexpected shudder of sympathy for the hordes in the Hotzone. All those stories I heard over and over about rampaging raiders must be wearing off.

It must be the ultimate torment to slowly starve.

Agar. It all revolves around this deceptively simple plant. Normally, agar multiplies so fast there is no need to line the shelves with stock. It's always been on a grow-and-ship basis. The way I figure it, the Ocean D factories only have a one-month surplus. To conserve this, I only shipped out half-orders before I left. Buyers from both Dominions, but especially from Land D, were aggressively clamoring for the other half of their orders. I don't know many of those clients, they're not starving yet, and their pushiness doesn't endear them to me. I can't casually reassure them like my father would have.

All the agar farmers are gasping for air in the same choppy surf. A few days before I left, I conducted encrypted online discussions with them to figure out what we'll do when the reserves are 100% depleted. After that computer scare with my dad's system, I was quite paranoid about our private listserv being hacked. But we certainly couldn't do a face-to-face at any old watering hole like at Tundra Squid.

Teitur Farms: Serge reconfirmed that blight has taken all agar. Thoughts on our best alternatives?

Perseus Agar Farm: We'll have to grind up that finicky Finnish blue kelp with lower-grade sea cabbage.

Arctic Wonder Farms: Lousy substitute. It grows slowly, and blights with every airborne bug. What about nu-corn?

Atlas Agar Farm: The DNA is weak, old. Fixers don't work well with nu-corn, so it's inadequate for building material. We should have built a backup agar seed vault in a second location! I'm kicking myself. I vote for Finnish kelp. We can't risk riots.

Teitur Farms: I'm looking into other comparatives.

Perseus Agar Farm: Such as?

Teitur Farms: Searching my father's files, some of his as-of-yet unexamined certs.

Arctic Wonder Farms: Can we count on that?

Teitur Farms: Not sure yet. In the meantime, shall we stall clients with half-orders? No whisper of this can escape.

After my incompetence with the workers and around Serge, it feels good to be regarded as one of the club. If only the circumstances weren't so dire. When I told Serge I was traveling to the Zone to search for Fireseed, he did his best to talk me out of it.

"Varik, sir, if you don't mind me saying, that is a very bad plan. You may get killed. The ZWC is a dangerous group. And if no one has found the Fireseed plant in all of these years, what makes you think you will be any luckier?" His narrow face wrinkled in concern.

"What other option do I have, Serge?" I held his gaze. "Dad

said he grew Fireseed. That it grew five feet tall."

"But then you said it burned up."

I bowed my head. "Yes."

"And no one's ever found it in all of these years," Serge repeated.

"I have to go. My father would have wanted me to."

"Perhaps we can breed these plants we have, sir, with seeds from the vault."

I was touched that Serge cared for my safety so much. I knew at this point, I'd have to tell him more to convince him. "One more thing." I took in a breath. "We had a break-in at the vault. They took many of the seeds, including the agar."

"Oh, God, no! Why didn't you tell me before? When? Who?" His eyelid was twitching and his face was wild with worry.

I told him about Marisa, about her connection to the ZWC, even that she'd revealed where their headquarters were. I insisted not a word of this could leak to the authorities or I could be killed by the ZWC. I told Serge everything except that Marisa would travel with me. He'd never understand. I would've argued with him for days over it.

"That changes the picture," was all Serge said. Glancing back into his steel-gray eyes, I saw a hint of resigned approval.

After all, I was his new boss. He promised to go every day to help Audun care for the agar, and to tell no one where I was—at all, for any reason. I handed him a copy of my key card, and we gripped each other in an awkward hug.

And now, closing in on Yellow Axe, I pray I can deliver back some promising news. Land Dominion's Stream bursts out in my head, breaking up my memory of the frantic listserv conversation. My bowels clench up. We must be close.

Today, real-estate mogul Melvyn Baron sent word that Baronland South was getting slowly back on track after he gave rioting workers 200-D stipends each to spend in his Baronland Emporium. When asked about the whereabouts of his daughter, Marisa, and if there was any truth to the rumor that she was the new spokesmodel for Ocean Dominion's Angel Bootery, he replied that he was happy for her, but would prefer she work at the Shoe Palace in Baronland's Emporium.

Brought to you by Baronland South, where pioneering meets style. Orders are filling fast to this luxe condoplex, so sign on today!

If Melvyn knew his precious daughter was with a guy from Ocean Dominion on the way to meet the notoriously ruthless ZWC, he would shit a golden fish. Despite the undercurrent of panicky tension, I chuckle to myself as I recheck the coordinates. We're almost there, and Marisa's still asleep. I tap her shoulder. She shifts in her seat and grumbles. When I gently shake her shoulder, she jolts awake.

She checks her map and advises me to decelerate. We plunge through the smog-tinged clouds and swoop into the gauzy air. I'm so used to riding undersea surrounded by brackish water and eels, the sight of an expansive leafy green canopy below us has me giddy.

"Last great wilderness," I whisper, thinking fondly of old-beard Thoreau on his Walden Pond, Audubon in his magnificent extinct Everglades, my relatives on their Iowa corn farm before the land dried up.

But Marisa's in a radically different headspace than I. "Decelerate, now!" she orders. "We're almost past it, Varik. Please, hurry! They'll think we're a fucking Fleeter and shoot us down."

Suddenly, this doesn't feel like a nature jaunt. My balls freeze up to the base of my spine.

I break out in clammy gooseflesh as I blindly lower the darter. "How do you land on these flimsy treetops? Don't they have a proper landing pad?"

"No, straight down. I've sent word," Marisa cranes her neck to see below the darter.

"Word? To who?" I ask. And then I see dozens of those awful vulture-cat birds parked in the trees. They're leering up at us with accusing eyes. Audubon would have a seizure in his coffin.

Piney spikes and heaving leaf clusters rush up. I brace myself to crash.

Then, out of nothing, a dark square of dirt opens up.

In fits and bumps, we land.

The forest seems to fasten itself back over us in a shimmering sea of green. I sit in mystified, if anxious, awe.

Marisa opens her door. "We need to get out. Find Nevada by the counsel tree. She has our suits. Come on. Before Bryan sees you, or some Land D flyover does."

I thought I was going to negotiate with the jerk. Little of this makes sense to me, but this is Marisa's territory, so I decide to follow her protocol. At least for now.

We climb out of the darter, which has landed perfectly—not by my conscious doing—in a grove of large-leafed trees. The scent of wet leaves and verdant earth overwhelms me. I imagine all kinds of life burrowing into its black gold: newts and beetles, ants and possums. It must be drenched with clean minerals. Relatively clean anyway. My nose doesn't prickle from the acidic brine like it often does on the sea.

I suck in glorious gulps of cool air as I follow Marisa through the underbrush. She's like I imagine a Native American girl would have been, zipping effortlessly around trees and under low branches, all with no obvious trail marker.

"Hurry," she murmurs, looking worriedly back at me over her shoulder.

Almost simultaneously, I'm aware that the lush greenery has eased my fear, while the concern on Marisa's face has alternately flamed it to dreadful proportions. I pick up a thick stick as I run.

Out of nowhere, a vulturous creature has swept down. It

lurches close to my head and then falls back slightly, tracking me like a guided missile. Is it attracted to the scent of sweat? Does it eat human flesh? What's wrong with these birds? I run faster, swatting at it as I go.

For a moment, I lose Marisa, but then I spot her dipping into the dark gap in the trunk of a gigantic tree. The thing must be a million years old, and as wide as my house.

"Hurry, Varik!" She peeks her head out and pulls me in.

One small light glows from within, sending down just enough radiance to see another person is huddled in further. Well, I see the person's face at least.

She's a green-haired vixen with leaf patterns tattooed on—two leaves on the left cheek, three on the right. Smoky kohl circles her eyes, and she wears a quizzical, strained expression, as if she's wondering what disaster Marisa has dragged home this time. Her hair, what I can see of it, is woven through with vines. She looks like a spokesmodel for those old eco-themed clubs popular in my granddad's day before the environment went kablooey. He told me about eco-clubs called Vegan Pleasure Dome and Blossoming the Bar with kids wearing sustainable clothes and hemp sandals crowding entrances, vying to get in. This girl is wearing those earrings with the three-pronged flame. It dawns on me—must be the ZWC logo.

I glance down at the girl and gasp. Before I remember my manners I blurt out, "Where's your body?"

Rude but valid question—I thought it was the dark that shrouded her, but now that my eyes are adjusting, I see it wasn't just that. Not even the top or back of her head is visible, just an eerie frontal facemask floating in the dank belly of the tree trunk. Is she simply a face, or is her body somehow camouflaged? I can't believe I'm even considering this question, it's so absurd.

Does this wilderness have laws too topsy-turvy for me to grasp? This is stressing me, and I'm already unhinged, thinking about meeting a deranged ZWC svengali like Bryan.

Marisa and this eco-girl laugh at my expense: Eco-girl a wispy laugh, and Marisa her husky one.

"I'm Nevada," says Eco-girl. "Put on your suit and you'll understand." With one hand, she holds out a bundle of fabric. "There's a photon sack for your pack, too." She hands another bundle to Marisa.

"A Robin Hood costume!" I announce, examining it under the dim glow. "No way am I putting on girly tights." Not showing my, ahem, family jewels.

All giggles stop and Marisa says, "It's the only way, Varik. We have flyovers. Land D Fleeters check for refs every few hours. They can't know we're here."

"We'll look the other way while you change," Nevada says helpfully. The girls must be doing an about-face, because even their faces disappear. I wriggle into the ridiculous getup. In the process I trip a few times because it's difficult to see the leg-holes. How do girls deal with these absurdities? I slip my pack into the other piece. And freak.

I've become invisible, too. More accurately, I am tree-trunk colored and as rough. The suit fabric is a perfect mirror of the environment! Chameleon skin. "Whoa. This is unbelievable," I say, running my hands over the fabric. My hand identifies cell-like structures—soft-edged angular shapes but ridged—almost like fish scales, and about the same size. Holding my arm up, the ridges are illuminated in the flickering light.

The girls whirl back around—rather, their faces do, because Marisa has changed into her suit as well. She flips her hood over her hair and says to me, "You'll need to stay here while I check in with the collective."

Squinting, I can see the edges of Marisa and Nevada's hips and narrow waists glinting. Okay, I can sort of see them now. But the me-hiding-in-a-tree-part while they run off is not a particularly funny game.

"I thought Varik was coming with us," Nevada says. Great,

she knows my name. Does that mean that Bryan knows I'm here? Do they know my eating and sleeping habits, too?

Marisa starts to talk to Nevada before deciding to walk her out of the tree for a private briefing. I overhear Marisa say, "I can't bring him in yet."

"You said . . . Varik . . . shifted alliances," Nevada insists, "—now one of us—"

"What?" I shout loudly so they'll hear me, and know that I heard them. I'm one of them now? Marisa better have a good answer to this idiocy. She may not be able to see me in my photon suit, but she can surely see my thumb on the InvisiTag toggle.

With a rustle and a series of glints ricocheting off their bizarro bodysuits, the girls duck into the giant trunk again. Marisa's warmth by my side jolts me. "Hold on," she says.

"Where's this Bryan guy?" I ask. "I need to talk to him. Oh, and by the way, I'm not one of you . . . you ZWC freaks."

"We're not freaks," Nevada says defensively.

Marisa says, "It's too soon, Varik. Understand?"

"Not at all," I bark.

"What's he doing here, then?" Nevada asks, her kohl-lined eyes narrowing.

Marisa sighs audibly and looks over at Nevada. "Trust me, Nevada, it's complicated. I'll bring Varik over after I speak with Bryan. Give us some time. I'll meet you back at the counsel grove later." Marisa can be very persuasive when she wants. I should know. I'm standing here in clingy man-tights.

"You've got fifty meters of fish line," I remind her. "And if I zap it longer than a few seconds it can do more than stun you."

Nevada screws up her face in confusion. She says to Marisa, "I stuck my neck out to get you the suits, so don't get me in trouble."

What trouble will she be in? I wonder. *Will the gallant ZWC guru beat her with a tree limb?* I startle violently when I hear a loud rustle, and then realize it's only Nevada slipping out. I know this because her face is gone. Glancing over at Marisa, I see a tangle of red hair has escaped her hood, and is sort of dangling in space. It's hard to wrap my head around the fact that I can't see her body. Or more accurately, it has become one with the tree trunk.

"I never said I'd hide, Marisa. I came to get my agar disks back."

"And to listen to what we do here, to at least try to understand how dire it is. But I need to talk to him first. You don't want to be killed, do you?"

Killed. Dead. The *dead* word. I picture my father, rotting in the invasive vines, and that bird, thankfully gone for now, eager to peck out my eyes. What was I thinking when I decided to leave my harpoon at home? "You said the ZWC wasn't into harming people, only into *token acts to prove points*," I hiss. "Your svengali proved his point. He already has my disks. What more does he want? Shit! I'm not hanging out in this mildewed tree all night."

Marisa puts a hand on my shoulder. Unbidden, heat rushes to my head. "I'll be back soon. Promise." With that, as quietly and swiftly as she raced through the forest earlier, Marisa disappears.

13.

I wait until the loose lock of hair streaking behind her as she runs is a distant orange blur before I follow. Freeze me! She's fast. And she knows the route. It's hard to avoid slamming into the trees as I madly try to keep up, while keeping quiet in the process. My suit is damp with sweat. Amazing the moisture hasn't blunted the suit's reflective qualities.

But it hasn't. I'm still a tree, then a crusty branch, and then a rugged boulder.

The ugly bird is following me again, flapping its ungainly wings just over my head. It's going to give me away. I throw a rock at it, which doesn't hit, but makes the bird veer off course and knock into a tree with a deliciously sharp clang. It's not a real bird. It's some kind of goddamn tracking device, isn't it? I'm tempted to go back and throw a bigger stone at it to bring it down, but there's no time.

"Flyover!" A man's cry echoes in wakes of sound that alarm me to the marrow.

"Hide!" a girl's voice—Nevada? There's the roaring crackle of underbrush nearby.

In a thicket of trees, each as wide as an AmphiTractor, I duck into a gaping trunk. These are the ancient trees caves my teacher told us about. Cool concept, except that it's pitch black in here and its walls are leeching slimy cedar mulch that sticks to my suit.

There's excruciating silence for about five minutes, except for my breath, which sounds as loud as a buzz saw. I'm imagining the moment the ZWC yanks me from safety, handcuffs me, or worse. The silence feels dangerous. I'm dizzy. It's hard to balance myself in this darkness. Try standing still in a midnight-dark simulation with a tilting carnival floor. Same deal.

More thwacking of branches outside, and loud voices boomerang my way again, a mere thirty meters or so from this trunk. *Hardly breathe*, I tell myself. After about five minutes, I smell some sort of grilled meat. A rumble of conversation follows.

I inch forward and peek out. Catch a flash of Marisa's red hair, her throaty voice. She's talking to . . . some guy, or really to his face, suspended in air. They must be sitting, because they are low to the ground. The guy's hood is down and his head exposed. He has on the same square earring Serge gave me from the loading dock, the same smirk and dark, heavy brows I recognize from the man in the frozen, grainy video image down in my dad's undervault.

A fury of adrenalin surges through me. It's Bryan, the head of the ZWC.

"So, you saw Varik. Big deal," Marisa is saying. "I left him somewhere in Yellow Axe. Call off your spies and you might see him later." *He saw me?*

"Yeah? Bring it on." Bryan has a deep, determined baritone voice that has me anxious. As my eyes become accustomed to the suit, I see the outline of his tall, lithe form flickering in the filtered light. The man seated on Bryan's other side is short, with the stumpy, weighted quality of a prizefighter who long ago stopped practicing. An oily sheen coats this man's wide baby face. He's got on the flame earring, too. He seems totally incongruous in this forest, where one must be light on his feet and ready to run. By process of elimination, this baby face must be Tornado, the guy Marisa said recorded their deeds.

They're all taking hunks of meat and tearing them with their teeth, as if they haven't eaten for days. Despite my state of wired alertness, my stomach rumbles.

I step out. Walk forward. They're huddled around the maw of yet another giant tree cave. Nevada emerges from it carrying a second plate of meat; apparently the grilling is done inside the tree. I notice that strung above the second tier of branches is a tarp of the same glinting scaled fabric.

Time to confront the tyrant. All conversation stops as I approach them.

Plunking his plate on the matted leaves by his stool, Bryan gets up and stalks over, rage coming off him like vaporized steam from the solar shield. "Hello there, Varik, how was the ride here from Vostok Station in your fancy red darter?" Marisa was right about Bryan's spy getting the goods on me.

"Just fine," I reply, holding my ground while he hovers over me.

Nevada shifts over to offer me the trunk seat between her and the greasy flubber-faced guy, who gives me a curious once-over before returning to his meat. As Marisa described, Tornado's gaudy blond dye job is slicked back with overbearing licorice oil. Yeah, it's definitely Tornado.

"What else do you know about me?" I ask Bryan.

He wastes no time in answering. "Fireseed," he says. "It's a beautiful plant—in concept, anyway. Tell me, does it exist in real form?"

"Marisa seems to be the expert on that. Marisa?" I want to see how much Marisa's in charge, or whether she kowtows to Bryan.

With a murky mix of fear and respect in her eyes, she turns to Bryan. "Tell him what we do here. I showed Varik the industrial video of his father." Bryan remains expectantly quiet. "Varik knew nothing about the Fireseed One project," she insists.

Bryan throws his head back and laughs. He lobs a bone onto a plate at the foot of the semi-circle of stools. "Give me a break, Farmer Boy. You're the Prof's son."

"I was only around five when all that was happening, so how would I know?"

"Liar!" Bryan jumps up and stares hard at me. Marisa tells him to ease off and he sits back down, but not without scaring the kidneys out of me. Marisa, for all her bravado, flinches as if she's scared of him, too.

"I have a sketch of the proposed plant," Nevada says helpfully. "I drew it myself."

Bryan throws Nevada a fierce look, as if he's promising a medieval punishment if she continues on this overgenerous track, and I can feel him poised to jump up again.

Nevada's hand hesitates over her pack. She nudges it back under the stool. "It's nothing. I drew it from some random notes a Zoner wrote up after seeing Professor Teitur's treatise. No one's ever found Fireseed. Everyone in the Zone's trying to track it down. Hunt of the century." She stuffs a handful of some charred leaf in her mouth with her grubby fingers, which forms an instant, cinematic image of Nevada as a cave girl in an extinct rainforest, leaping over palmettos and grazing on wild chard, her leaf tattoos moving to the rhythm of her jaw.

Tornado says through a mouthful, "You'd think we were back in the Stone Age. I heard that clans in the desert worship statues of Fireseed as if it were a god."

"A goddess," Nevada corrects him.

"And those notes weren't random," Marisa counters. "They were written up by a professional geologist, a serious interpreter of early research data. Why else would his spec notes fly like wildfire around the last scientists in the sectors?"

Bryan wags his hand dismissively. "Geo Man's been selling a bill of goods."

I think of the word *mimetolith* in my father's cert. Some kind of rock formation, I'm sure. It would be helpful to talk to this Geo Man. I'll ask Marisa where he lives. "Why would a professional geologist want to fool people?" I ask Bryan.

Bryan sneers at me. "Idiot! Everyone wants to find Shangri-La. Geo Man's collecting lots of cash for his maps and lectures."

"Geo Man knows what he's talking about," Nevada whispers.

"Where does he live?"

Bryan ignores both of us. He gets up and starts pacing so close to me I can feel the meat-laden breeze when he whips by. "If Fireseed's real, it could feed people and provide shelter from the killer sun," he says. "They say it could live without water in two-hundred-degree temps. Zoners are killing for water pellets and for a bunk in a sector where the sun can't bake them." He stops pacing and regards me with a look of pure animal hate. "You have no idea up in your snooty water paradise. I was born here, in an old swimming-pool shelter covered by car parts. And that was better than most had. We ate beetles, dried twigs, anything we could get to fill our stomachs." Bryan takes a swipe at me, clearly trying to intimidate me rather than make contact. He's a gigantic muscle clenched for battle with a hungry, crazed, and desperate expression. I picture that same look on the Zone creep who left my mother to die.

Yet, it's not what Bryan's saying that's cruel. He's right that I have no clue what it's like in the Zone, and that I live in a relative paradise. I can imagine he would be a go-getter organizer if he used all of his energy for the good. I'm sure the people need a leader, any help they can get. But there's more to this ZWC gathering than altruism. There's something murderously brutal here. I feel it in my bones.

Marisa gets up and touches Bryan's forearm. "It's okay, settle down. I'm sure Varik will see what we're trying to do here if we get him up to speed." She eases Bryan back down to his seat in a way that makes it seem like they've been lovers.

This might be calming Bryan down, but it's agitating me. What is my problem? If she left off this maddening boyfriend detail, what else did she neglect to tell me?

Averting my gaze to the wet rug of leaves underfoot, I watch finger-long white newts with rows of golden spots skitter about. There must be dozens in this patch of woods. Most are flicking their heads over the slimy pile of bones. They must congregate here for ZWC food droppings.

When Bryan's slightly calmer, and he's sitting so close to Marisa they're practically touching, I note with repulsion, I again ask Nevada to see her diagram.

"Look, Farm Boy, you don't get to see the goods," Bryan shouts. "I have a mind to take you out in these woods and—"

"Yeah? Try it," I say. My whole being is tensed to fight.

Marisa presses her arms on Bryan's shoulders, holding him down. "Let Nevada show him the diagram," she says to Bryan. "If it sparks Varik's memory of his father talking about Fireseed, we'll all benefit."

Bryan nods reluctantly for Nevada to proceed. So there are more important things to Bryan than hurting me. Nevada dives back into her pack, extracts the diagram. Pointedly avoiding Bryan, she unfolds it and hands it to me.

She's quite a decent artist. It's drawn in colored pencil. As before in my father's hidden chess video, I see a red plant with six pointed petals on the blossoms. Three side branches bend at mid-juncture like elbows. Each branch ends with four spiked "fingers." Nevada's drawn prickers on the stem larger than those on a sea rose. But, unlike a sea rose, these are of the same red, fleshy material as the stem, unless Nevada was careless with this detail. This seems unlikely, since she's meticulously drawn the thing on graph paper, and recorded the size.

Fry me! If I were standing in front of one, it would graze my chest. My dad wrote that they grew over five feet tall. If they're that conspicuous, why hasn't anyone in the Zone found any? I refuse to accept the logical answer, that they don't exist.

That the first crop of ten was the last.

"So," says Bryan, "Are you sure you haven't seen anything like it?" He chuckles. "With all your clout, surely you could've gotten a day pass to the Hotzone to hunt for it like all the other speculators." He stares hard at my face. "But I bet you wouldn't dream of burning your tender skin down there." At this, Marisa shifts away from Bryan.

I examine Bryan's face. His skin has a crackled, grainy consistency. And like antique tar that swelled and then shrank, there are buckles and narrow gullies around his cheekbones. Nevada's skin, too, is grainy and dull under her tattoos. As if she's gotten burn over burn over burn.

"I asked you a question, Farm Boy!" Bryan shouts.

"I told you, I haven't seen it."

"Some squirrel?" Tornado asks, as he lurches down to reach the plate on the low tree stump . . . and avoid my scrutiny? Unlike the others, his skin is dolphin-soft through the sheen. I was too busy trying to adjust to the whole weird environment to see the obvious.

Tornado hasn't spent time down in any Hotzone. Who is this guy?

I make a mental note to discuss this with Marisa as I rudely choose the piece of squirrel Tornado was reaching for himself. From the corner of my eye I see Bryan try to kiss Marisa on the cheek. She pulls away.

"So, Bryan, talk about the group. Why what we're doing here is so important," Marisa persists. Bryan doesn't comply. He frowns at her and looks back at me. I see who's in charge here. It makes me think of Lionfish, that deranged guru who had girls leaping to their death in hopes that they were saving the world.

Marisa said she needed to find a god, after her disillusionment with her father. This guy, though, is no god. I almost feel sorry for Marisa. *Almost.*

There's the matter of the agar disks. I'll have to breach the subject slowly. If I pretend to be interested in their world I might reap more benefits. "Let's put things on the table here, Bryan. You want something, and I want something, yeah?"

Small muscles twitch on Bryan's hard face as he considers my sudden offer. "What do you want?"

"First off, tell me about the sectors."

Tornado reaches into his pocket for a HipPod. Flicks it open and starts taking notes. Is there a flourishing black market for HipPods in the Zone? Doubtful, I think wryly. For sure, he's shopped in Ocean or Land D stores.

"After the disasters and the killings," Bryan says, "there weren't many of us left. Just the wily ones used to fending for themselves. You wouldn't have lasted a second."

"Tell me how the sectors communicate," I insist.

Bryan shrugs, toys with his earring. With a thick rush of hatred, I recall Serge handing me the earring from the loading dock. Did one of these thugs have something to do with what happened?

"Runners like Nevada carry things," Marisa explains.

Nevada takes over. "Folks cobbled the Net back together from dead computers in dead cities, but only in the few stable sectors, and it times out."

Bryan makes a noise between a clearing of his throat and a grunt. "A dust storm knocks things out for weeks. But I've dealt with that. I've worked on distribution for years, building drop-off centers in each sector for when we grow crops." He jabs me with his glare.

Nevada chimes back in. "Some sectors fare better than others. The one up in South Dakota where we get the suits is doing okay. People blasted for tunnels there, in the Black Hills. But in most sectors?" She shakes her head sadly. "They're fighting, stealing. The stress can drive you crazy. Last year, a desperado blew up two hundred thirty people in his sector, including his own family, before he was offed."

"You don't have to deal with things like that, do you?" Bryan stares at me. "What do you really want?"

I screw up my courage. "The seed disks."

"Don't know what you're talking about."

Now it's my turn to snort. "Don't BS me. My father's under-vault monitor took a video of your face just before you crashed it. I *saw* you down there."

Bryan pounds on his chest. "I need to feed my people. They've been waiting years for some edible greens to actually pick up from those distribution centers. In the meantime, they're living on cave moss, beetles. My people are ruined. To you I'm a terrorist. To them I'm their savior, Farmer Boy." Tornado and Nevada nod in solidarity. Only Marisa is still.

"Debatable," I mutter. If the people down here are mostly like Bryan, no wonder my father rejected them all. "Besides, you can't plant those seeds in that sun with no water."

Tornado has started taking furious notes. Nevada gets busy cleaning up the plates.

"Underground will work," says Bryan. "We've dug out a few plots. It would be a helluva better bet, though, if we could crossbreed them with a Fireseed plant. That's where you come in, Prof Son. That's what *I* want, even though you haven't had the manners to ask me."

At that, Marisa nods eagerly.

"Look, I'm no scientist like my father. I know nothing about Fireseed and I'm no expert on creating new Hercules plants. Tell you what: keep some of the seed disks. Just give me the agar disks."

"Impossible," Bryan bellows.

"Why?! They're mine. Give me those—" I'm out of my seat

and ready to kill him.

Marisa grabs me from the back and tries to hold me. "Let's talk calmly, Varik."

With Marisa still pulling back on my photonic suit, I repeat my question. "Why can't you give me those agar disks? You think we have utopia up in Ocean Dominion, but we have a serious, serious agar problem. It will spill over to the Zone. You think your people are bad off now? You eat *our* food that we ship *you*, fool. So, all of your people will starve and—"

"That's why I came back after Marisa went down," Bryan insists. "We reject your control. We don't want your miserly rations. I scored a big seed haul, but the agar disks weren't part of it. Must've been carried off by sea monsters." He sneers.

"Liar. Where are they? I'll mess you up." I surge forward, blood crowding my head.

"I said I never took those." He gets in my face. "Do it. Punch me, spoiled boy. You ain't worth the boots on your feet." He turns back to Tornado and winks.

Marisa weasels between us. "Bryan, come on. We need to keep our heads. Let's take a walk. Just you and me." Doesn't she have any self-respect? Can't she tell this live grenade off instead of trying to placate him?

Nevada breaks out in a relieved smile. "We'll hold down the fort, won't we, Tornado?" Tornado nods as he continues to scribble notes.

Bryan glowers at me. "We ain't done yet, Farm Boy."

Marisa latches her hand through his and urges him forward. She turns around and gives me a nod, saying silently that if I only hang tight she'll get him back to talking like a wise leader. Fat chance. I watch with a curious aching queasiness as they disappear into the forest.

14.

"What about your father's land down there?" Tornado asks the minute they're gone. He pauses from his writing to unfold a packet of half-eaten candy whose brand name, "Quell," I don't recognize.

"What do you mean?"

"I heard about your loss," he says with overdone sympathy. "I caught it on the Hotzone news one of the rare days the feed was up and running." He catches my look of disbelief and adds, "The northernmost sectors around Baron's construction site don't time out as much."

"Oh, uh-huh." I nod slowly. "What about my father's land?"

"It's just that . . . I assume it goes to you now. You hold the deed?"

"I suppose."

"Have you seen it? The deed?" He leans forward, causing the fat around his waist to bulge.

"Why would you care?"

"I . . . we may want to make you a deal."

"Why, Tornado?" Nevada asks suddenly. Now that she's finished clattering dishes, she's so retiring, and so hard to see in her suit, I almost forgot she was here. "Who needs the deed?" she says. "We can explore that land any time we want. No one's down there except that Fireseed cult." She glances over nervously, as if to get my approval.

All I do is smile back. *Stay cool,* I tell myself. *You'll learn more that way.*

"I have a copy of the deed," Tornado says, ignoring Nevada's question.

"How'd you get that?" I ask.

He chuckles, revealing teeth threaded with squirrel. "The ZWC doesn't believe in centralized government, so . . . We have our ways, don't we Nevada?"

"I suppose," she says, almost reluctantly. Unlike the corrupt but somewhat orderly governments of Ocean and Land D, the Third Dominion—the Zone—is pure anarchy.

Tornado claps once as a sort of punctuation. "Mr. Teitur, sign it and be done with it," he says. "It's not as if you'd ever vacation in that desert. There's no guest pool, no hotel, no buttery lobster dinner in any fancy restaurant." He wipes squirrel grease off his face with his cuff. When I don't answer him, he adds. "I . . . we could pay you in disks." He nods to another tree nearby. How stupid can the guy be?

"Pay me with something I already own, how ironic. Do you really *not* have the agar disks?"

"We don't. That part is true," Nevada exclaims. "Maybe they were swept far away in one of those recent monster storms. Bryan looked hard. They're lost."

Oh, Lord, no. I'm forced to find another solution. Fireseed, I've got to search for it. If that turns up empty, well then . . . God help us all.

During the painful silence that follows, I happen to glance

up at the trees. Those predatory birds are sitting in a row, staring down with a glassy emptiness. I make a face at them. Before I have time to comment on their presence, Tornado seems to remember what he was doing before this conversation. "Have a piece of candy, Varik, while you think about my offer." He hands me the reopened package. In it are squares of pink caramel, some with a tracery of fingerprints. He watches as I take one.

"I won't sign the deed," I say, "but I'll take a look at it." Tornado seems disappointed at my response. He tells me he'll be right back, and waddles into the tree trunk.

I toss the candy behind my seat and study the newts that quickly skitter over it. One by one they slow their pace until they're stumbling in slow motion over their padded feet. My stomach goes queasy at the sight. *I didn't mean for you to run toxin control,* I say silently to the poor newts.

Nevada sees them and gasps. "Sorry. I guess he wanted to force your signature," she whispers. "If they ever find that plant the land could be valuable." It seems it wasn't a group decision to poison me.

"You should get away from this Bryan guy," I whisper. "If I don't return, it was nice to meet you."

She startles, but settles quickly, as if she knew things would end this way. In her face I see sympathy for me, and a sense of defeat, as if she wasn't so bad off in her former life as a simple postal runner; as if working for the ZWC has drained her of hope. Though that could be my wishful thinking for an ally.

"I know Bryan's hard to understand from the outside," she whispers, as though she's trying to justify his cruelty to her. "But you were never a nomad like he is, going for days without food. You never saw your brother murdered for a handful of dried beetles like Bryan did, you never heard people moaning because their skin was shriveling up from the heat."

Sounds horrendous—like pure frying hell.

Warm fingers burrow into my hand. She deposits a folded

paper, as she puts her tattooed face close to mine. "My pager times out a lot in the Zone but . . ." Nevada whispers, "will you give the number to Marisa?"

I nod, then duck into the neighboring cave tree for as many latchbags of disks as I can find, and then I'm off just as Tornado clambers out of the tree.

It takes me longer this time to find Marisa. She can't be more than fifty meters in any one direction, but I'm frustrated, circling and circling. Just when I'm considering pressing the toggle to find her, I spot her up ahead. Lowering the three bags of disks I found as quietly as I can, I crouch behind a boulder. She and Bryan are standing in a grove of wide trees a stone's throw from me. They're close enough to kiss. I'd like to throttle Bryan, but I remind myself a spy plays it cool for good reason.

Information.

Marisa's talking in a hushed tone, almost as if she expected me to follow, and wants to ensure I don't hear this time. Or maybe Land D flyers pick up loud conversations.

I strain to hear her. "What I need to . . ." she starts, ". . . did you murder Professor Teitur?"

Shock clenches my throat closed. I struggle not to cough.

"Didn't do it," Bryan insists.

"I don't believe you." Marisa again.

"Come on, baby."

"Don't 'baby' me, Bryan. Tell me the truth. All of it."

"I was about to dock at the agar place," he starts hesitantly, "when I saw the Prof arguing on the loading dock with Tornado. He was holding some papers," Bryan starts.

"With Tornado? Did you authorize that? What papers?"

"No. I don't know. I asked Tornado later and he played dumb. He won't do that again."

I can only wonder what he did to Tornado. Must be talking about that copy of the land deed Tornado pushed on me. Bryan doesn't even know about it! Is Tornado working for himself or someone else? My head is spinning, trying to align all the odd angles.

"The Prof took them and Tornado grabbed them back," Bryan continues. "Looked like they were arguing about those papers. I hid until I saw Tornado's boat go out. Then I docked. I asked the Prof a few simple questions: Where's Fireseed One? Is there a secret crop? And what are the krypt codes to the vault? He refused to answer. Maybe I roughed him up a little, but I didn't kill him. When I left him on the galley floor he was breathing. His nose was bloodied up, and I had the krypt codes; that's all." A pause. "What do you think I am?"

My temples throb. This stinking rotfish smacked my father. That explains why his nose was broken. The urge to slug Bryan is overwhelming, as primal as breathing. I'll hear more, though, if I force myself to stay put.

"Who then?" Marisa asks. "Who killed him?"

"How should I know? Maybe Tornado came back. Me? I just came to do the plants."

My heart turns to stone. He poisoned all of our precious farms. Our lifeblood. His own food source too, the fool. Because of him we'll all starve. Because of one thoughtless idiot who thinks it's heroic to terrorize an entire Dominion.

"You poisoned the plants?" Marisa repeats, as if she wishes he'd tell her a different answer this time.

Bryan says, "Yeah, what of it? Did you get any real information from this Varik guy?" He's shouting now. "Is he really that clueless about Fireseed, or is he playing us?"

I want to coil a twine around Bryan's neck until it slices him in two. I'd stand there and spit on his seizing body.

Marisa avoids Bryan's question by launching into another track. "My assignment was to take a *latchbag* full of disks so we could seed crops—a token sortie to make a statement. Taking them *all* wasn't the plan. Raiding the inner vault wasn't the plan. And poisoning the agar fields was definitely not part of the plan.

How are you going to fix this one, Bryan?"

"A token sortie, that's lame," he sniggers. "I never promised to stick to that if we could get more seeds. That's like a starving person taking one carrot when he needs the whole bag."

"But Bryan! You wrote about the wisdom of *controlled* sorties in your own handbook."

"Sure, when I was young and wonky-eyed. Besides, what're you whining about?" Bryan throws up his hands. "I only *did* one floor, two at most. It was just to make them feel our pain. A *token* sortie, just your style," he says in a mocking tone.

Ocean Dominion and its wonderful, innocent people, as well as all the other people in the world, will now slowly starve because of this . . . this evil incarnate.

"No," Marisa says, "you killed off the *entire supply*, all of the agar farms in the Dominion. Ocean D sends the Hotzone food shipments, always has. They feed *us*, too, Bryan!"

"I know that. But a stingy amount." He pauses. "You're joking about the crops, right?'

"I wish." The finality of Marisa's two words destroys me all over again.

"We've got lots of their seed disks," Bryan reasons as he starts to pace. "We'll figure out how to grow them in the Zone. We already have garden plots dug underground in three sectors. We don't need squat from Farmer Boy." He bursts out in frenzied laughter. I duck down as he paces my way.

"Bryan, what's so damn funny? You can't grow enough underground in a few plots to feed the Zone. Plants need sun, so you need something to fortify the seeds against the solar rays and lack of water. You need Fireseed, or something as powerful." Marisa goes on. "Plus, you could've been more careful with the disks, Bryan. They were all over the seabed."

"We'll dig more plots. Organize more workers. Hey, whose side are you on? You have a crush on that rich geek."

"No way."

"I see the mushy look in your eyes. Some operative you are. Guilty as charged."

"I was a good operative. I only took a few disks, as per the plan. But you freaking drained that vault. We wanted to make a *statement*, not ruin the guy's life, and the entire world."

"Who cares if we ruin his life? His father ruined the refs' lives."

"His father isn't him. I thought you had ethics." Her voice is thick with disgust.

"I do, baby." His footsteps stop. There's silence and a smacking noise. I peer out over the rock. He's trying to kiss her but she's shifting her face away. It's sick. I want to smash the guy's head with a stone.

"What's wrong?" It's Bryan's voice. More silence. I imagine them communicating through facial expressions or . . . touch, and the question of what they might be saying—or doing—is driving me mad.

"No." Marisa's whispering. "Don't. No more. Never!"

I peek out. Good Marisa. She's shoving him away.

"You're a weak operative, falling for the enemy," Bryan roars. "You looked *us* up. You said what a revolutionary you were, how you hated all the crooked, rich rats, especially your father. You said you'd do anything for the cause. You cried crocodile tears over the refugees' situation."

"You're wrong, Bryan. The refs are why I got involved. That hasn't changed."

"You don't care about the refs. Why should you? You have everything you need up in Baronland—fancy food, fast darters, luxe condoplexes. Your rich dad to shell out cash by the fistful."

"Just because I wasn't born a ref doesn't mean I don't care deeply, I—"

"Little Miss Activist got bored, is that it? Wanted a hot hookup from the enemy she was supposed to be getting the goods on. From a bloated pig in Ocean D, who hogs all the farms—"

"Not *all* the farms."

"Varik represents every cause we're fighting against. Closing the Beltway to refs, hoarding all the best food, ignoring the human devastation in the Zone, holding out on new science that could help us, like Fireseed. It's criminal. Yeah, I killed his father. I rolled him over off the loading dock after breaking his nose. Wanna know why? He called us scum. He said the people in the Hotzone weren't worth the slime on his boot heels. Yeah. Go comfort your spoiled boyfriend, you slut. I should—"

I watch Marisa slap Bryan hard, and then his fist hits her flesh with a meaty thwack as I fly out of the tree and plant my own curled fist, bull's-eye, in his mug. He stumbles backwards and falls, scrambles back to his feet.

I punch him again and again and again. My fist is dripping with his blood and I keep on.

When Marisa pulls me off him, I see, with grim satisfaction, that I've broken his nose like he did my father's. I hope he's dead. Leave him here like he left my father, and like some ref left my mother to die.

Marisa's cheek is bruised. Tears blot her iridescent eyes. "I'm sorry," she says to me. "So very sorry. He killed your father. Oh, God. I was crazy to get involved with him, and the whole ZWC. Way too idealistic. Misguided. He hypnotized me, or something. It's so screwed up. *I screwed up.* I ruined things. Forgive me, Varik, please."

"No." I watch blood drip from my fist and wet the leaves by my feet. "Don't know if I can."

"Try. Please try. I'm so sorry, so sorry," she murmurs over and over.

"I'll do one thing," I say, shaking off my hands. "Lift up your hair."

She does it without question.

I take out the toggle decoder and graze the nape of her neck with it. A blinking light on the device tells me that the InvisiTag is dissolved. "It's done. Over. You're free to go."

I'm shaking, partly from rage, partly from the recurring memory of seeing my father's battered, swollen, and waterlogged face undulating in the current.

She reaches out her hands to touch my face.

The sun, through the filter of the trees, glints green off the cells of her suit, outlines her soft curves. I'm overcome with visions of my father poring over his books, and the wet, verdant forest floor, and newts pausing over toxic yellow candy, and leaves flying up from the impact of Bryan's body hitting the ground. Another, confused part of me hears my father's voice calling the refs scum, trash, slime. With flashes of fury at Marisa, mixed with a sad, all-consuming longing that feels dangerously like love, I pluck her hands from my face and push her away.

15.

We hoof it back to Yellow Axe to discover gouges in the side of the darter, and a nasty chip in the rear porthole the size of a sea apple. Looks like someone tried to smash it with a sizable rock. It must not be common knowledge in the Zone that pressurized agar's resistant to almost anything. I can deal with the rock damage, but the thing that truly bothers me is the "ZWC" someone scratched in the paint by the driver's door. Audun would blow a gasket over some weed tagging his custom job. I pack in the seed-disk bags. Taking cover on the far side of the darter, I gladly peel off the girly leotard and get back into my clothes. Although Marisa cautions me to leave it on, I notice when I come back around that she's taken her off camouflage in favor of her street clothes too. I study her body in the tight blue suit, though I'd never tell her that. We throw our gear in the back hatch.

What she says next catches me way off guard. "I'll prove it to you."

"What're you talking about?" I know exactly what she's talking about, but I want to put her on the spot.

"I'll prove that I'm not a shallow, impulsive fool. That I'll help fix the mess I helped cause."

"Ha! How?"

"I'll help you get down to the Hotzone. Turn you on to my contacts down there."

"Contacts like Bryan?" I snort. "Who needs contacts like that? You have the worst taste in guys."

"He wasn't my boyfriend."

"What was he, then?" My rage over Bryan flames up again into a giant firestorm. I scream, "Do you make it a habit to go around pawing criminals who aren't your boyfriend? Who frying murder people? You picked the wrong god, baby."

"Yeah. I know. Very wrong! I'm so horribly, horribly sorry about your dad. Look, I told you. I have a lot to learn."

"You sure do, you clueless girl."

"Don't rub it in." Marisa's crying now. Good. Let her feel as deep a pain as I felt over my dad.

"I'm going down to look for Fireseed," I announce dryly. "Or *something*." I lock eyes with her. "I suppose you need a ride home. I'll drop you in Land Dominion."

"Let me go with you," she says, wiping her tears with her sleeve.

"Why? I mean, you don't want to be impulsive, or anything like—"

"I know where we can get heat-shield clothes there. I know where Geo Man lives. I want to help make things right."

I burst out laughing. "You have a terrible way of showing it."

"True." She shoves dry twigs around with her boot.

So, maybe she's still half on their side. Who knows? Fact is, I do need to talk to Geo Man, and I need clothing to keep me from burning up. I can have a secret life, too. I think of the Fireseed cert, and that second cert I found, and it gives me hope.

"Look, it's dangerous," I say. "You heard your great, wise ex-ZWC guru."

"Shut up, Varik," she says softly, in a tone that, despite my fury, shoots a different kind of flame through me.

"On one condition," I say.

"Yeah?" she says with an upturn.

"Stop being impulsive."

"That's what I'm talking about."

We soar over Yellow Axe toward the border, sharing a weighted silence, probably both of us still smarting. I know I am. The view is so spectacular, though, that it's hard to brood. From up here in the clouds, the tree clusters below form abstract pools of green. It reminds me of the way the ocean changes color whenever I sail from shallow reef to deep water.

"We should've asked Nevada how the ZWC hacked through the border here," I say. "But since we didn't, we could try crossing the border to the Zone out over the Pacific Ocean. Out there, there are probably fewer aerial border guards."

"From what insufferable Melvyn used to tell me, I doubt it." Marisa finishes rubbing her sore feet propped on my dashboard, and slips her boots back on. "Oh! Good news, though," she adds. "When Bryan was trying to grab me, I jacked his hack-code to the border." She fishes in her pocket for a scrap of paper. "My first attempt to make it right. Hack-code to sector 9,570 to be exact."

"No kidding?" The devilish gleam in her eyes confirms it. "Marisa, you are fryin' unbelievable!" I pound the steering wheel for emphasis. Got to give the girls props, even though she's a wicked one.

Turns out that sector isn't far. The ZWC only trekked in about fifty kilometers to set up their counsel grove. Even though in this remote area the guards may all be robos, it's no wonder the ZWC wear the photonic chameleon suits. Who wants to be caught by a border guard! If everything's ruined down in the Zone, how does their contact in Dakotas get fabric? I make a note to ask Marisa later.

After punching in the coordinates, we auto-coast toward the mythical Herculean border that I've never actually seen. As I stretch back in my seat to rest, Land D's Stream buzzes in my head. It gives me pause, and reminds me of the precarious nature of the two agar plants in my father's office. I pray that Audun isn't too busy partying to baby them.

Land Dominion uplink: Supplies of agar have become scarce since it was revealed that Ocean Dominion's production has fallen way below expectation. Farmers from Ocean Dominion are tight-lipped about this, yet we have learned from Stream sources that a serious blight has occurred, similar to the White Spore of 2081. That blight killed off one-third of the agar crop. With the devastating loss of Professor Teitur earlier this year, the likelihood of quickly hybridizing a blight-resistant strain is slim. In the meantime, restaurants in Land Dominion are substituting agar with Finnish kelp. Because of its scarcity, they are forced to raise prices. Both Dominions urge people not to panic, as they are working hard to solve this.

Brought to you by Baronland Emporium, where total hair reorg is as easy as shopping for blintzes or skygolf clubs.

"It was only a matter of time before the rumors started swirling," I say darkly.

"At least no one's sure of the hard facts yet," she replies.

"The border!" A welcome, but unsettling distraction. "Sweet, sullied ice, we're here."

It's the total intimidation I imagined and more. From the approach, I see a white, monolithic partition, taller than the trees and blinking red and blue, snaking on beyond either side of the horizon. It's a nightmare agar conglomeration of all the historic barriers that kept people out and people in; a Berlin wall, a Great Wall of China, the Mexican borderland of the old Southwest.

We land in a forest just north of the border. Even though it's spring and leaves should be at their greenest, many of the leaves on the tall, thin trees have crumpled to the ground. It's almost as if they recognize this as a death zone, and have withered in response. It takes us about fifteen minutes to hike to the wall, and we're concentrated on the task ahead.

"Brace yourself," Marisa warns.

"What do you mean?"

"You've probably only seen photos of it, but I've *lived* by the border in Baronland. I just mean, prepare to be overwhelmed."

"Ah. Okay."

Closer now, from about sixty meters away, I can see the wall is much taller than skyscrapers on Tundra Island, or any condoplex in Restavik, the only Land D city I've traveled to. If this wall were a condoplex, it would have about two hundred floors. But this thick wall has no windows, only a gigantic holo image of a Fleet guard on each forty-meter-wide section. The sections connect seamlessly, to give the impression of one continuous line of impenetrable soldiers. Halfway up the wall a flashing yellow news crawl travels horizontally along the beltline of each guard, as far as the eye can see.

In a commanding male voice, the wall broadcasts slogans that appear on the crawl: *Bliss is a tight Beltway; Bake Below the Belt; The Hotzone isn't Healthy for Living Things; Chaos Rules Below the Border; Refs are Armed; Shoot on Sight; Root out Refs; Hell is the Hotzone!* They are ingrained brain worms; I've heard them so many times on the Stream since childhood I can recite every word without thinking.

At only twenty meters from the border, peering through the final line of trees, I gasp. Its enormity up close takes my breath away. I'm microscopic plankton flitting on the open jaw of the Loch Ness Monster.

The holos projected on the surface of the sections show bold graphic guards: their helmets and dark glasses, heavy mustaches, navy uniforms, and maroon storm boots. Each holo soldier's helmet is branded with its own sector number.

I see, with a hard pulse of fear, the numerical match to the border section Bryan hacked through. *Section Number* 9,570 is emblazoned on the giant helmet straight ahead.

Each section also has a guardhouse. The guardhouse is a boxlike structure about the size of my outdoor storage shed. Four mobile GuardBots stand at attention in front of each guardhouse. The bots wear the same threatening uniform but are only about seven feet tall and seem to be on OFF. Who knows what activates them. I see no live guards; still, that doesn't fill me with confidence.

There's something peculiar about the last line of trees running along the front of the Beltway border. Aside from the fact that they are white and leafless, they are peppered with holes. I point them out to Marisa.

"They aren't trees, Varik, they're killer lasers," she whispers. "They'll shoot down any flycar. And if they sense a refugee, they shoot."

"Will they sense us?" My gut pinches in terror.

"Yes, but we have Stream implants that ID us as full citizens of the North, you know? If refs have implants, they're phony IDs. They're not registered on this side of the border."

Oh, please. I hope this trip to the Hotzone is worth risking my life, and I hope it's not too late to save that agar. I wonder what Audun's doing now. Is he helping Serge care for the plants, or dancing with Brigitte at the clubs?

We advance through the white "trees." Marisa's given me the hack-code. It starts with BORDERVAPORIZEREFS—and then launches into a series of numbers and letters it took me an hour to memorize. The plan is for me to plug in the code at the BotLink guard station up ahead. It's the last thing holding us from the mythic passage to the Zone. This hack-code will supposedly crash the four BotLink guards, now activated, standing at attention in front of the station, blinking and reciting border phrases to the rhythm of the crawl. Then, the hack will supposedly release the lock to the access tunnel. Hopefully it will remain open for enough time to run for the darter and zip through.

I worry that we haven't packed supplies. This is ill planned. I was so busy trying to figure how to get *through* I didn't think of what we would eat—or drink. What if we can't find food or water for days? I curse myself for not thinking of all the details.

And now we need to do this.

The bots are only slightly taller than me and only machines, I remind myself. Still, I'm so flummoxed I'm afraid I'll space out the code. I worry they'll detect the motion of my trembling hands as easily as a shark detects the scent of blood. As I march forward I picture my body blown into gushing holes from the laser trees. Marisa follows, though I recommended she stay put behind the laser trees. I still have misgivings about her, but I'd be upset if she were hurt.

I reach the station. The guards are still motionless, babbling fools. *This will work,* I tell myself as I approach one. *I can do this. Yes.* I raise my arm toward the keypad on the guardhouse.

An earsplitting alarm sounds. All four BotLinks seamlessly glide over and surround us. "Citizen Varik Teitur," one blares, "what is your business in this sector?"

"I'm uh . . . taking a vacation?" I squawk.

"The Hotzone is presently one hundred forty-one degrees over the south wall. Passage is denied. Citizen Marisa Baron," it adds, "an all-points Fleet stream is out on you. Report to Fleet in progress."

She steps forward and brashly flicks back her tangled mop of hair. "Abort the report. Your system is infected with a bad virus, because I'm not *that* Marisa." Her bravado amazes me.

"Your implant reads Marisa Baron of Baronland," pipes up another. "Access denied. All-points bulletin is active at this time. Sending message to Baronland Fleet. In addition, border crossing is impossible at this Section Number 9,570. Section is under repair."

"You heard the lady, she's not *that* Baron," I insist, as I stare into the bot's insensible brown eyes. "If you don't revise that Fleet message, I will report back that you are seriously malfunctioning, and recommend your immediate takedown."

A third bot guard adds, "BotLink malfunction, affirmative. Three weeks ago ZWC hackers crashed this section."

"Have any of the hackers been apprehended?" Marisa asks in a voice that sounds a bit too concerned. We just left the ZWC, so it's unlikely they were, but I'd certainly be overjoyed if Bryan's skeleton decorated this stretch of forest for years to come.

The fourth bot says in a loud monotone, "We are hunting the hackers. We will apprehend them. Anyone using hack-code starting with BORDER will be terminated on sight."

Marisa and I exchange horrified glances. I'm sooo glad I didn't type in that code!

"You've been very informative," I assure the bots. "We'll totally rethink our vacation, and good luck in finding those hackers." Marisa and I back away, facing them.

"Varik Teitur," a bot drones, as it starts to follow us at a frighteningly fast clip, "the Stream informs us that you are to return immediately to Ocean Dominion. The Stream says—"

"You need debugging," I yell back. "The hackers royally wormed up your mainframe!" Marisa and I jog steadily backwards as they continue to zoom toward us, babbling about the Stream, and Baronland, and Melvyn Baron.

Just after the white tree line we turn and run, as casually as possible, despite the fact that my blood is pounding through the roof of my mouth.

We're back in the sky, and miraculously no Fleeters have tracked us, and the bot guards are about fifty kilometers below and behind us.

"That was really, really bad," I say. "I have another idea, though."

"What?" Marisa's pulling at her tangles, and yelping when she tugs too hard on a knot.

"Your father goes down to his construction site in the Zone any time he wants, right?"

She stops tugging at her hair and glares at me. "Not that. Don't even think of it."

"What other options do we have, Marisa?"

"You heard that bot guard. I'm, like . . . *wanted*."

"Maybe if you spoke to your father?"

"Not an option." She rips apart a knot with particular malice. "I may have been impulsive in joining the ZWC," she admits, "but my decision to testify against the megalomaniac they call my father, well, that wasn't done on any mere impulse." She looks hard at me. "Varik, I told you, the man doesn't care about me, or anyone. He uses people as slaves."

Marisa looks more dejected than mad, and I have an odd urge to tuck a curl behind her ear and promise I wouldn't hurt her like that. Instead, I say, "Just because you're working on your impulsiveness doesn't mean you have to throw away your good impulses. You wanted to help people . . . even if it meant hanging out with Bryan."

"Guilty as charged," she admits. "But I have limits. You have your limits, too," she argues, louder. "You're just going down to hunt for Fireseed. Not to help the refugees."

I pull back. "Now wait a minute . . ."

"See? You hate the refs." Her narrowed eyes gleam. "If you're willing to suspend judgment until you're down there and try to connect with some of them, I'll consider your plan."

The refugees. Mistrusting them is so ingrained in me I can't help suspecting they're all a bunch of cons and thieves like Bryan. Is that any better than Marisa assuming Bryan is an eco-guru? Fair is fair.

I groan. "All right, I'll try."

"Deal." She goes back to pulling out her tangles, less roughly.

16.

It takes us six hours to reach Baronland. Even from a distance I can see it's a carnival of blinking lights, swirling buildings, and elaborate holo banners floating in the sky that spell out *Baronland*. We enter under cover of night and park in a seedy outdoor lot for an exterminator called "Bug Off!" on the edge of the city. We'll have to take the air-train in. Marisa reminds me that every Streamerazzo would kill to interview not only her, but now me. It's annoying to have to avoid them again. Before I curl up in the darter seat for the night, I manage to scratch away the ZWC tag on my door with my small fish knife. It wouldn't do to have some grunt bug killer turn us in to the Stream. We rig up disguises for tomorrow's trek into Baronland for supplies—sunglasses and bandanna over braided, pinned up hair for Marisa, sunglasses and light jacket for me.

Now that we're back in range, I call Audun on my HipPod.

It rings and rings. I'm about to click off when he answers, out of breath. "Hey, Drifter! I just sailed in from SnowAngel. How the heck are you?"

"Fine, fine. Hey, thanks for sending the you-know-who on a wild-goose chase."

"Just say the word and I'll . . ."

"Yeah? You friendly with some news guy?"

"Better, dude. Working angles."

"How are the . . . you know?" I won't use the word *agar*. Big Brother was watching way back in 1984, and the Fleet continues the ignoble tradition. Plus, Marisa still knows nothing about them.

"Still hanging on," says Audun. "A couple of the, um, appendages dropped, though."

"Oh, no." My mood crashes.

"Sorry to say."

"You and Mr. S. on the case?"

"What do you take me for? I'm a doting mommy, and Mr. S. is the pro. Where are you?" He's silent for a moment. "No, I won't ask."

"How's Juko?"

"'Fraid I haven't seen him."

"Keep looking, okay? Will you send the you-know on another . . . you know?"

"No problemo." A pause. "Drifter?"

"Yeah?"

"They're freaking up here."

I gulp hard. "They know?"

"'Fraid so."

"Taking care of biz. Call you again soon." I feel flat and dead when I click off.

"What?" Marisa asks, leaning toward me.

"The people know," I whisper. "They know about the agar."

Audun works fast. The morning air-train to Baronland ends with an uplifting Stream:

The latest on the "Snorkling for Gems" show! Audun Fleury, friend of Varik Teitur, the young proprietor of the now-troubled ocean farms in Vostok, claims to have spoken to both Varik and Marisa Baron, daughter of Land D mogul, Melvyn Baron, on two separate occasions.

Marisa and Varik may have met at L'Ongitude and shared one sim-ride, but there's zero truth to the rumor they're an item, Fleury insists. Marisa has journeyed to the Bering Sea for design inspiration in the unique wave formations there. She says that the arching turquoise plumes have already begun to inspire her next boot design, the Bering Booty.

Fleury also reports that Varik took off on a Chinese desert expedition to track extremophile bok choy to replace crops lost in the blight. Teitur stressed that he would very much appreciate being left alone.

Brought to you by Fleury Darters, where a ride isn't a ride until it's a Fleury WaveRyde.

"Working angles, no shit."

Marisa and I collapse in weak, relieved giggles.

The air-train deposits us on the twenty-fifth floor of the Baronland Emporium.

It's a mind-boggling conglomeration of shops in a condoplex disguised as an old Euro-style castle. It does have a Medieval feel to it. Mutton, rabbit, and Restavik boar hang with staring eyes and flagging ears from dangling clamps. Cooks, in front of their respective stores along the hall, sauté up fragrant goodies for the onlookers. Funny, I had almost begun to see Marisa as a grizzled Zoner, but it hits me all over again: she grew up in luxury. This place has far more amenities than whatever Ocean Dominion offered.

People flow by us, staring at our get-ups, probably wondering why we're wearing sunglasses in this rather gothic environment lit by thick fake torches set in wall sconces. I notice that Land Dominion grows its folks tall and ruddy. Must be all that meat.

Marisa and I gulp down brewed coffee and freshly fried nut-meg donuts in one shop. They taste like manna after the tough, sinewy squirrel I choked down in Yellow Axe.

On the next tier up we amble by the Shoe Palace, where, according to the Stream, the great Melvyn Baron wistfully wishes his daughter would work. After that, we study the Emporium's map designed like a Crusader's battle plan. What is this bizarre fetish for castles? We search on the map for which tier the camp store is on. We'll need supplies for the grueling trip ahead.

Next to the map is a large-screen holo of a man with small, determined eyes set far apart in a pumpkin-shaped head. He's chattering on about the Emporium. The guy has a receding red combover despite the obvious facial reorg that's smoothed out his skin. His mouth wears an almost girly pout. It's heart-shaped like . . . Marisa's.

"Let's go." Marisa pulls me away the second we finish reading the map.

"Whoa, whoa." I yank away from her grip. Fascinating. I've seen the combover guy on the Stream, but never up close up like this.

"Want to look like a true Baron?" The man booms. "Shop at the King's Throne." He winks. "Take it from me, Melvyn. Whether you're shopping for a gold-threaded tie or a luxe con-doplex, at Baronland Emporium you'll score a royal ransom."

I break out in loud guffaws. "That's your fryin' dad!"

"Shush! You're blowing my cover." Marisa pokes me in the side. "Plus you're so not funny," she growls, as holo-Melvyn repeats his jingle. She fumes silently all the way to the airlift.

On the fifteenth tier, in the camp store, aptly called *Journey Beyond,* we collect enough vacuum food packs for three weeks. Also two silvery-celled burn suits that are more substantial than the photonic suits from Yellow Axe. We find moleskin for injured feet and Sonic Blast Sunbloc, which will surely be a lame joke against the roaring sun.

A colorful display of water pellets catches my eye. *New product!* it brags. I pick one up. It's a round, blue tablet the size of my fist with an etched-in logo. "Look, Marisa, this says Vegas-by-the-Sea. Does that mean this tablet was *made* in the Hotzone?" That would require much more Zone organization than I ever imagined possible. She says she has no clue. "How many times have you actually been to the Hotzone?" I ask her.

"I've been to Ye Old Blowhard's construction site in Dominion South a bunch," she says.

"Beyond that?" I ask. Marisa's hard enough to read without sunglasses, near impossible to read under her shades.

"No-oo," she admits reluctantly.

So, Marisa's never actually met any refs deep in the heart of the desert. She's a frying novice, too. *Fitting,* I think darkly.

I throw three-dozen water pellets in the basket and find a tank of oxygen and smaller ones of hydrogen, required to actually *make* water. They're cumbersome, but there's no way we'll venture down there without them. If we dragged down the amount of real water equivalent to the pellets and tanks, the darter would be too heavy to fly.

The checkout guy, an outdoorsy type wearing hike shorts, gives us the once-over, as if very few folks actually buy the oxygen and hydrogen tanks or burn suits. Or maybe he's gawking at my spray jacket that screams, *Waterlogged tourist from Ocean D!*

"You going hiking in the Hotzone?" he says, as if it's a big blubbery joke.

"Yeah," says Marisa, "It's a hobby of ours to get fourth-degree burns!"

The guy laughs raucously. I'm half afraid he's going to report two crazies to the Fleet, but we get out of there without incident and struggle down the hall with our loaded packs.

"You should call your father," I tell Marisa. "We need access to the construction entrance. And what about that all-points bulletin out on you?"

"That's a problem," she agrees, but doesn't open her HipPod to make a call. Further past the camp store we see a hair-reorg shop, and then a mood-reorg center promising to elevate your mood for an entire year or all your money back. After that are a string of simulation rides, which seem to attract ninety percent of Baronland's under-twenty-one set. They hover around the entrances, more interested in chatting, sipping drinks, and trying to strike poses than in riding sims.

Audun has way more panache, I think, than these drones with their preppy Land-style pants and clubby shirt logos.

Marisa's the exception. I won't flatter her, though.

One sim game does have an eager line snaking clear back to the hair-reorg shop. I read its advert:

Hotzone Expedition! Feel the lethal heat, see roving murderous refugee tribes up close and personal, witness the primal rituals of the Fireseed cult, survive monster-beetle attacks!

An unwelcome preview of the hell we're about to plunge into? The holographic cult guy has on a witchy red cowl. Okay, but monster-beetle attacks? A stretch, or what? I certainly hope so. We step up our pace to pass it when my eye catches on a head of gaudy yellow hair and a wide greasy face ducking behind a throng of teens.

I nudge Marisa. "I saw Tornado!" Without moving my head I roll my eyes toward the spot behind the kids. "He's over there."

She scans the throng. "I don't see him. How could he have gotten here, and why would he?"

I explain how he tried to drug me and wheedle me into signing a copy of my deed to the land in the Hotzone. "Bryan probably gave him orders to do me in because I found out too much. As much as you hate to, Marisa, you have to call your . . . father. We need to get across the border fast, to start looking for Fireseed, or answers to what's on that land."

"Don't make me call him." She sounds like a fretful toddler.

"At the very least we need him to call off the all-points."

Marisa's expression is drawn yet stubborn. She slows her pace, pulls out her HipPod, flips through the numbers and taps one. "I did promise to help fix this." She sighs. "I'll call Freddie instead."

Her father's infamous spokesman booms clear through the earpiece, "Miss Baron, you're back! What an honor you thought of me first."

"I need a face-to-face."

"You get right to the point; I appreciate a lady after my own heart. Meet me at the Sky Turret in say—"

"Five minutes," says Marisa, as if she's aware Freddie was onto our landing at the "Bug Off!" lot and is now trailing us through the Emporium. Disturbing thought. Is he right behind us? Watching us walk as he chats us up on his HipPod? Whipping around to confront him, all I see is an elderly couple sharing a cookie and a flock of kids strolling along near them.

"Freddie, we're wearing sunglasses," Marisa adds, and then clicks off.

17.

Freddie Vane is a real piece of work. We've only been sitting at
the Sky Turret Bar for a mere three minutes when he strolls in. I
recognize him from the Stream. He's on there a lot. Other people recognize him too and shift in their seats to study him. His
nails are manicured and glossy, his high-cheeked face is inscrutable and flawless. No visible pores; he's had facial reorg for sure.
A tattoo of a snarling Restavik boar with its funny square ears
pokes out from under his impeccably cuff-linked suit-sleeve.

"He's a master manipulator," Marisa warns. "He's used to
being a hard-core player, and it irks him that he has to treat me
with kid gloves. But he's devoted to my father and he'll do anything to get me back with him," she adds just before he reaches
us. I nod, take it all in.

With a snap of his finger, Freddie scores us a seat in the VIP
area by the floor-to-ceiling windows. Astonishingly, it overlooks
the border wall into the unfinished condoplex, and the Hotzone
beyond. Enormous construction project, with AmphiTractors

and upcranes and scaffolds and then nothing more than flat, dull brown ground that stretches on beyond where I can see. I flinch. We could soon be treading on that dry expanse of nothing.

I order Restavik rye beer; Marisa, an Emporium Ale. Freddie orders a highball. With his pinky out showing off his chunky diamond ring, he tips the drink into his mouth.

Quite a piece of work.

Marisa, sitting next to Freddie, plunges in. "Why the all-points bulletin out on me?"

Freddie eases into a slick grin. "Can't Melvyn Baron be worried about his only daughter?" He leans close to her and says in a confidential tone, "It's your seedy involvement with the ZWC."

"Melvyn can stuff it," spits Marisa. "Report me to him, what do I care? Tell him I'm here and I have no time for him. He disinherited me, I disinherited him, so why does he give a good . . ." More than a few customers whirl around in their seats to stare, trying to figure out who the rude stoners in shades are, upsetting high-end mover–and-shaker Mr. Vane.

Freddie sighs loudly, as if he's trying to reason with a stubborn child. "He's not well. Your father had, uh, an episode."

"What're you talking about?" Marisa asks sharply.

"He had a minor heart attack a few weeks ago. It slowed him down, made him think."

Marisa plunks down her drink. I try to determine whether or not she's upset by this news, but her face is unchanged. "Get the Fleet to call off the all-points bulletin," she says, as if she totally disbelieves what Freddie Vane said about her father and won't even consider it. She did warn me that Freddie is a seasoned manipulator. One would have to be, to survive as Mr. Baron's publicist.

"I can't. The wheels are in motion." Freddie flicks an olive onto a cocktail napkin.

"Stop them. You have the power. You work for my father."

Freddie shrugs. "Why should I upset him in his delicate

condition? Should I tell him his daughter was here, but left yet again without seeing him? Are you going to move back, stop your wild ways? Make peace with him? That's the only way I'd even consider it."

Marisa groans. I never thought of her as a brat, as sadistically torturing her father. But there are two sides to any story—at least two sides.

"She'll cut you a deal," I blurt out. Then I glance at Marisa to make sure she won't resent me for butting in. She raises her sunglasses and stares at me.

For the first time since we've been here, Freddie runs his eyes over my spray jacket, my scruffy hair. "We were never introduced . . . you must be the Professor's son."

"I am," I answer. "If Marisa's willing to speak directly with her father, will you promise us clear passage over the border to the construction site? No guard ID, everything anonymous."

"Marisa?" Freddie waits for her response.

She snaps her sunglasses back down and snorts derisively. "I don't need a chauffeur. I've gone back and forth a million times. I'm the boss's daughter!"

I point to myself. "But I do," I say under my breath, because more people are starting to gape at us. "Guards will ID me. How will I pass? And the all-points out on you."

Marisa's mouth tightens as she turns to Freddie. "You heard Varik—no press, no Fleet, drop the all-points, just usher us through and I'll speak to him," she says sharply. Things might be easier if she would relax. If she doesn't blow up when she sees her father and abort our whole precarious plan.

Freddie says, "I have your absolute word that you'll speak to Mr. B. after his lunch meeting with his architects?" Freddie sounds stressed. It's obvious that however suave and take-care-of-biz he is, he cares deeply about his boss's personal welfare.

"Call him now, Freddie," I blurt out. "Tell him Marisa's in town. That way she can't back out."

"Hey!" Marisa jabs me. "That's unnecessary."

"I want to hear Freddie tell him."

"It's not up to you," Marisa hisses.

"It's partially up to me," I counter. "We need this to happen."

"Yeah, okay. Let's do it," Marisa remarks with a sigh.

Freddie looks from me to Marisa. For a moment he drops his blasé pose, sagging in confusion. But he must think I make sense, because he flips open his HipPod and runs a finger over the keypad.

"Mr. B. Me, Freddie. Got a hot hunk o' news here. Your daughter's in town."

Melvyn starts yelling, "Where is she? Get her over here! Did you talk to her?" Freddie must've forgotten the thing was on speaker. He turns down the volume, but not before more people look over. I get up, too, and stand off to one side of Freddie in order to peek at Melvyn on videophone as Freddie explains that Marisa's not here but she promised to speak to him following his meeting.

"Did that ZWC worm mess her up? I'll murder the guy!" Melvyn rants on lowered volume. All the while Marisa's sitting squarely out of video range with her arms crossed, staring straight ahead.

I must say, Melvyn looks bedraggled, almost jaundiced compared to his holo-advert. White roots are poking out of his scalp under the red dye. So even a Baron can look like a train wreck. I sit back down next to Marisa, who stares at the bar with a melancholy gaze.

Freddie sets a meet time, clicks his phone closed and pockets it. "Toast to the meeting?" he says tentatively. Marisa barely raises her glass, but I clink Freddie's glass with zeal.

Marisa tells Freddie in a flat, robo tone, "We'll meet you in two hours in the ground-floor Emporium lot closest to the border entrance. You'll need to give clearance to a dinged-up red darter. Can you do that, Mr. Vane?"

"No problem," he says, shaking our hands as we hightail it out of there.

"Marisa, over here." I wave as I lead her into an alcove outside of the Sky Turret Bar, where there's some cool, dark privacy. "I want to tell you a secret."

"What?" Her eyes, that a minute ago looked so sad, glint with curiosity.

Don't know whether I'll regret this, but sometimes being impulsive is a good thing, too. She's delivered on the hack-code, the meeting with Freddie, and the meeting with her dad. Somehow, these acts have uncorked in me a frenzy of bottled-up feelings for her. I lean in as if to whisper in her ear. Instead, I wrap my arms around the small of her back, draw her close and kiss her. She presses her lips on mine, shooting flames all over me. She's feeling it, too. We're combustive, like Fireseed. I taste her mouth, her tongue, breathe in her earthy scent of violets.

She pulls away and softly flips her hair behind her.

"That kiss," she whispers. "Um, what're you—?"

She's cold. I should never have touched her. "Casual pity kiss," I blurt out, not wanting to say that, but not knowing how else to get back at her. "I certainly wasn't thinking of getting together with you. We're absolute opposites. I'll find a pretty girl in Ocean Dominion who gets me." What I did was insane anyway, kissing a girl who robbed my farm, whose ex-boyfriend killed my father.

She touches my palm, and unbidden, another tiny flame burns through me. "It's just that . . . I don't want to be impulsive," she says softly, "like joining another demented cult or . . . I don't trust myself. I need some time, that's all."

"Yeah, whatever." I need her contacts. I'll focus on that.

By the time we fly back that afternoon, Freddie's waiting for us in the lot in his white, tricked-out uplimo. I see sections of a plush red interior, curving agar wings on the back, and purple detailing above the back fender that reads: *Freddie Knows the Score*. I may be totally misguided, but the narrow pipe-like things protruding from either side of the front fender look a lot like guns. I gulp back a ripple of fear.

He gives us a perfunctory wave as indication we should follow him, caravan style. Streamerazzi have already flanked both sides of the border entrance. As we pass, they point their probe-like videos at us.

"Freddie!" Marisa screams into her HipPod, "The Streamerazzi were strictly *not* part of the deal. Call off your minions or I won't ever talk to my father ever again."

"Not my doing. I already called off the all-points," he insists. "You must've blown your own cover with someone else in the VIP Lounge. You're going to talk to your father, or else all bets are—"

"Yeah, yeah, thanks a lot, Freddie." Marisa slaps the HipPod closed. I've never seen her more agitated. Tendons in her neck are bulging, and she's practically gyrating with anger. They have each other over the proverbial barrel.

"Marisa, the Streamerazzi won't go beyond the border, will they?" I ask softly.

"I doubt it," she says, still not willing to look at me.

"So, be brave. Let them take a few shots, yeah?"

She motions to Freddie in front of us, who glides his uplimo forward. Here we go, into the hell my father warned me about. The place we heard bad stories about. I think about my mother stranded in that desert and feel a long, deep tug of sorrow.

But it's not time for that. Not now.

Hungrily shooting footage, the Streamerazzi jog next to the darter. I make a monkey face at one, and overdramatically wink at another. I open the darter porthole and yell, "It's not really us. Aren't we perfect clones? Of course, the real Ms. Baron is sailing on the Bering Sea and the real Varik is on expedition in northern China!"

For the first time in hours, Marisa giggles. She opens her porthole and shouts, "We're part of Freddie Vane's publicity stunt for the opening of Baronland South condoplex!"

"Brilliant!" a Streamerazzo in a navy suit and pink neckerchief calls back.

"They're lying, it's them," a tall reporter says to Pink Neckerchief. "Clones aren't that real."

"Sure they are," Neckerchief snips back, thrusting her camera closer to our darter.

Let the vampires feed on extra-special footage for the gossip mills. What do we care? Audun will hopefully send them off on another tail chase. I'm almost looking forward to his next installment!

We glide closer to the towering border entrance with a BARONLAND SOUTH holo flashing on the top of the gate, a gate gigantic enough for giant construction equipment to pass through. The gate opens! A magical passageway between all the linked sections of holo guards beckons; except this part is guarded by a phalanx of live guards.

There's a frightful moment when we stop while the guards ID a group of workers ahead of us. Will they arrest us? Freddie Vane has set a trap, sure he has. No wonder Marisa was so cynical. We look on with grave worry. But then Freddie's white uplimo in front of us, and behind the workers, slinks forward again, and we follow as swiftly as possible. The guards, with cordial smiles, usher us through.

"Sweet ice!" I breathe out a relieved gust of air along with my exclamation.

"Now comes another hard part," Marisa mumbles. She's curled in on herself, hugging her ribs, ignoring Freddie, who is motioning from his air-conditioned uplimo for her to get out and come over. I shut the portholes and turn on the extra air vents that Audun installed. Already the heat is oppressive. It must be a good one hundred thirty-five degrees! How is that possible? We're only on the south side of the *wall*!

It's sinking in. We are over the border. *In refugee territory.*

Marisa calls Freddie on speaker. "You can go now, thanks. I'll talk to my father by myself."

"Can't do that."

"Those were my terms," Marisa snaps.

"I never agreed to that." Vane is more of an obstinate barnacle than Marisa.

"Go anyway," I urge her. "Get it over with. For the mission," I remind her. She sends me a look filled with fearful reluctance. Her father must've really hurt her. No wonder she fell sway to a malicious guru like Bryan. I've heard that girls fall for guys like their dads unless they consciously avoid it. Parking behind Freddie in the spacious Baron lot, I wish her well. She brushes off her suit and cracks open the door.

Marisa and Mr. Vane walk toward the construction office where her father's finishing up his meeting. This gives me time to look around. When it's complete, this condoplex will be as big as SnowAngel Island! It's a series of interconnected half-finished buildings with jutting geometric tiers and angular walkways thrusting out in all directions. Workers in jumpsuits and hoods the color of the dry, bleached soil, hang from scaffolds; others steer power cranes and AmphiTractors.

Even from this distance it's clear that their skin is burned dark with patchy red areas. Still, these refs who work for Baron are the luckiest ones, even though Marisa told me some work twenty-hour shifts for no more than room and board. Their rooms are in the north Zone, though, nowhere near as lethal as in other Hotzone areas.

I spot a guy with a crude wire arm. There are risks even here.

This heat has reminded me to check my pack for my Skiin sharps. I text Audun, and beg him to send out another misleading gossip gem. I take a miserly sip from my thermos and recheck the coordinates to the Black Hills sector in South Dakota, where Marisa says the lady who makes the photon suits lives. That sector will hopefully be a safe one-night perch to points south. I'm halfway into my silver burn suit when Marisa comes racing out to me, tripping over the cracked dirt and bumping head-on into a worker laden with tools.

"Sorry!" she yells, without stopping to help him pick them up.

"Move over!" she orders breathlessly, when she sees I'm hopelessly tangled in the suit. I somehow twist-scramble-hunch to the passenger side as she powers up the darter and swerves upwards.

"What happened? I thought you'd be a little longer. Why were you running?" I ask, but I see now. Freddie is hurrying after her down the path and climbing into his fancy uplimo.

We lurch into the sky in fits and starts. I wonder if Marisa even has a license as I struggle into the armholes of the blasted suit. I belt up and stare in the side mirror at Freddie, who's giving chase with rabid determination.

We soar west over a deserted town and veer up into cloud cover. Freddie disappears from sight, and then suddenly reappears through the gauze, closer than ever. Marisa's HipPod rings off the hook. Freddie wouldn't dare shoot his boss's daughter down, but he's obviously determined to talk Marisa out of this.

Now that my hands are free, I help Marisa turn a hard left and we lurch east again, and down, nearly slamming onto a roofless, ruined mall. We see people down there run from a jimmy-rigged shroud over one corner of the mall and duck into a hole for cover.

In a burst of terrible energy that I half hope will pulverize his uplimo, Freddie copies us in a nosedive. He manages to narrowly avoid a crash into the mall, too. His inscrutable face is finally spooked.

As we ascend, Marisa's HipPod rings again.

To the sound of the incessant ringtone, I help navigate the darter back into deep cloud cover and head for the Black Hills of Dakotas. We're inside this latest river of dirty yellow clouds for at least fifteen minutes. Bursting out of the cover, I scout for Vane in my rearview.

"He's gone! We lost him, Marisa."

We both murmur a "Thank God."

I reach over and set the darter on autopilot. Marisa slumps back in the driver's seat and picks out the sweaty tufts of hair that, through the ordeal, have gotten stuck in her mouth. Then she clambers into her burn suit. These Land D burn suits are thicker and clunkier than the photon suits, but at least they don't make you invisible. Marisa and I are leery of each other after that awkward kiss, but I sneak peeks at her sexy body anyway. It's a relief to see my body, too. This suit is oddly cool to the touch, yet on the inside it sticks to any exposed skin.

After some time, Marisa says, "Freddie hates it when his lily-white limo gets all skuzzy."

"Hear, hear to being a clean freak," I say, still trying to humor her out of her funk.

We gaze down at the dead cities, one after the other. Roofs and walls have long blown off, revealing the skeletons of houses. Overturned vehicles have been scavenged for parts. Everything lies under a thick layer of dust, as if the Creator decided to pile sand and dirt over his project to hide it. I think of Bryan's lament about dust storms. Anyone in those doomed cities must have suffered horribly when the storms hit. How many years has it been like that, I wonder, how much dust upon dust upon dust, like the crackled layers on Nevada's shy face?

We pass over yet another highway of gutted cars, as if the drivers had barely enough time to park and flee with the shirt on their backs before some weather calamity hit. A river long-since dried near one highway leaves a Martian-looking dried canal, from which smaller sets of cracks wheel out into the horizon. We pass Mount Rushmore's infamous carved faces. Their stone noses and lips have been flattened by multiple sandstorms, leaving their faces curiously blank.

Loneliness hits me. I'm not used to soaring in an empty sky with no other flycars, and only a pensive girl and the psychedelic, piercing needles of sun for company. I wonder if our sun was like this before they put up the solar shield. I can't even imagine.

"The refs working on the construction site," I start. "Their skin is so messed up. Nevada's too."

"It's been dimed," says Marisa matter-of-factly.

"What?"

Marisa chuckles low in her throat as if it's supremely unfunny. "Varik, that's a euphemism for a skin-cancer lesion—a dimer. Sometimes they cut off part of a ref's face, other times they just sand it down." She shrugs. "What do you think happens if you spend time out here? No wonder the refs gave it a less-scary name."

"Wow. I'll keep my mask on, except at night," I say. A long silence breathes its stale air on us as I wonder if my recipe for Skiin would help heal them.

"How well do you know this lady in the Black Hills?" I ask Marisa, breaking the quiet.

"Her name is Rain and she has a kid. That's what Nevada told me. She's kind of a friend of Nevada's." Marisa glances over at me. She's crying softly. The soft skin around her eyes is pink. I'm filled with a sudden tenderness despite my humiliation over her pushing me off at the Sky Turret. I shoved her away in Yellow Axe. *Reality balances itself.* That's what my father used to say.

"I never saw my father," she admits. "Freddie and I were almost to the office door, and I said I was going to be sick. He showed me to the bathroom. And I . . . I climbed out of the window and ran," Marisa says through her tears. "I *was* sick. I couldn't do it. My stomach was full of hate."

"Smart way to ditch Freddie Vane," I say simply. "I feel bad that your father is such an operator. But Marisa, at least you *have* a father. He might be a megalomaniac and a seriously bad dresser . . ." I add to try and humor her. "Those ties—ack!"

"You forgot sadist. I swear he enjoys mistreating his workers."

"Yeah, well, that's wrong. So, he's messed up in the head, so he's got a slick assistant that would throw anyone under a flycar for a deal. At least your dad cares about you."

She grunts, brushes her tears away.

"You told me he sent you to the best private school and bought you a flycar at sixteen. He worries about you. Even after you testified against him."

"Shut up." She raps the door handle with her fist.

"Look, I saw his face on that videophone. He looked horrible."
"What do you mean?" She stops punching the handle.

"His skin was the color of a rotten yellow squash. There was fear for you in his eyes."

"Varik. It's too late," she says wearily. "I don't believe it. He never paid any attention to me until I was gone. I'm like a condo deal he got outbid on. It all reflects back to him, his power."

"Okay. I give up." It's obvious she's got her father's temper and stubbornness.

The auto coordinate pad utters a short bleep, and a guy announces that we've reached the sector. I power down, surfing the heat waves that crash off the darter. We land in a wide swath of dried sediment. I figure the valley will be slightly cooler than the hills. The Black Hills may have once been covered with fragrant green pines, but they've turned into hard black ash.

The heat. Even sealed in this vehicle it's searing my flesh, instantly drying out my mouth and nose. The external thermo that Audun rigged up reads 148 degrees. Marisa crawls back into a ball in her seat and hugs herself, as if she's in no mood to explore. We'll have to get out at some point, just not yet. We decide to wait for the sun to shift down from its zenith.

The Stream jolts us. Who knew it would play down here, even in this relatively northern area.

Land Dominion Uplink: News from Ocean Dominion is worse than expected. All agar crops have perished, and panicked people are rioting. Serge Casparin, the Teitur Farms farm manager from Vostok Station, was trampled to death during yesterday's riots. Pyotor Sigurd, the manager now in charge after the strange disappearance of Varik Teitur a couple weeks earlier, declined to be interviewed. He has ordered a twenty-four-hour Fleet guard shield around the beleaguered farms.

Brought to you by Restavik Chophouse, where the boar is better than home-grilled and the ladies drink free on Saturdays.

Serge is dead! I go numb as I rest my head on the steering wheel. He's been part of our family for so long. "Poor Serge," I mumble. I remember him showing me how to load the fertilizer hoses when I was a boy, and him fixing me raspberry blintzes in the galley. I can hear his Russian-edged English, and see his chapped hands working the feeder lines and plant beds. How can he be gone?

"Omigod! Varik, are you all right? Your farm guy!" Marisa gently rests a hand on my back.

Serge, the farmer from old Kirov, is no more. A man who was practically illiterate yet was all knowledgeable about when to plant and when to harvest, about how much we needed to grow each year to keep up with global demands. Crushed in one of the very factories that fed the world. I lift my bleary head and stare at the bleached-out sky.

Marisa gazes at me with deep worry in her eyes. "God, I'm so sorry," she whispers, stroking my shoulder. I'm so numb I can hardly feel it.

"The situation's deadly serious now," I mumble stupidly.

"Completely," she says.

"Serge was like an uncle to me. More farms will be looted and torn apart, Marisa."

"God, I hope not," she whispers.

"We need to get this mission going fast, before the people get hungry and storm my island looking for food that isn't there."

"Before they murder Audun," Marisa reminds me.

"Don't even say it." I think to myself that Audun's the only one left to care for those two agar plants. And I wonder whether it's time to tell Marisa about it. Not quite yet.

Great ice, is there no peace?

18.

It's mid-afternoon when the sun lowers enough to exit the darter. We grab the thermoses and lock the vehicle. We can't afford to be robbed by some starving desperado.

Even with the sun at half-mast, that first step outside is a heart-stopping shock to the system. The heat hits like a slap. My first intake of air feels as if I'm smothering inside tightly wound burlap.

But we're determined to negotiate our new environment. Moving slowly helps, one cautious step ahead of the other.

The sun truly roars. I don't literally *hear* it, still it roars on my burn hood, roars on a crudely painted sign that says *Black Hills Sector*, on the decrepit bikes chained to a metal pole. Walking toward a row of blackened hills with carved-out entrances, we pass sculptures made of scrap car parts, broken computer monitors, and office chairs. A chassis from an ancient truck creates a face with dangling wheels as eyes. The totems mark our walk up the hills. Up closer to the cave entrances in the hills is another sign. A ring of stones suggests a counsel, some metal buckets chained to a pole suggest vital liquid is available, and more pathways marked with totems suggest order and art.

Marisa stops walking. She scans the various entryways into the mountains. "Shall we walk up the hill and see if anyone's around?"

"It's a plan." I spin around slowly and survey the sky. "Didn't Nevada say people have homemade flycars? In Ocean Dominion there'd be a serious aerial traffic jam by this hour."

"Yeah, you'd think. On the other hand, Nevada said most people stay inside during midday." Marisa, with an arm over her face to protect it, searches the sky, too.

Something flits by the corner of my vision. "Look, Marisa, one of those horrible birds. It's a tracking device. I just know it!" The thing flaps down closer to our level. It seems to be treading water as its vacant eyes stare at us.

Marisa gives it the finger. "Go fly into a lava pit!" she shouts, and then starts to power walk up the path. "Let's go, let's get out of this goddamn sun."

I do a breathy lock step to catch up. We pause at the next sign, which lists the sector's inhabitants in alphabetical order by first name. My eyes scroll down to Rain and a guy named Armonk. They're in Sector 3, Bunks 15 and 16. The bird's flapped over and is sitting on a totem to one side of us, too far away to grab it, but too close for comfort. It almost seems to be reading the sign, too. How creepy is that?

We reach one of the inlaid metal doors in the mountain, Sector 5, and knock. We do this for a good five minutes. Then we pound on it. Nothing. We trek about fifty meters to the next door: Sector 6, same thing.

I'm losing any strength I had. Marisa, too, is red-faced and dripping sweat. The burn suit doesn't help cool things, but I'm leery of removing it. If we soldier on any further south we'll need to use the oxygen tanks.

After another twenty minutes we find Sector 3. Knocking and kicking the door for ages does not arouse the apparently catatonic dweller within.

"Even if they're asleep, you'd think this would wake them," Marisa mutters. "Maybe this Black Hills sector was abandoned."

"What if we sit down under this overhang?" I suggest. "It's shady under here. If there is anyone around, they have to come out sooner or later."

We crouch in the shadiest part, a few steps to the left of Sector 3's heavy metal door.

We must've nodded off, because when I wake up the sun is hugging the horizon line. And the temperature is noticeably cooler. Still unbearable by Ocean Dominion standards, probably around one hundred thirty-five degrees, but at least I can breathe without my lungs hurting and the fear I'm burning alive.

Marisa's still dozing, leaning against the wall, her head lolling to one side, when I hear the first distant sound of a door creaking. Then a young girl's cheerful yell, as if she's being let out for recess. And more sounds of people, and people wandering down the hills in groups, all as the sun continues its furious descent below the hills.

These are night folk. Of course! They only come out when the sun leaves them. I hear a loud creak and the door to my right opens. A small boy of seven or so, with a deep, crackled tan and long, shiny black hair leaps out. He jumps back upon seeing us, and props himself against the door staring at us with his big eyes. Like Nevada, leaf tattoos decorate his cheeks and a metal leaf dangles from a twine necklace. He's dressed in a raggedy pair of hike shorts and has only one healthy leg. Where the other should be is a metal post. *Post-apocalyptic prosthetics*, I think.

"Hello," I say cautiously. "Is Rain here?"

The boy peers at us as if we've come to rob them. He runs

inside. "Mama!" he calls.

I wake Marisa. She rubs sleep out of her eyes and slips her sunglasses back on.

Rain and her boy emerge from the dark entrance. Rain's a big woman wearing a quilted dress of the scaled fabric that the ZWC wore, except this version is visible to the eye. She's sporting the same leaf tattoos as Nevada and Armonk, and has on a necklace with a handful of metal leaves that clink when she moves.

We explain, as best we can, where we came from, how we got her address, and that we know Nevada, without mentioning Bryan. We tell her we're on a mission to search my father's land in the Southwest, which is now mine. No mention of agar, or the ZWC, or any of that.

Her eyes still dart suspiciously from Marisa to me. "You say you know Nevada? Tell me what she looks like."

"She's thin, with blond hair. Her hair's wound up in twine," I say. "She has leaf tattoos on her face." I squint to help me retrieve a picture in my head of our first meeting in the forest. "Two tattoos on her left cheek and three on the right."

"She wears lots of gray eyeliner, and um, she's a runner," Marisa says.

Rain comes alive. She steps forward and offers her hand. "Any friend of Nevada Pilgrim's is a friend of mine, that poor child. You're looking for Fireseed One, eh?" She grins, revealing a mouth that could sorely use some dental care. "That's almost always why folks come through here, looking for Fireseed. Most speculators go down south there in the desert," she says. "They've been looking for decades." She brushes hair from her son's forehead and makes a derisive clucking noise. "Between you and me, it doesn't exist."

I know better, but don't say it *did* exist.

"What makes you think that?" Marisa asks.

"I don't believe anything that Fireseed cult believes. They're a bunch of crazies." She laughs. It almost sounds like the tinkling of rain, and I wonder if that's where she got her name. "Ever read about their rituals?" she asks us. We shake our heads. "Well, they reenact the supposed historic Fireseed planting every full moon. They seal their unions in front of Fireseed statues." She winks. "Unions, know what I mean?"

Marisa and I look pointedly away from each other.

Sending Armonk off to play, Rain invites us to sit in her circle of stones on the side of the hill. A few people glance over with curiosity and wave. We wave back. Rain brings us out some liquid that looks thick and moldy and pours out two small mugs of it. It tastes like minerals and it's sour, but after I get over the texture and manage a few gulps, it does refresh. Rain explains she makes it from dribbling cups of precious water into rock crevices and scraping off the ensuing moss. Marisa asks her how they get water.

"It used to be a real ordeal to make a quart," Rain says, "but now the runners deliver the pellets every month. I trade for my handmade clothes."

"You mean those pellets that say *Vegas-by-the-Sea?*" I ask.

"How'd you know?" she asks me, generously refilling our cups.

I tell her about seeing them in the camp store. "Are the sectors that organized?" I ask. "I was always told that it was real chaos down here, constant murders and such."

"It was bad, very bad. That's why we never answer our doors in the day, especially alone. That's why we congregate together at night." She waves her hand over the people who are talking and beginning to cook. I notice lots of them are wearing the photonic suits, only *this* fabric is visible. There must be various kinds, I decide. I wonder where she gets the fabric. Perhaps here and there people weasel through the border for goods.

Rain goes on. "Slowly, it's getting better. Vegas Sector's the richest one. It'd be nice to live by the ocean. Cooler. The pellet company was started by a guy in Vegas Sector we call Geo

Man. He had lots of family money to invest, came from a line of old Texas oil-families. Geo Man knows about rocks and how to use the ocean water for the pellets." She pauses. "He's got lots of Fireseed theories, too."

"Really!" I exclaim. "So, he's that same geologist that Nevada mentioned, right?" I glance at Marisa, who nods. "He must know about rock formations and such."

Rain studies me. "Who did you say you were again?"

"The famous Fireseed Professor's son," Marisa tells her before I can make something up. I throw Marisa a frown. No doubt these Zoners are scornful of the professor who turned his back on them.

"Ohhh." Rain draws out the sound as she scrutinizes me. She's silent so long I get paranoid that I've made her angry. Finally she says, "Nevada told me they were thinking of doing a sortie on your sea farm."

"They sure did," I say, holding Rain's gaze to let her know just how devastating that sortie was.

"Sorry, kid," she says. "I told Nevada to steer clear of Bryan. She lost her whole family in a dust storm when she was twelve. I take her in and feed her now and then. She works so hard running the mail from here to points west. She fell for that Bryan's line of radical mumbo. I think the girl's sweet on him."

I peek at Marisa to see her reaction to this mention of Nevada's crush. Nothing. Marisa's face is blank. I quickly look back at Rain. "I thought he was organized, and had a distribution plan," I say, as much to get more information out of her as to see where she stands.

She fingers her leaf necklace. "Yes. Bryan used to be respected. He put together distribution centers for underground crops he had planned." Rain looks at me nervously as if she figures that the seeds he was planning to sow in those fields might come from my farm. But that could be my imagination, and I'm not in the mood to press her on it. "Bryan was smart, and he cared, but something happened. He became a really angry man," Rain continues. "Nevada told me he saw his brother torn apart for some food. People down here feel ignored by the richer folks on the north side of the border."

I feel a hard pull of guilt when she says this.

"Lots of folks have calamities." She shrugs, which makes her leaf bangles clink. "It doesn't give them the right to kill. I'll sell my photon suits to other folks trying to cross the border, but not to the ZWC anymore. More and more folks around here don't approve of Bryan's politics. They say he's killed dozens of border guards. Blew up a Fleetcar, too, the last time he pulled some stunt up north. It's no way to open the border. That only makes it more impossible to cross."

Rain turns toward the open plain, to watch her son struggle to keep pace with another boy. "You can't get your rights from bashing someone's head in." She picks up a piece of lava stone and rolls it in her hand. "God knows we've already tried that down here."

Marisa and I nod silently, each in a lonely space of our own. It's a lot to take in, knowing all of Bryan's terrorizing was only a preview of what he did to my father.

Rain smiles at us. "We've been cooped up in the cave all day. My boy needs exercise. Got to keep his one good leg nimble."

"That's important," I'm curious as to what happened to his leg, but don't want to pry.

Rain must sense this. "It burned clear off one day after Armonk got his other leg stuck in a rock crevice, and was trapped outside too long. I was crazy with worry. A guy from Sector 5 found him. Had to cut that part off," Rain says brusquely as she winds her photon cape around her. "We were going for a walk. Will you join us?"

I tell her that sounds great. Marisa admits she could use a walk because her legs are cramping. Rain calls Armonk, who comes limp-hopping back and then inside the cave. He emerges

with an old metal box with a handle and a thin, flat-edged metal rod about the length of my arm. It has a pointy crab-claw-type pincher on one end.

"I'm catching beetles," Armonk explains, balancing the rod on his shoulders like a fishing pole.

Rain leads the way down a stony path that winds behind the caves. The view is spectacular, with endless rocky black whorls and hills. There's no vegetation other than an occasional tan, thorny weed pushing up between the rocks that seems to live on thin air.

Armonk limps eagerly ahead. He pauses by the side of the path, and leans his bony elbows against an upward-sloping boulder. By the time that Rain and Marisa and I catch up, I see he's examining a crevice in the rock.

Rain puts a finger over her lips to warn us to keep quiet.

Armonk dips his scooper into the crevice and waits. Then he slowly waves it back and forth. When he pulls it up, the pinchers hold a shiny blue beetle, madly cycling its legs. Armonk plunks him in the rusted metal lunchbox that up close I see must be from around 2025, because the faded cartoon characters of a stylized windmill and a nuclear reactor blowing steam from its ears are ones I don't recognize. Armonk snaps the clasps shut.

Turning to look up at me, Armonk cocks his head to one side, and squints against the bright sunset. "Wanna hunt with me?" he asks.

"Sure," I say, flattered and surprised.

Rain gives me an approving nod as I head off with Armonk. He lets me hold the scooper as we go, which I'm sure is a big deal for him. I make sure to carry it high off the ground so it won't get scraped as I stop by the next big boulder.

"Not that rock," Armonk says, and points to another rock some twenty paces beyond the first, and on the opposite side of the path. "That one," he says. Clearly he's memorized all of the populous beetle spots. Just before he reaches the rock, his peg leg catches in an uneven section of path. He puts an arm out to catch his fall, while he manages to cradle the lunchbox with his other arm so it won't clatter on the ground and unlatch.

Before I can help him, he's already up and by my side, his little lungs pumping hard.

"So, how do I do this?" I ask him.

Armonk makes a swiping motion with one hand. "Pretend the rod is beetle food. Put the scooper in and move it super slowly like a crawling ant," he whispers. Armonk's dark bangs dangle forward as he leans over the rock to watch me lower the scooper in the cleft.

After a few clumsy tries where I lose hold of the pinchers, I manage to pull up one of the blue beetles. "Got one!" I say.

"You got one!" Armonk repeats. He unlatches the lunchbox and waits ceremoniously while I pop it in. I hear clapping, and turn, just in time, to catch Rain's and Marisa's broad smiles. Suddenly shy, I look away.

Before Armonk and I reach the lowest part of the path, we've caught about eighteen more beetles. We follow the curve of the path as it loops back up toward the cave dwellings. Armonk's chest is puffed out and his eyes are gleaming pools of brown joy. *Little hunter*, I think. That's what my father used to call me when we went on scavenge dives.

"It's like fishing," I tell him.

"You've fished? For real fish?" Armonk asks me.

"Yeah, real fish."

"What kind?"

"Oh, dogfish and grouper and sometimes a shark."

His face lights up as if he's picturing himself in a boat. I don't have the heart to tell him that mostly we collect farmed Flyfish from the vine instead of taking the risk to fish for toxic ocean fish. He limps off behind me to tell Rain I'm a fisherman, while I wind my way up the hill.

Something grazes my hand and curls around mine, giving it a squeeze. At first I think it's Armonk, but glancing up, I see it's Marisa. A huge wave of emotion catches me off guard. It rolls me around and around, almost knocking me off my feet.

"You were cute," she says softly.

"Huh?"

"I didn't know you had it in you." Her face is ruddy and sweaty and she's looking rather boldly at me, as if daring me in some way.

I unlatch my hand from hers. "What does that mean?"

"Your heart. You have a big heart. And you were only trying to help back there with Freddie and stuff." Now she sounds on the verge of tears. She switches moods so fast she's hard to figure out.

Heat rushes up my neck and into my head. "Thanks." I fumble for her hand and latch back on. No rebellious comeback from Marisa. We're just quiet and feeling each other's vibes. For once, hers feel undefended. I wonder if my vibe feels like a beetle hunter-gatherer.

We walk up the hill like that, matching steps, listening to Rain and her boy discuss fishing and what they should fix their guests for dinner. They're a good ways behind us, giving us our space.

"Are you being impulsive?" I can't help asking Marisa.

"No. I've thought this through." She pauses. "Do you think we're too different?"

"To different for what?" I won't make this easy for her.

"Too different to, you know . . . to be together?" I look over at her. Her skin's lost a bit of that ruddy quality and looks delicate now, lace over blue veins. Her expression's doubtful . . . . afraid of the possibility that I might turn her down this time? I imagine her feeling that way around her father, and how he must have continually disappointed her.

I smile inside. "Different is good. Don't they always say that opposites attract?"

There's an edge of danger to Marisa. I think I like the edge. It's less boring than being with a good girl with mousy hair from Land D who reads all the right books and stays out of trouble. I only had that one other girlfriend. Even that felt nervy, although all we did was grope each other at the Stream flicks. What will happen next with Marisa? I picture kissing her again, stroking her wild red hair that smells of violets and sweat, her pressing against me under the night sky. Not knowing how it will unfold, especially down in this untamed Hotzone, makes my breath come fast. She could've killed me, she could've run, she could've double-tricked me. But she's done none of this, and now she's helping me with her contacts. Audun was right—she was mesmerized by Bryan like those Lionfish disciples were. Conned by the clever rant. It's scary how even smart, rational people fall into traps. Our earlier argument seems far away. We're both growing out of our old skin, like two desert lizards, and the feeling of connecting is amazing.

Up at the crest of the hill by the cave entrances, we turn to each other at the same time and find each other's lips. Hers taste of salty sweat, yet of sweetness. Her skin brushing against the palms of my hands feels like plush leaves.

She's spring sun after polar night.

When Rain and Armonk reach us, we wheel around to greet them. A slight wind cools my face as Rain invites us to sit back down on the circle of rock-seats in front of the caves. The barren hills ahead are elegant in their vastness. Riding along the hills is a radiant orange glow deepening upward into starry ink.

More dwellers emerge from their caves and settle on their set of rocks. Their chatter is friendly, their outlines fringed with torchlight that they set up in various spots along the hill. We're quiet for a time, enjoying the peace and the view.

Armonk has run into the cave and come out with a homemade bow. Reminds me of the Native Americans my father told me stories of. It's nice to imagine how a tribe might have broken out of those reservations and taken back this land, however barren. They, of all people, would know how to negotiate this fierce, untamed place.

Armonk limps over to Rain and points toward the night sky. "Look, Mama, there's a bad bird coming."

My stomach drops. That evil device is homing in on our gathering, almost as if it's jealous of us having a conversation without it. It loops back around toward the Second Sector sign.

The boy hobble-hops down the hill after it.

"Armonk! Watch yourself," calls Rain, in a tone so different than during our hike it sends a shudder through me. "Those things aren't native to this sector," she warns, holding out a torch to light the hill.

We walk toward Armonk to watch him track the metallic bird. My instinct urges me to protect the boy giving valiant chase on his peg leg. Armonk shoots an arrow, but it misses. The bird then charges and tries to peck Armonk's head. Armonk ducks. He shoots a second arrow as the bird veers away.

Direct hit! The bird crashes onto the hard ground.

Armonk lopes over, grabs it, and sits down with it for a closer look. By this time, we've all reached Armonk and are panting for a good breath in this thin air that's given me a sour taste in the back of my throat. There's a whirring sound, as if a machine is stuck in a loop.

Armonk grasps the bird's hook beak, which is convulsively snapping. His mother yells for him not to touch it. "Mama, it's not real!" shouts Armonk. "It's a machine."

Rain hurries over. "Well, I'll be scalped!" she exclaims, bending over for a better look.

I crouch down, and stare into its mirror eyes. "I knew that thing was fake."

Marisa's quiet, guarded, almost as if she knew all along what this was. I remember her giving it the finger. I'll ask her about it later.

Armonk and I yank off the bird's "face."

"It's a video camera. It's been taping us!" I shout. And it took the little hunter boy to call it alien and hunt it down. "Armonk, you're a frying genius," I exclaim.

We drag the bird inside Rain's house to play the video.

It's Marisa and me streaking through the forest to the ZWC fort in Yellow Axe, it's us failing to hack the border, us parking at the skeezy Bug Off! lot in Land D, it's us sitting on the air-train to the Emporium. Oh crap, it's Marisa taking over the wheel as we lurch over the buried cities.

"Did you know what this bird really was?" I ask Marisa while Rain's busy putting Armonk to bed.

"I suspected." She studies her hands. "But I was afraid you'd hate me if I told you I knew. It was like a part of my old, bad personality stalking me. I kept hoping it would get lost."

"Don't withhold information. Don't ever do that again," I insist, knowing I'm withholding my own private piece about my dad's ten burnt-up Fireseed plants, and where they grew, and about the two seedlings in the solarium.

"I won't. I'll tell you everything." Marisa rises up to give me a hug, her hair cascading around me like a silky, crimson cape. Her new honesty gives me a twinge of guilt, but it passes. Her weakness was her impulsiveness, I decide, but she's trying to change.

We watch the video a second time, to let it all sink in. It's the whole long trek.

"I resent my life being made into a show." I slam the bird head back on its body.

"We'll get them back. Somehow," Marisa replies.

I text Shin. I don't care how many times my HipPod crashes down here; I'll keep texting him until I get the tek info I need. I'm going to boomerang this video-bird torpedo right back to sender.

One nice thing, even if the birdbrain was still "alive," it couldn't video Marisa and I cuddling in the dark of the cave under Rain's clean covers, with a candle to better see the magical trees and leaves Rain's painted all over the walls.

"Her trees are like Ocean Dominion's nostalgia for ice," I tell Marisa. "Because trees are gone from the Zone. They're extinct, gonzo, you know?"

"Exactly," she murmurs, half asleep on my chest. "Or like Land D's nostalgia for a normal, happy Euro past, with all of our fake castles and palaces and tavern-on-the-greens." She props her head on her elbow and declares, "I want to do something real, something good, and not find out it was all for nothing."

"I hear you. I want to be a doctor. Make prosthetic limbs. How about you?"

"I want to work for refugee rights, help these people down here. Try to get them access to Land and Ocean Dominion, and to more goods, protective housing from the sun."

I'm so confused about the refugees. Things are changing so fast in my mind from what my father said. It's hard to forgive him for only concentrating on their inhumanity, hard to reconcile all of the inconsistencies. But it's not over yet. He may still be right about the refugees being criminals. I mean, my mom . . .

"There's something I haven't told you, Marisa," I say out of the quiet.

She studies me. "What?"

"I found a Fireseed cert on my father's laptop. He *was* trying to develop it."

"Eee! That's incredibly important. Did he ever grow it down here?"

"Only in the lab," I lie. That last cert I found is too private—my last secret. "But there's one more thing."

"Yes?"

"Back at the sea farm, after Bryan poisoned the agar, I found two live seedlings."

"What?" Marisa jolts up, her eyes wide. "Are they still alive?" When I tell her yes she wraps her arms around me and hugs me tight. "That's such good news. Great news!" She knows better than to ask me why I never told her.

"Audun's taking care of them since Serge died," I add slowly.

She loosens her grip and stares at me in horror. "Do you think he can—?"

"Take decent care of them?"

She nods.

"God, I hope so. We need to trust that he can."

"Right. Trust. We'll trust him, that's all."

"Fireseed—if we ever find it—we can try to interbreed it with the seedlings."

"Yes! Genius, Varik, we'll just do that. We will!"

If we can.

It's good to instill the idea in her head. It'll help me believe. And that last cert, that private cert, gives me faith that if my father grew it once, it might still be growing—somewhere. I kiss Marisa, and she gives me a longer one back.

"I secretly liked your first kiss back at the Emporium," she whispers in my ear, and kisses me again.

"I admit, mine wasn't a pity kiss," I say, folding her in my arms. Her body is perfect, miraculous, healing. Caressing each other is a drink of sweetness, a swim in pure, blue waters.

Afterwards, we drift off, wrapped up together, putting to rest the lost past, and praying for a safe future.

19.

I wake to a sausage smell and to my HipPod glowing. My pulse is galloping as I click it open.

"Hey! I can't believe it. I got through to Shin," I tell Marisa, who's stepping into her burn suit. "He sent me directions of how to reprogram the video and put in a loop relay. If I do it right, it'll fly back to the sender, video them, and fly back, repeatedly."

"Excellent idea!" Marisa gives me a thumbs-up.

I read the last part of Shin's message:

You got wacked enemies. Pay me 2,000 Ds for bird job. Big one, dude. I'll chant you guys zen travel koan for auspicious luck. Peace, Space Strawberry, Shin Kaskade.

Out in Rain's kitchen, Marisa and Rain have been talking about what organizing a ref union might entail, about writing letters to the government of Land D and Ocean D with a proposal to share more goods with those in the Zone. Gee, I guess Marisa's wasting no time in thinking up political strategies. I just hope she gives it the time and thought it needs, instead of jumping into another crazy stunt. Rain serves us something that resembles meatloaf. I take a tentative bite, reluctant to ask what it is, for fear I won't be able to eat it.

"It's good," I say doubtfully, as I crunch the stuff gingerly with my back molars.

"Black Hills specialty—beetle loaf," Rain announces.

Beetle as in those crawling blue things with wings? I thought Armonk caught those for fun. I nearly spit the mess out. Marisa's also having trouble swallowing hers, but we need nourishment for the next leg of the journey. After a few more crunchy mouthfuls, the loaf starts to taste better, slightly nutty, almost like peanut brittle.

"Can I help you send the video bird back?" Armonk looks hopefully at me.

"Of course. You shot it down. You're the big man!"

Rain gives Marisa a food pack for the road, and two of her special padded photonic heat masks that cover everything but the eyes, while I send Shin his credit-card payment and program in his codes. I'm hoping there's food aside from beetle loaf in Marisa's pack. We help Rain scrub her few dishes with damp cloths. She has little water and no kitchen bots to help. We give her our largest water pellet as thanks.

She insists on taking a smaller one and thanks us. "You kids better hurry," she says, hanging up the last pot on its hook over a stone side table. "Sun's on the way up and we'll have to lock up soon, so Armonk can do his home study." Armonk makes a vinegary face, and then carries the unwieldy brown bird outside as fast as his gimpy leg can take him. I think of Juko. If I ever return, I'd like to make Armonk a more sturdy prosthetic. With a pang of sadness, I wonder again how Juko is.

The cauldron of boiling air takes me by surprise. I almost forgot from yesterday, and the sun is only halfway over the sea of hills. We hike down past the last Black Hills sign into the valley, where I open the video contraption and activate its relay. Then we snap shut the ugly bird-face. Armonk takes it and throws the monstrosity as hard as he can. It wobbles overhead, and I worry that it'll torpedo down and smash. But with a low whirring, it flaps its brown wings, and begins to navigate up and north.

Rain utters what she says is a Lakota prayer for a successful mission and return.

"Let me learn the lessons you have hidden
in every leaf and rock.
I seek strength, not to be superior to my brother,
but to fight my greatest enemy—myself."

I've asked Rain for the coordinates to Geo Man's storefront, and she says she'll try to patch him a message, but warns that the feed out here is spotty, that it crashes for months. Marisa and I thank her. As we take turns hugging Rain, I notice Armonk is hanging back.

His radiant face has lost its light, and I realize it must be lonely for him under this infinite sky without a dad or sibling. It would have been for me. I crouch down. "Big man," I say, "Take care of your mom." He nods. "Here's my good-luck shell from Vostok Station," I say, pressing it into his little palm, "so, you'll know I'm thinking of you." His hand curls around it.

Clutching my neck, he leaps on me and gives me a squeeze.

As we head out west to Vegas-by-the-Sea, we fly over an immeasurable flatland. There's not even one rock or lousy dune to distinguish it. I wonder if the wind keeps whipping up weather calamities whether every mountain and hill on the planet will be razed. I think of those old presidents carved in the mountains near Black Hills Sector without noses, foreheads, or chins.

We do pass a few flycars. The ones we see are decades old, perhaps from before the border was built. I wonder where the people are flying to, because I haven't even seen a single brave nomad yurt, much less a town. Maybe pioneers burrow in tunnels under the sand. The thought makes me lonely and frightened. Marisa must feel the vibe, too, because she takes my hand and holds it for a long time without speaking.

After about two hours, we're forced to make a pit stop. The darter's on solar mode, which works great down here, but its master system is overheating. I never thought a solar flycar could get too much sun! We land in an empty basin of parched, splintered dirt to make a gallon of our precious water for the tank. Inside the darter with its custom coolant vents and insulation, we can supposedly withstand up to one hundred eighty degrees if we wear our burn suits. Outside is a different story. I forgot to wear my mask, and by the time I make it back inside Marisa tells me my face is blistered. She puts a salve on it, but it's already raw and swollen. I'd use the Skiin formula, but I want to save it in case we go through a worse patch. There's also the worry that it's too old, and never tested, and will somehow poison us.

As we approach Vegas-by-the-Sea, air traffic gets heavy. Vehicles cobbled together from antique helicopters and satellite dishes chug past us. Others are fresh models in clean agar curves.

Even from this aerial view, the sector looks surprisingly prosperous. It's twenty times the size of Black Hills. Buildings shaped like domed obelisks shimmer in the sunset. Flying closer, I see that humble nomad yurts and lower-lying domes hug the city's majestic structures.

This is a relatively new coast, since a fiendish quake and its following tsunami ate up California when I was a baby. Seeing the mighty Pacific lap on the shores of Vegas-by-the-Sea gives me a powerful yearning for Ocean Dominion. I'm overtaken with the desire to leap out of the darter after our long, stressful ride, and dive into the surf. But I'm sure it's too polluted.

We are flying over the buildings now. A few ultra-modern buildings mirror the rise and curl of the surf. They're of modest height, with only three or four floors. Still, I'm impressed, even shocked, to see that the architects had the nerve to build upwards toward the sun rather than cower underground. The new buildings have few windows and thick, glowing, sun-protective walls. Is this Hotzone actually a potential rival to Ocean and Land D? Is that why so many myths are spouted about the Hotzone crawling with primitive, bloodthirsty thieves? Is it actually filled with normal everyday people who just had the shitty luck to be here when the last holo section of the border wall went up?

I look again at the cityscape. Vegas figurines—of Elvis and Houdini and a fat guy labeled *Wayne Newton*—and the gaudy theme hotels I've heard about—like the antique Luxor with its crumbling Sphinx—rise up from the old city under a matte glaze of sand and dust. It looks as if the fake Manhattan skyline, the Eiffel Tower, and other copies of "wonders" have been repaired so many times they're stuck together with spit.

Marisa and I land according to the coordinates Rain provided. People scurry about in trendy versions of Rain's photonic protection suits, with flared pants and angular fins coming off their shoulders. Some glance over at our darter, and then away. It's clear they don't want to spend any longer on the baking street than necessary.

We park, suit up, and exit the vehicle in front of Vegas-by-the Sea Water Pellet Company. It's a rambling showroom with an arched door and one tiny porthole in front. The walls are of thick blue agar. *Built when the agar still flowed,* I think sadly. We used to ship agar to Land D, who, in turn, would ship down here. But there was always a strict quota for each sector. Geo Man must be truly wealthy to have far surpassed his. Or was there a black market before the blight? Marisa and I exchange puzzled, bemused glances and a quick kiss. Who knows what to expect here? Certainly not me!

20.

After the second round of knocks, Geo Man answers the door. He doesn't match the image in my mind as a rugged explorer in faded work gear. This guy looks like a windsurfing, sun-blond, forty-year old Audun. Dressed in a smart coral shirt with shell buttons and white photon pants, he's the essence of neo-coastal chill. He promptly announces that the store is closed.

Marisa says, "We heard you're the expert on where Fireseed might grow. We heard you have special maps."

"Look, I was just leaving." He clinks some old style keys in his hand. "I sell pellets, not maps. I used to sell maps," he says in a more wearied than hostile tone, "but I'm concentrating on the pellets now. You are?"

We explain that we're friends of Rain's from Black Hills Sector, and tell him an abbreviated story of what's happening up north to the agar. I figure it's time to let on how deadly serious this all is. Rain assured us that Geo Man would understand. I drop Dad's name, figuring he might have heard of him.

Geo-Man's leathered face changes from weary to worried. He tells us to sit tight. We perch on hollowed-out egg-shaped agar chairs in the showroom.

Marisa starts to snoop. I might as well, too. It's not often I get to visit a water-pellet company in a freaky refugee nation.

Bins full of pellets line Geo Man's walls. There are basketball-sized yellow pellets; medium-sized blue ones like we have; small purple ones no bigger than a pill. Others resemble pink ice cubes and orange diamonds. The overall vibe is rainbow festive. I guess knowing you can make water when you've been dehydrated to the point of death makes you pretty darn happy. Normally I'm no klepto, but I'm tempted to pocket a few, as we have no idea how long we'll be down here and just how parched we'll get. But the guy could be coming back here any second, and I don't want to piss him off. Besides, he might have hidden cameras, or some ugly, melon-headed video bird flying around. You never know in the Hotzone.

Geo Man returns with an armful of rolled maps. He opens a briefcase and carefully loads them in. "I was just going for a drink at the Shark Bar."

"Really, we need to talk quickly and press on," I say, even though my secret wish is to take a long nap. I'm woozy from the constant heat, and the blisters are throbbing. I'm definitely running a fever.

Marisa sends me a look of longing. "I'm sooo thirsty." She rests a light hand on my cheek. "Besides, a cold drink might bring down your temperature."

"Don't think so," I say stubbornly. "Alcohol dehydrates. We can't afford that down here."

"Let's go for an hour. Varik, I'm drained."

Truth be told, I could use a frying drink myself. And we need that special map, and some advice. I need to ask the guy where those mimetoliths are.

"I've gotta go." Geo Man jingles his keys.

"Yeah, we're in," I say. We suit back up and put our facemasks back on, brace ourselves for the blast furnace. Geo Man offers to chauffeur us in his vehicle, but I'm not leaving my darter unguarded no matter how flush this sector is.

We follow his flycar past a collection of low-lying warehouses, a war-torn fifteen-meter-high statue of a goofy clown with puffy hair labeled *Carrot Top,* and a much newer one of Vivienne Froth. She was Cherry Froth's ultra-famous mother, who, I must admit, was a far superior actress than her daughter. We zip into an underground lot and take the stairs down into the belly of the Shark Bar. It's a defunct aquarium that Geo Man explains was connected to one of the casinos until they were destroyed by flood.

There are no fish in tanks, but there is an ocean theme in this deep cavern under the streets. There are faux reefs and coves and agar-sculpted neon coral as big as two of me. Waitresses dressed as sharks, with short spiky-edged skirts, serve us hissing blue drinks. Light shows shift the walls into heaving waves, where holo fish play. Reminds me of the cheesier clubs on SnowAngel Island. My pulse jumps when I spot a flyer behind the bar announcing the construction of ZWC crop plots in a warehouse on Crab Street. So, the ZWC—and Bryan—have infiltrated down to this sector. I'm tempted to ask Geo Man how he feels about the ZWC, and Bryan, but think better of it. We need information, and a conversation like that could easily flare into a camped battle.

"I'm shocked a club like this exists," I tell Geo Man as I check out a group of well-heeled clients in flowing gear, with their photon jackets draped behind them on their chairs. They're laughing and generally having a cheerful time. "I mean, up north they told us—"

"That we're a bunch of primitive killers living in raggedy tents?" Geo Man claps me on the back, which makes me flinch to protect my blistered face.

"Pretty much." I chuckle nervously. "Can we see the map?"

Marisa takes a more relaxed tack, with a toss of her freshly combed hair. "Rain tells us you've walked the Fireseed perimeter, that you know it like the back of your hand."

"That's right. I know all the rock formations that seemed likely ground for Teitur's project." He clicks open his case and unrolls one of the maps, points to a spot in the area labeled *Chihuahua Desert* that stretches through a few of the old states, including Texas. He's marked off a square in green pen. I pay him for the copy.

"Is that the focal point?" I ask, pointing to the square.

"Yup, that's it." He looks up at me. "Your father distributed a video on Zone TV, oh, almost two decades ago. He spoke about wanting to grow Fireseed next to a protective wall of metamorphic rock."

"Metamorphic?" Marisa asks, peering at the map.

"That's rock reformed under intense heat," Geo Man explains. "The plant would have to have some protection from the sandstorms that rip through the area. Teitur's theory was that hybridization of a heat extremophile with a temperate plant would create a super-plant that would survive invasives, CO_2 poisoning from climate change, and any amount of heat."

"Any particular area of interest in the green square?" I ask, poring over the map. "How about mimetoliths? A cup mimetolith, for instance?" I drop this in as casually as I can.

"Huh?" Marisa gives me a quizzical look, arching her brows.

"Funny you should mention," says Geo Man. With his index finger, Geo Man draws a rectangle in the bottom half of the square. "If Fireseed grew anywhere, it grew there, among the mesas or the mimetoliths." He slugs the blue drink, which hisses as he swallows.

"Mimetoliths, what are they exactly?" I ask.

"Rock formations that resemble objects, like giant water pellets or beer mugs." He grins.

"Or like cups . . . or flowers?" I persist.

"Sure." Geo Man runs a hand through his over-bleached hair as he looks at me. "Funny you should say. There is a cup *and* a flower one."

"Something you want to tell me?" Marisa says under her breath.

I shake my head in all innocence, while inside, I'm prickling with excitement. *So, there is a cup mimetolith!*

She shrugs and looks over at Geo Man. "You talk about Fireseed as if it's in the past."

He nods. "The thing is, I've trekked that area many, many times. I've taken crack geologists and botanists out there. Nothing. Fireseed plants are *just not there.*" He leans in toward Marisa. "I never met Professor Teitur, but I did know *your* father, Melvyn."

Marisa's eyes glint with a combination of curiosity and scorn. "What was your verdict?"

"Baron contacted me after Varik's father shut down the experiment. He wanted to know where the best part of the land was. Wanted to buy it. Professor Teitur had already refused him."

This news jolts me. Thus the private phone numbers. There's so much my dad kept secret, it's hard not to resent him.

"So you're saying that my father thought the land would become incredibly valuable if they found Fireseed," Marisa nudges.

Geo Man nods. "Baron was furious that he couldn't make that buy."

"Of course," Marisa says wryly. "He's used to getting everything he wants." She slugs back her hissing blue drink and asks for another.

I think of Tornado pressing a copy of my deed on me. Amazing that people still want that sterile land. Even Geo Man is convinced there's no Fireseed. My spirits drop slightly. It probably never grew back after it burned up. My stomach is empty and burning like everything in this freaking zone, so I grab a handful of blackened cocktail nuts. Or are they beetles? I try one. It's not a nut or a beetle, but something salty that melts in my mouth. I'm afraid to ask; I simply chew, gag and swallow.

The glitzy group sitting near us rises en masse to dance to the twangy beat.

"I'd love to get some exercise," Marisa says wistfully. I'm too feverish to ask her, but Geo Man does. She curls her arm around his and they stroll over to the dance floor. With her wavy hair freed from the braids, and wearing one of Brigitte's short, striped smocks with hike shorts, she's a fluid, sexy dancer. The sight of her dancing has me feeling all kinds of things. I bet she had lots of admirers in those dark, gothic-themed Land D clubs. Bryan, for one.

She's weaving on her feet, though. I feel woozy, too, and I've only had two drinks. The heat must accentuate the effect of the liquor.

Taking a second look at the crowd, I see that even though the setting is upscale, some of the clientele at tables on the outskirts are grimy-faced and emaciated, as if they only score beetle sandwiches and murky water every few days. One particular bunch of guys at the bar is gawking at Marisa over their drinks. Clearly they're the sun-scorched working class—that, or frustrated speculators. I wonder what downtrodden factory they slave away in.

The ZWC warehouse on Crab Street? I shake off a wave of panic.

Marisa flounces back, out of breath, and throws her arms around me. She plants a wet kiss on my neck. "C'mon, Varik, let's see what you're made of."

"We've got to push on."

"I can't bear to go out to the desert yet. Just another hour." There's true pain in her voice.

I'm so feverish that I can't say I disagree. Creaking out of my chair like an arthritic sailor, I slog over to the dance floor. Thankfully, the music has slowed down to a rugged ballad.

I slide my arms around Marisa's waist and pull her close, her sweat mingling with mine. God, she's sweet. Soft, broad curve out, just under the small of her back, her chest pressing into mine, hair that smells of heat and sun block with a fading hint of violets. Her face is still blessedly pale, and I pray she never gets burned. We kiss just as the song ends.

A kiss of shared adventure, of longing and protective friendship. We look at each other with a realization that we're in this deeper than ever. Reluctantly we return to the table.

"Why not stay the night?" says Geo Man expansively. I see he's ordered us more drinks. He seems delighted to be the arbiter of our renewed cheer.

We share another round. By now, everything has taken on a fuzzy, melodramatic patina: the oversize blue drinks the waitresses balance on their trays, the archetypical cowboy honky-tonk, Geo Man's frequent, wide lizard grins and larger-than-life brags about the grand future of Vegas-by-the-Sea.

"We'll be the capital in five years," he promises. "We've already set the bar for new industry. We'll build a Vollywood-by-the-Sea with the most drop-dead gorgeous video stars. We already have people planning out farmland that's safe from the sun—in warehouses, caves, underground shelters. Only need some good seed stock. I'll detoxify that ocean and drill for hidden lakes. After all, I've got drilling in my blood. We'll find those suckers even if we have to drill down to the center of the earth. We'll rival land Dominion for ballsy real estate. Hell, those snooty northerners will be stampeding the borders to come down here. Ha! We'll put up a goddamn border of our own and charge a staggering toll." And so forth.

At some point Marisa stumbles out of her seat to the "Sharkettes" powder room.

"So, what's the deal with the Fireseed cult?" I ask Geo Man as

I roll and pocket the map.

"Watch out for them," he warns me. "They think they own that desert."

"Who started the cult?" I ask.

"Oddly enough, I heard it was an old assistant of your dad's."

Someone I never met. "An overzealous assistant, huh? What's their doctrine?"

"They think the Fireseed will come back to earth to feed the world. They think the sky talks, and that the plant will fall from the sky or something. Word is, they do some pretty odd rituals." Geo Man knits his bleached brows. "Don't tell them who you are. They might try to fry up your brain and dole it out, thinking that eating the founder's DNA will mystically help Fireseed return or some bullcrap." He's taking pains to say it in a clever way, but I cringe.

Shark Bar takes on an unsettling and spooky feel, as if the ghosts of the fish forced to endlessly lap swim in this crusty aquarium are back here spinning indignant webs around us. It's not my imagination that the lone hardcore lug still on the barstool is leering at me. And Marisa is still not back from the ladies' room, even though it's been a good fifteen minutes.

I reel out of my seat. Stumbling over to the bathrooms, I pound on the shark-shaped doors. A disgruntled lady coming out of one stall tells me to watch it. I crash into one stall after the other. No Marisa, just liquor-drenched air.

Clambering up the steep, slippery agar-gel stairs, I clutch the banister and curse myself for getting trashed. My head is throbbing so badly I can hardly see. At the top landing, a steroidal bouncer in a blue Shark Bar T-shirt asks if I need a cab. I say no. He says I forgot my burn suit, says no one ventures out there without it.

"I'll get it later," I say, rushing past him. It's nighttime. I won't burn at night.

He throws me a spare burn jacket a size too small for me, says some tool left it there last week. I thank him and lurch out the door. It's nighttime, but, still, without a full suit the heat instantly reheats my scalded skin. I swallow hard. Got to find Marisa. Where? Where?

Across the street, the flickering ash from a man's smoke illuminates a row of hastily erected nomad tents. To my right, a man in a filthy burn suit is crouched against the sidewall of Shark Bar. "Some cash for a man out of work?" he croaks, holding out his gloved hand.

I step back and stumble the other way when I hear loud arguing ahead. My insides drop when I hear Marisa yell, "Get off me!"

I see now. She's being accosted by two of the withered thugs from the bar. One of them is in front of her, holding down her arms. The other guy is behind her, doing something I can't see. Shit! Is he trying to rape her?

A seawall of adrenaline knocks me out of my stupor as I race over.

Marisa screams when she sees me. "Varik! Get them off!"

I pull out my fish knife and spin behind her, jab the guy in the right side of his back. He groans and whips around with a clump of Marisa's severed hair in his fist. Frying ice! He's wearing that square-flamed ZWC earring.

"Back atcha, blowhard!" he yells. A stabbing pain streaks through my arm holding the fish knife. I cry out as it clatters to the ground.

Bending over to pick it up, I almost fall on my forehead as I overshoot it and have to pivot back to retrieve it. By the time I'm on my feet and ready to destroy them, they're a long block down the street. With fists raised, and waving the clump of hair, they yell, "Stupids, we know who you are!"

Marisa shouts back at them. "I'll set the Fleet on you, jerks!"

"Try it. By the way, Bryan says hello!" one yells, before they evaporate into the night.

I fling the bouncer's jacket around Marisa and hug her tightly. "You all right?" I ask, now holding her at arm's length for a look. Her shirt is spattered with blood, my blood. She now has short, jagged hair like a psycho elf.

"They cut my hair off, Varik. Why would they do that? Damn that asshole Bryan." She pulls at the stubs. "And look, you're bleeding." She pulls out a bandanna and ties it around my injured arm. "Poor baby."

From my peripheral vision I see nomads in front of their yurts stumble up. One yells at us. "You, rich boy! Give us some cash." I swing around for a better look. One of them, wrapped in rags like a mummy with a slit for an eyehole, is charging across the street toward us. He's got a frying homemade dagger.

"Let's get out of here," I say, wrapping my non-bleeding arm around her and guiding her toward the darter, down the street.

Panting and bleeding through the bandanna, I unlock our vehicle and practically shove Marisa into it. I race to the other side and slam the door just as the guy with the dagger thrusts it at me. The blade gets stuck in the crack of the door. With trembling hands, I rev up the darter. The guy yanks at the door handle, but he's thrown off by our sudden acceleration. I slam the door and we lift up, leaving a throng of angry, famished nomads cursing up at our darter.

I hardly know where I'm going, only that we need to get away fast.

"Let me help you." Marisa takes a second bandanna out of her pocket. I hold out my arm so she can wind it around my wound. She knots it. Then she gives my arm a soft, lingering kiss.

I decide to zoom to a parking lot on the south edge of the city. Anonymous lots seem to be our safest temporary perch. After a few false tries, I contact Geo Man and tell him what happened. He expresses his condolences, but adds, in his grandiose way, that the city is still gentrifying!

Marisa and I lean into each other and hold hands. We stay like that for a good five minutes. It helps calm me down and I even imagine that my fever is lower. "Varik," she says, "I'm really sorry I insisted we stay too long. They got me outside the bathroom with a knife in my back."

"No apology needed. We're alive," I tell her. "That's all that matters."

Just as we're settling in to sleep, a large object rockets toward my porthole. "Incoming fire!" I shout, and instinctively compress into a tight ball. Did the yurt people—or Bryan—fly after us and launch a homemade grenade? With a thunderous bang, the thing hits. I wait for smoke, fire. Realizing we didn't explode, I cautiously open the door to inspect.

"What happened, what is it?" Marisa unfurls from her own crash position.

It's brown and dirty . . . and has wings. "Fry me in the Hotzone! It's the video bird." How ironic that I blindly repeat that saying. Because I *am* in the Hotzone and I *am* frying.

We pop off the ugly bird-face and press *play*.

It's Tornado, no shocker. But he's with Freddie Vane! With Freddie, and they're not in Yellow Axe. They're standing on the luxe penthouse roof deck of the Baronland Emporium.

"I knew I saw Tornado in the Emporium!" I punch the armrest before realizing I've used my jacked-up arm. I moan as it starts to leak blood.

Marisa applies pressure through the bandanna. "I can't believe Tornado was a spy for my father!" she spits, and then says in a softer tone, "Let's listen to it."

"The Prof's son wouldn't sign the deed," Tornado is reporting to Freddie. "He wouldn't eat the doped-up candy Bryan wanted me to feed him, he wouldn't do nothing he was supposed to do."

I flush with a warped pride that I was so completely obstinate.

"Why should I pay you then, huh?" Light glints in Freddie's narrowed almond eyes.

"Because you hired me to track Marisa, that's why," Tornado says. "I kept tabs on the little lady. I gave you full reports." His gaudy dye job has transformed to a more subtle golden brown. His goatee has been freshly trimmed. Must've spent time in the Emporium's hair-reorg center. "Having Varik sign the deed was an afterthought," he adds.

"An *essential* afterthought," Freddie counters.

"Whatever." Tornado cracks his gum loudly for effect.

Freddie slaps the gum out of Tornado's mouth. "Do better!" he orders. "If you want to get another payment, get Bryan put away."

"Did you hear?" Tornado rubs his jaw. "Varik beat the tar outta Bryan in Yellow Axe."

Starvation can create monsters. Still, I'm sorry I let Bryan live back in Yellow Axe. If my father had met Bryan and heard his tale of woe, would he have had any sympathy? Probably not for Bryan.

"Not bad," Freddie offers, "but I want Bryan arrested. Melvyn Baron's beside himself since he found out his daughter has a relationship with that sickly parasite."

"But Marisa got away from Bryan." Tornado flings up his hands as if it's taken care of.

Freddie snorts. "As if I don't know that Marisa and the Prof's son are in the Zone."

"But I heard Varik was in China." Tornado's oily mug wrinkles in confusion.

Marisa gives me a playful elbow poke.

"You mutant!" Freddie yells. "You believe everything you hear on the Stream?"

"Hey, what's that?" Tornado points up at the sky. "Isn't that your bird? Why's it flying over us? And why's it flying away now?"

The video cuts out. Marisa and I howl until tears are running down our cheeks.

I'm still flying high on the laughter that lessens the throb of my stab wound when we cuddle and press close. I'm heating up, but it's not just from my fever.

Afterward, in my dream, amusement turns to a queasy disquiet when I stumble upon two Fireseed cult members in the desert. Their witchy red cowls are hiked up around their shoulders as they fornicate under a huge Fireseed statue to celebrate the anniversary of the original, mythical planting.

21.

The next morning, with wretched hangovers and our backs in paralytic cramps from sleeping another night in the darter in fetal position, Marisa and I curse the fact that we left our burn suits in the Shark Bar. We can't go back there, though. I insist that Marisa wear the bouncer's burn jacket.

"You need a burn suit, too," she says. "I know! I'll tear off part of Audun's custom insulation and make you one."

"Under no circumstances," I tell her.

Under no circumstances until we've been in flight for three hours over high desert and my facial blisters have popped and new ones have formed over the popped ones, and I'm developing nasty burn streaks down my arms and the exterior thermometer reads 162 degrees and my body is literally being parboiled.

"Do it!" I tell her.

She starts ripping the lining in long strips and cuts pieces with my fish knife. Sews it together with dental floss. I must admit, the floss is an ingenious touch. During the last part of the flight she's already got the body part done and pants for her, and she's stitching my new hood onto the body of the suit as we land on the shaded side of a pointy butte. It's about three kilometers from the mesas in the Chihuahua Desert just inside the key area Geo Man marked in green. I want to search straight away for the mimetoliths, but this is on the way, and Marisa's insisting we look here first. I'll play along. For one day.

Our hangovers are slightly better after drinking a thermos of Rain's awful green mixture and forcing down slices of beetle loaf. It's my injury that's ailing me, threatening infection as it swells.

"What now?" Marisa peers outside the porthole with a dread that's leeching into me.

Outside—the real deal. No cactus or shrub or even an insipid weed. No laughable patchwork darters from old cars, no Shark Bars, no nomad yurts or even a rusty, dinged-up bike chained to a pole. Just a million kilometers of sand interspersed with large irregular dirt patches.

I'm overcome with a recurrent nightmare I had when I was a tiny boy that started after we went out on deep ocean and the moment came when the last jetty melted away. All I saw was endless water, and my breath stopped in my chest and tears sprang to my eyes, because I was certain that I would never see land again, that I would be devoured by sharks or drown after a storm sunk our AmphiDarter.

Marisa's here, but we're really each alone, and lost. The agar will perish, its last black leaf will drop off, and there's nothing I can do about it.

I don't tell Marisa all of my nightmares. No doubt she has her own.

Instead, I suit up in her ingenious creation. She zips up her bouncer burn jacket, and wriggles into her new pants. We clip on our oxygen tanks and give each other the thumbs-up.

Then, at sunset, we climb out into the oven. Hike up Rain's burn masks higher on our faces and our hoods further down over our foreheads until there's only a narrow gap for our eyes.

We scour the ground in sections and mark off each grid as we go.

Grid 1: Dry metamorphic rock with sedimentary striations. No sign of life.

Grid 2: Dry metamorphic rock with sedimentary striations. No sign of life.

Grid 3: Dry metamorphic rock with sedimentary striations. No sign of life.

And so on.

We hike around the lone butte just inside the area of interest. Geo Man said it was highly unlikely that Fireseed would grow around a butte. "The buttes are mostly too pointed to offer shelter from sandstorms, and outside the area I've marked. They're too few and far between to offer any protection," he had said. Still, Geo Man may be wrong, even though he's hiked this land numerous times and he's a rock man and he had access to my dad's instructional videos.

But the thing is, he's not wrong. After about eight exhausting hours of this, we crawl back to the darter and collapse. My knife wound is infected. My fever has surged. I'm tempted to get out the Skiin injections, but Marisa advises me to save them for a worse emergency. Hard to imagine a worse emergency, but who knows? Marisa helps slather antibiotic lotion on my wound and I coat her cheeks with burn salve. We're a frying mess.

"We can't even do this at dusk," says Marisa.

"We'll explore strictly at night."

"And before dawn," Marisa adds.

"During the day we'll sleep," I decide, as I rest my throbbing head on the headrest. "And we should only trek in the green area that Geo Man explicitly marked."

Marisa cools her purple face on a damp towel. "True. If we waste time, we're dead."

We spend six days searching for the mimetoliths in the southern plot of the desert Geo Man marked on the map. This part alone is three hundred square kilometers, and contains a dozen concentrations of mesas in petrified sand. Each day we wake well before dawn. If we hit a mesa, we exhaustively circle around it from various altitudes. Whenever we hit a crevice that deserves further examination, I idle the darter and latch onto anything solid so we can climb out and explore.

In one crevice, we find spiders, which make us hopeful of other life in there. No plants in the crevice, but we dine on the lemonade-tasting spiders for lunch. Who knows what the creatures eat! On the second day, we stop at another breach, seeing, with huge excitement, what we think are leaves twirling in the wind, only to realize they're thin, dangling rock shards.

Our food packs and water pellets are dwindling, and we always wear the oxygen masks because the air contains dangerous levels of CO_2. My wound is slightly better, though my blisters upon blisters are raw. Now Marisa's developed blisters on the soft skin under her eyes.

Our spirits are still strong, though. At dawn when it gets too hot, we climb back into the darter, which we park on the shady side of the last mesa we studied. Then we sleep until the raging red sun charges under the horizon to torture another part of the world. At that point we start circling the next mesa we hit on the search for the mimetoliths, as we shine our infrared beams on its clefts and fissures.

There's endless variety in the surface of the rock. Some grooves are vertical, some like pockmarks, and others like S-curves or irregular amoeba shapes. Aside from the spiders we've identified as Wolf Spiders, we see no signs of life.

In between our forays I'm getting to know Marisa better. Marisa's mother, Melvyn's first wife, had an untimely death from Cutters' bacteria during a seaside vacation.

"It fired through her body, killed her almost instantaneously.

I woke up late at night and found her on the bungalow porch, with a book still in her hands. I was eight at the time."

"Awful."

Marisa goes on. "Melvyn married and divorced twice afterwards. My first *stepmother*," she says with real bite, "was a dancer with a penchant for live-eel accessories. Kept them in cages in our breakfast nook. Smelled like stale farts. The second was obsessed with winning beauty pageants. She screamed a lot about my so-called slutty clothes. Ironic, since her boobs practically fell out of hers. My dad likes 'em wenchy."

I'm not sure how to respond other than with a limpid, "Wow."

Ultimately, Marisa says she was groomed as I was, to run her father's industry. "Do you like sea farming? I mean, *really* like?" she asks me.

"I wouldn't have chosen it, but I do love the farms, the crops, the sea. And the farmers—a crusty, but loyal folk." I pop in a handful of dried peas and chew, careful not to break a tooth on one.

"You would have preferred to study medicine, right?" She turns to me expectantly, stroking my matted hair.

The desert's a world beyond—a world where if we're not careful we could lose our lives—so why not pour myself out? "Yeah, cure people. Kids, stuff like that. But now I'm not sure I can. The farm and all."

"Do it," she says as if we're back in Vostok. "Do what you want. Everything else will fall into place."

The next afternoon as we share our last pack of dried peas and rice in the darter, Marisa's back to complaining about her father, and it feels as if she's taken a few emotional steps backwards.

She shrugs. "Real estate can be interesting, but my father's never satisfied with his holdings. That turned me off, so I thwarted his hope of me taking on the family business. I mean, how could I work with a guy like that? There was never any question that I would tell the truth at the trial about how he handled those workers. The fallout was that he disowned me. Whatever I do, I'll have to raise the money myself." She toys with some peas in her upturned palm.

"Not such a bad thing."

"No, I suppose not. He's questioning all that now. But it's too late. I'm starting to do my own thing, something for the good."

Again, I wonder about her interpretation of her father, but don't challenge her on it. Challenging her clams her up, and she's finally talking.

After the trial," she says, "I went wild, hanging out in clubs all night. Like I said, that's where I met Bryan." She peers out at the mesa, the heat waves blurring its square bulk. "Bryan had a good line; I was naïve and he signed me on before I could change my mind. I fell for his *earnestness*." She toys with my ear and whispers in it, "Not trying to compare you to Bryan but . . . that's what I like about you, too."

I scratch my ear. "I guess I fell for your rash impulsiveness."

"Lovely of you to remind me." Marisa puts the clean silverware in the food bag, tosses it in the back, and we recline our seats. We're quiet for a while, and then she says, "When Freddie told me my father had a heart attack, do you think it was true, or was Freddie just trying to scare me into seeing him?"

"You know Freddie better than I do," I answer, sliding my arm around her. "We'll do the best we can down here, and when we get back, we'll swing by Baronland so you can see your father, okay?"

She leans away. "I wasn't saying I want to see him."

I pull my arm back. "Okay. Whatever." I snap my seat to upright position, grab the facemasks and the oxygen from the cargo hold in back, and hand her one of each. We've got to find those mimetoliths. Time's run out. "Let's motivate. Sun's going down."

There's only so far you can pry into someone's soul before they protest. But I have to say, Marisa builds her walls faster than anyone I've met, and, as close as I've gotten to her, it still brings me down.

22.

We've explored most of the southern section of the area marked in green and still haven't found the mimetoliths. Geo Man's map isn't all it was cracked up to be. I'm frustrated. I'm itching to see stone fishburgers or whatever, but mostly to see the cup and flower mimetoliths. I need to scout for charred stubs, or maybe . . . something more miraculous. For what it's worth, Geo Man said the cult around here believe the flower mimetolith holds the key to Fireseed, probably just because it resembles the flower. Does the cult even speak English, or do they have their own "flowerspeak"? I forgot to ask Geo Man.

I worry that down this far we're cut off from the Stream, and, for the most part, our ability to text Audun and Shin. Now that Serge is gone, I worry constantly about those agar seedlings. Is Audun taking proper care of them? Does he remember all I told him? The noise of the Stream always bothered my head, but I almost miss it now. Here, there's only the occasional pop of rocks imploding from the heat and the low hiss of the poison sun.

We still have the video bird, and we're debating sending it back for another spy session. For now, we've propped it up in the back porthole so it stares out, doubling for good luck and scarecrow mascot.

Marisa pilots the darter while I scour the land through a special infrared magnifier gadget we nabbed last minute at that camp store. The sky is overcast and seems to be developing into a storm system. Yet, no matter how overcast it's been out here in the Southwest, so far it never develops into rain.

"Oh, my God. Look!" I shout, as I crane my eyes to see. "Must be . . ." Through the dark, the mimetoliths emerge in the distant horizon. They form a semi-circle of bent and arching shapes, as if something froze them in mid-dance. I'm vibrating with excitement. They're as tall as the border wall, and they look man-made, although Geo Man insists that they're naturally formed stone. I'm about to tell Marisa about them when she starts yelling.

"Yeah, look! Fire down there!" She points to a ribbon of smoke far off to the right.

"Life!" I shout. *Or else spontaneous combustion,* I think, my heart rapping against my ribs. "And see? The mimetoliths are over to the left." I hand her the magnifier so she can see for herself.

"Wow, double jackpot," she exclaims and hugs me.

I'm eager to explore around the mimetoliths, but we decide to take a low-lying approach to first determine what the smoke is without anyone seeing us, especially after that near-disaster at the Shark Bar. Gliding over the ground, with our lights and infrared off and only the jumping sparks in the smoke up ahead to guide us, we inch closer. From two kilometers away, it's apparent that there's more than one jet of smoke, and a circle of people around a fire. There is an enormous red-cloaked throng, and they are bunched around two gigantic torches. Luckily, they're too preoccupied by whatever they're doing to gaze up in the sky, plus we're shielded by some wide buttes. I glide behind one and land. Inching open our doors, we slide out.

The trek to the edge of the butte takes a good eight minutes, as the thing is wide as a Baronland airport. It's fortuitous that the rowdy crowd camouflages any noise we're making. When we get a look at what's going on, it's hard not to emit a cry of alarm at the sight.

"Oh, man," Marisa whispers in my head mic.

"Unbelievable," I whisper back.

There must be about a hundred and fifty people in the mix, all in red cowls with red masks. Oh, man. They're no run-of-the-mill masks, they're made of metal and some have spikes sticking out to the sides. Only their eyes are visible, and it looks like they have tattoos on their foreheads. They're stomping around the fires, which are shaped like funeral pyres—tall columns with flat tops where the flames burst through. They're chanting. I make out a few phrases: something about a "special night" and "our founder" and "sacrifice."

I hope that doesn't mean they're about to throw one of their own on a pyre.

What really gets me is that in front of the two pyres is an ancient green flycar with a white stripe over the roof suspiciously similar to one my family used to own. I even see some stickers on a side window where my parents always stuck them. The sight makes my stomach churn. My eyes shift to either side of the fires, where enormous, spectacular stone carvings of the Fireseed plant stand. A score of children in the same red uniforms are stomping single file around them.

Uniforms give me the creeps. People should be free to wear what they want.

I can't put my finger on it exactly, but the vibe here reminds me of other demented cults I've heard about: the Nazis, James Jones's cyanide Kool-Aid cult in Guyana, and loony old Lionfish in Svalbardia. I could see how my quest to save the world from starvation could seem, to someone else, as grandiose as Lion-fish's deadly vision. But I can't afford to equate the two. I'm not a nut. I can't despair.

Marisa, crouching by me, points over to a scratched-up video screen on the podium between the fire pits. I gasp inside my oxygen mask. On it, my father is lecturing about plans for his experiment. It's that same frying video Marisa showed me. So the mysterious Shadow Man *is* my father. My skin breaks out in gooseflesh. I'm thoroughly spooked.

"They've pirated my family," I whisper to Marisa in my helmet mic. "I'm sure that green flycar with the stripe was my mother's."

"Oh, God." Marisa reaches out and hugs me through our padded suits. "That's so perverse. What's wrong with these people? I feel so bad for you. Are you okay?"

I nod, though I'm definitely not okay, and we turn to watch the cult. Did the guy who left my mother in the desert to fry join this cult? Was the overeager founder her murderer? Or did the cult buy her flycar at some renegade auction?

"They're frying parasites feeding on our family name, Teitur," I tell Marisa.

"No shit."

My father's saying on the video, *"I plan to sow the Fireseed crop around the flower mimetolith. This mimetolith offers protection and auspicious tidings."*

So, this video was before he grew those ten plants up. Before they burned down. "Strange," I whisper to Marisa in the head mic. "I've never known my father to be superstitious. He must've really doubted it would take root."

"If it is successful," continues my father on the video, *"I will plant crops all over my desert land to feed the refugees."* So, it's true. He did once feel for these people.

Marisa and I exchange glances and I give her a smile. "You were right," I admit. She presses my shoulder through my suit, and then we continue to study the scene.

Someone's created an audio loop of his last phrase: *"Feed the refugees! Feed the refugees! Feed the—"*

At that, the screen goes blank, and the entire tribe cheers their face off for a good five minutes, with various melodramatic lulls and swells, while the children bow down to the video as if my dad was some god.

Through our oxygen masks, Marisa and I again exchange glances—this time shocked ones. Mine suggests that I really want to avoid being thrown in those fire pits as a sacred sacrifice. Judging by the whites of Marisa's eyes and how fast her chest rises and falls under her suit, she's feeling the same.

"We'll come back here tomorrow when these creeps are gone," I whisper in the headpiece. Marisa gives me a hopeful thumbs-up.

We turn for a last long look. A look that provides concrete evidence that this is no cute airy-fairy cult contemplating the future in a perfect grain of sand—evidence that makes my blood stop in its veins.

The cheering has finally ended and the adults have herded the children, in three lines, to the podium. The guardians are now raising the sleeves of the three children in the front. Three adults with much bigger masks approach the children with a metal device resembling a fireplace poker. While the crowd chants, they start to apply the devices to the outer wrists of the children. The children start to scream. Branding irons! *They're branding them.* Even through my mask I detect the sickening stench of fried skin. The next three children come to the front, and the next. Some of the children are stoic during their ordeal, but the younger ones, some as young as about three, wail inconsolably.

I get out our magnifier to make out the brand on the arm of one child. It's . . . it's a frying Fireseed blossom. Apparently the kids have multiple brands in various sizes.

I'm deeply ashamed and appalled that my father's project inspired all this. He would've hated it. He hated any kind of abuse. Overcome with disgust, I lurch back behind the butte and slink to the ground. Marisa crouches down there with me. Her energy, like mine, feels as if it's wavering between shocked anger and terror. After a few minutes, we tiptoe back to the darter and fly to a safely remote spot for the night.

"These people are nuts," Marisa murmurs as she rests her head on my chest. "How can they do that to their own kids? I feel so, so badly for the little ones."

"I'm with you, it's beyond horrible. Even if Fireseed turns out to be the savior of the world, no child should be branded for it." I hold Marisa tight to help her stop trembling. She's in way over her head. "When you dreamed of being an activist," I whisper, "I bet you never thought it would get this menacing."

"That's for sure. This place will take a long, long time to fix." We sit in silence for a while, thinking about all that means.

"So, we'll hike to the mimetoliths before dawn," I say.

"Sounds like a plan."

Sweating from the heat and horror, I wake every couple of hours.

23.

Dawn is still an hour away yet it's already one hundred fifty-five degrees when we lock and secure the darter behind a small butte and hike the flatland toward the mimetoliths. We've mixed water and filled our thermoses. We've taken a food pack, the infrareds, and climbing gear.

We consult Geo Man's map. According to it, there are four mimetoliths: a cup, a flower, a fishburger, and a goddess. I can't help looking forward to seeing the goddess. As we start our trek, I notice that the ground is no longer seamless petrified sediment. It alternates with sand and brownish cracked dirt, separated into bone-dry circles. Some of the cracks are hard to cross without a running start.

"Let's hope those cult freaks sleep late," Marisa says. "They certainly drove themselves into a frenzy last night."

"Yeah, I'm not into being branded," I say, cringing.

"Me neither." Marisa kicks at a fissure in the ground and high-steps over the next one.

It's hard to negotiate the broken fields of dirt, with some sections as large as L'Ongitude's dance floor and others as small as a floor mat. It's what the last polar bears must've felt, leaping from one isolated patch of ice to another, and continually risking injury. The impending dawn turns the sky into swirls of blood-orange and red. It wasn't quite this color yesterday, but I guess the atmosphere is unpredictable when it contains near toxic levels of CO_2.

"How do people live with this constant level of poison air?" I ask Marisa through the headset.

"That's probably why they're warped. Their brains are pickled!"

"So . . . did you ever picture yourself down here?" I ask, changing the subject. "With me?"

"Not at all. When I first came to Vostok I was still under Bryan's spell. By the time I was starting to think for myself, when you showed me your dad's solarium, and I played you that video of your dad, well, I was sure you'd never trust me."

That whole early time with Marisa floods into consciousness: her as archenemy, then leaking secrets of the ZWC plan, us being evil to each other, me locking her out of the room while I hacked my father's chess file, me beginning to feel a confused attraction. "I had a dream way back then. You and my dad were walking through a field of puckered-up red plants."

She pauses by the edge of a wide precipice. "You should've told me about it."

"Why? I didn't trust you."

"Do you now?"

I think of that cert information I'm still holding from her. "Yeah, pretty much."

"Good." We leap over the crevice together.

The wind's picked up. It's whipping around us, making a high-pitched screech. I hope a storm's not in the works. The last burst of wind nearly knocked us over. At least we anchored the darter by a butte that should shield it. I worry that the cult might find it.

I'm so absorbed in an image of those red-suited cult members creeping around my darter that I forget to look up, and suddenly we're approaching the mimetoliths. Omigod! They are mammoth, misshapen hunks of stone, and they take my breath away.

The one on the left looks like a gigantic fish sandwich with a piece of wilted lettuce dangling from the bun. The stone goddess to its right has long, wavy hair like Marisa had before hers got chopped off. It also has a tiny waist and vixen hips under a long, stone skirt. The goddess is extending an arm as if to lure us to her. The stone cup to her right is like a wide-sloping mug of good coffee.

And the flower on the far right, well, it's the pinnacle of nature's sculptures. It has five spiky petals and two stone bumps in the blossom resembling eyes and a winding stem containing three stone leaves at inclined angles. One leaf almost seems to be waving in the wind.

How did nature get this so perfectly?

I almost understand why a cult formed, at least in part, from the sheer quirky majesty of these mimetoliths. Looking up at them is dizzy-making. Exhilarating! These accidental icons are like the four brand-new wonders of the known world.

"We're going to find Fireseed, Marisa, we're really going to find it! It's not a dream anymore, it's right here. Now. I can frying smell it." I'm ranting into the headset.

"We're going to save the agar, we will," she says a little less hopefully than me, and then she hugs me over my burn suit. We even try an awkward facemask kiss, clinking them together while puckering our lips.

Bracing against the ferocious wind, we hike up the last few meters to the cup mimetolith and reach out our arms. Even through my burn mitts, its reddish stone feels magical. An electric jolt zings up my arm as I picture my father down here in his farmer jeans and jacket, sowing seeds. I picture him seeing the first red seedlings sprout, grow tall, spread their leaves toward the open sky. And then burn up. Scouting around on the ground for charred nubs, or tiny red sprouts, I wonder where he camped around here, and how in God's name he survived this heat. On some energetic level, can he see us now? Does he know that I'm trying to carry on his work? I wonder if he's sensed enough through me in whatever realm he's in to know that not every ref is bad.

"They're not *all* scum, Dad," I whisper. "Did you see Rain and Geo Man? How about Armonk?"

I'm not sure I feel his energy coming through to me. Not sure. Perhaps he still doesn't approve of the refs. But he would approve of me trying to save the food. I'd like a sign, though. A sign would be good. All I hear in my head is Rain's voice reciting that Lakota prayer. *"Let me learn the lessons you've hidden in every tiny leaf."*

Another thing I *do* sense are all the excited and frustrated speculators who ever walked this patch of land in the last hundred years; I imagine mythical red Fireseed blossoms unfurling, stalwart through sandstorms and sucking up CO_2 like stubborn little warriors. We're so close.

We start to inspect the flower mimetolith, bending down to shine our infrared hand-lights at the point where dirt meets stone, when, from the extreme right, I see a moving flash of red. Legs approaching. My insides freeze up.

"We're not alone, Marisa," I hiss into the headset. "We need to get out of here."

"Huh?" Confusion is etched in her face as she bolts upright.

We wheel around to see that we are completely surrounded by about twenty-five Fireseed cult members in hooded cowls and red triangular-shaped masks covering all but their eyes, just like in that close-up poster in Baronland Mall. Each one has a Fireseed brand on his forehead, and each is supporting a section

of red net. The net snaps in the high wind, as they move en masse inwards. So this is what it's like to be a fly caught off guard in a spider web. My panicked mind rifles through a flipbook of unrealistic escape plans.

"What do we do?" Marisa groans.

"Follow me." I charge forward, aiming for a space between two figures, and frantically try to lift the red net. Before I can lift it up enough for us to duck under, the men on either side forcefully grab me. Judging from Marisa's curses behind me, others are manhandling her.

"Shit! Varik. What do we do now?" she gasps in the headset.

"Talk our way out." I jerk around to help her, but the men holding me down have other ideas. One of them shoves me forward while the other yanks off my mask. The blast of heat instantly scalds my recently healed blisters, and I have to bite my tongue to keep from yelping in pain. After that I start coughing from the bad air.

The dude's hollowed-out eyes bore into mine, plus his breath reeks of rot mouth. "What are you doing on our land?" he demands. "Were you conducting a ritual?"

I'm not about to tell him the land is mine and I own the deed. Like Geo Man said, if they find out who I am they may grill up some Varik brain loaf and feed it to their spawn.

"We're adventure hikers from Vegas-by-the-Sea," I lie. "We heard about how amazing the mimetoliths are." I draw my brows in a threatening manner to accentuate my right to be here. "What's it to you?" I ask, before gasping for some decent air.

Other cowled men and women are crowding around to hear what I have to say. I see they've left Marisa's mask on. At least she won't bake or choke on too much CO_2. But we won't be able to talk to each other anymore through our head mics. Not good.

They're having trouble holding onto their net in this frenzied wind. The net is tacking all over the place like a Tern in a hurricane. I'm suddenly hopeful it will blow away and we can make another run for it. But they've obviously planned ahead. We're being tied up, arms behind our backs, by a shiny red binding. Not agar, so maybe destructible.

"You speak untruth," exclaims the other man who grabbed me. He's tall yet hunched at the same time, as if he's suffering from scurvy or a bone disorder. The thought occurs to me that I could crack his brittle backbone with some fast kung-fu footwork; except that there'd then be twenty-four stronger cult members up in my face.

Marisa yells something in her headpiece, but it comes out all garbled.

The hollow-eyed guy wags his finger at me. "We've heard of your journey and we know who you are," he insists. Other cult members are solemnly nodding as they edge closer.

How is that possible? Do they get the Stream down here? Did Nevada tell them, or what? "You have no idea," I shout back. "My mask. I need my mask."

Hunchback steps over with an overzealous smile. "We know. Fireseed tells us."

"What? Fireseed talks to you?" I ask incredulously. "Have you ever actually *seen* your Fireseed god?" No one answers me. Ha! No easy answer for that query. "Where's Fireseed? Where's the actual flower?" I yell.

"Fireseed is in here." Hollow-eye taps his heart, and the others all copy him.

"And Fireseed is up there." A smallish female, who's weaseled her way in to the center, nods up at the sky.

They're no better than Lionfish's disciples, all spouting chapter and verse from the bible of the loopy sea king. I was hoping to get information from the cult here, but it would be a useless measure now that I understand the unfortunate depth of their lunacy.

Marisa struggles to loosen the guy's grip on her rope. With a momentary flicker of hope I recall her amazing knot training. She screams a few other things, but again, it's garbled inside her mask.

"Okay," I shout indignantly at the crowd, "if you're so fryin' smart, tell me who I am."

"You're the founder's son," Hollow-Eye says reverently. "You are Varik Teitur, and you've come home at last." He holds his palms face up and waves them over me, as if I'm an important foreign ambassador.

Home? My skin prickles. I'm hacking and choking. I can't pull a decent breath of clean from this crap air.

After this, a bunch of them start shoving fellow members out of the way for an up-close-and-personal glimpse of us. They pet us and poke at us. My claustrophobia's triggered, which makes my breathing even more labored. I'm trying to push them back with my shoulders. Through all of this, I try to keep track of Marisa, and stay close to her, because it's obvious from her expression that she's unhinged.

"Look, this is all a big mistake," I choke out. "We're just some kids from the coast who saved up Ds for a really polar vacation and—"

One particularly ardent guy leaps at me and gives me a sloppy bear hug. That's it. I charge him with a hard chest knock. He flies to the ground, gawking up at me with a hurt look.

This is getting more sinister by the second. First they're hostile and ready to rip our heads off, and then they're telling us we're home? I'm so upset I'm about to piss my pants.

Hollow-Eye starts pulling on our rope, leading us out of the circle. "We're taking you to the children," he says robotically. "They need to see the founder's son in the flesh."

"Hold on!" I shout. "If you think my father started your crazy cult, you—"

Hunchback storms over and clamps his big paw over my mouth. "Blasphemy!" he screeches.

"How can the guru's son speak blasphemy?" I roar. No one answers me. Instead, they have us walking single-file, like some refugee chain gang doomed to scrape sand off petrified rocks with a toothbrush for ten hours under the wrath of the red sun.

Red, this whole godforsaken place is red: from the blood running from their branded children's arms, to the CO_2-poisoned sky, to our re-infected blisters, to my crimson fury I can no longer contain.

It rises up in me like a blowtorch. Arguing is risky. But I can't help reprimanding them. "Speaking of your children, we saw that branding ceremony last night." I scowl at Hunchback, then Hollow-Eye, then at the entire lot of them. "You have no right burning your kids' arms with brands. You claim to be holy, or spiritual, with your, your Fireseed statues and all? Well, my father, the one who invented the plant your whole religion is based on, would've turned your red rumps into the Dominion Troopers for child abuse."

For my efforts, a hulkish cult guy, who was already edging toward me, elbows me hard in the back. "Blasphemy," he repeats. Clearly, I'm not immune to abuse just because I'm the Prof's son. I guess they like to mix it up pretty rough with their lesser gods, like in ancient Greece. From Marisa's loud groan, it sounds like she's also getting punished for my insolence.

"Leave the girl alone," I yell, but they drag Marisa forward as if they didn't hear me.

We hike for about twenty minutes. By the time we finally reach a red barrack with a long front porch, I'm gasping for an ounce of good air. The compound looks as if it's built in blocks of sand treated to harden. There's no storage shed, no greenhouse, no stockpiles of supplies in sight. I'm trying to imagine what in heck the people eat here, when a bolt of lightning strikes soundlessly in the near distance, and another hits down, closer.

The others look nervously at the lightning and then quickly rush past Hollow-Eye and Hunchback, in their haste to get inside. We're led down a hallway lit with floor candles in red sconces. Hollow-Eye pulls down his mask and turns to check on us. He's an ugly guy, with beetled brows and a pointy nose poking out of a badly shaven face. His skin has that Zone look of worn cowhide. The men pause at the double doors of an auditorium. I try to weasel close to Marisa but they create a blockade with their bodies.

I crane my neck to see inside the space and nearly lose it when I see a gigantic mural of Fireseed on the back wall. It's not the plant that alarms me. Standing in front of the plant are renderings of my father, my mother, *and me.*

Holy freaking Ice! The contents of my stomach push against my throat and I almost puke. I swallow hard and take a tentative breath. These people are bloodsucking sea worms sucking out their hosts' organs. Do they have chapter and verse of my childhood, too, in their holy text? What about the story of my mother, burning in the desert? Did they make that into a cautionary parable for their disciples? Do they have a final chapter, in which my father abandoned them? I suppose they left that chapter out.

Marisa's motionless, totally stricken as I am as she stares at the mural, and I lament the day I asked her to come down here with me. If *I* die by the hands of this freak patrol, so be it. Ironically fitting: three Teiturs done in by the very cult that worships and adores them. It's another matter entirely if Marisa dies because of me. When she looks over at me there are tears running down her face. I mouth the words I love you.

Scanning the room, I see the kids are here, arranged neatly in rows of red desks facing toward the center of the room. They look joyless and bored. One of them is absently picking his nose. A teacher's giving them what seems to be the day's lesson plan.

"When Fireseed bloom in your heart, you must give your soul to the cause," he's saying.

I sneak a closer glimpse of the kids. Their burn suits are off and they're in stretchy red jumpsuits of a thinner and cheaper material. Besides being emaciated and having the same kind of hollowed-out expression as one of the men who grabbed me, there are other unsettling things about them.

They have blue lips—oxygen deprivation and malnutrition for sure. Pieces of their jaws and cheeks are gouged out. I remember Marisa telling me about dimers. Were these old dimer sites or what? A little girl who's raising her hand is missing three fingers, and many have nasty third-degree burns, which have melded parts of their features. The doctor in me longs to fix them, no matter who, or what they belong to. I look over at Marisa. She sees it too. Through more tears, she mournfully shakes her head.

In fact, the entire room has a starved, stingy feel to it. The shelves are almost bare, the kids have no books on their desks, there's no rug, no curtains softening the line of flower-shaped portholes. The portholes aren't made from agar; I can tell by their dull quality. I wonder what they're made of.

The girl with the missing fingers glances over and we lock eyes. She must be only three or four yet her expression is almost lifeless like the men who caught us. But as I continue to smile at her, her face changes in increments; first into a nervous, fearful look, then into an aching gaze, and finally into a faint grin. You're still human, I think, with a surge of joy. You haven't lost it yet. If I ever make it back here, I'll help these kids escape—somehow.

Through one porthole, a second bolt of lightning bursts forth, followed by a thundering crackle. Daunting weather. I'm relieved to have a roof over my head, even this one. We can try to make a getaway after the impending storm.

Hunchback begins an announcement. "The founder's—"

A teenage boy streaks in and over to the lecturer. He twitches as he shouts, "Fireseed is speaking! Fireseed is sending a strong warning."

"Warning! Warning! All in receiving position." A lady from the crowd that has followed us in wags her hands wildly. "Fireseed is sending messages!"

Marisa and I give each other pointed looks that ask, *What are these nuts talking about? The lightning?*

There's mass pandemonium. The kids start screaming as they scramble out of the room through an interior door. The lecturer gathers up his notes and flees through another door. Hunchback pulls us, hog-tied, back down the corridor and out to the porch as he debates with Hollow-Eye over which one of them will escort us to the storm chamber. I'm not sure which is worse! Staying tied up out here, exposed to this lightning, or being tied up in some hot, airless cellar. I picture desert creatures nibbling on our exposed skin.

Meanwhile, a hundred molten arteries of light transform the sky into a streaky firestorm. My strategy is to press close to Marisa and hatch an escape plan using sign language while the two zealots argue about our welfare. She cocks her head at my arms, and then makes a circular motion. I turn so we're facing away from each other.

Surreptitiously, she works at my binding. She's nudged her mitts off, but she's doing it blindly, because her hands are also tied behind her. I try hers next, but these are no normal knots. There are no ends, just a seamless looping back of a tough, yet pliant material I can't identify.

Perhaps these people aren't as dense and retro as they seem.

Marisa makes a frustrated face through her mask and we give up on that possibility.

I tune into our captors' conversation. Hollow-Eye's saying to Hunchback, "Fireseed is sending a warning that the founder's son is not to be treated roughly."

I shout, "If I'm so sacred, why am I tied up?"

Hunchback glances my way, then, without answering my question, he moves further down the porch. I might be sacred, but on some level he obviously senses I'm an unwilling prophet.

I hear Shin in my mind. *Play the game, dude. Play it.* Shin's good at tek. My father worked his Chess. Now I must excel at strategy. No other option.

I study the two men. Figure out an angle. Hunchback glares at Hollow-Eye and pulls his cowl further over his forehead. "Your interpretation is misguided. Fireseed is saying that the time is wrong for the manifestation. It is not time for Fireseed to descend to Earth."

Huh? As in their cracked Fireseed god will appear out of nothing and flap down on its leaf-wings to bless and feed them all?

Why are they only talking about the founder's *son?* Marisa's here, too. What? Are they planning to dispose of her and make me king? These worries are scared out of me when a thick vein of lightning hurtles down mere steps away, and is followed by a cluster of new light columns that electrify the yard *right in front of us.* They come close to singeing off every toe on my foot.

Marisa loses it. She clings to me for dear life. There's never been lightning like this up in Ocean D. Never, ever. No matter how massive a hurricane blows through.

Play the game, my mind keeps yammering.

"What exactly do you mean, *manifestation?*" I yell over to where they're still debating.

Hunchback walks over and frowns at me wordlessly as if I'm a normally brilliant student who's been getting trashed and skipping class.

A few cult members have begun to peek out the door, until a new torrent of bolts that scorch the edge of the porch send them back inside screaming. Smoke wafts up. Even the two head guardians of the faith freeze as they stare fitfully at the smoke.

Sensing a chink in their holy armor, I yell over at Hunchback, who seems to be the alpha zealot. "Listen up! I, the founder's son, have correctly interpreted this pure and true warning from Fireseed."

For the first time since being hauled out in the lightning, Marisa raises her head.

Clearly trying to usurp the hunchback's power, Hollow-Eye

rushes to my side. "Yes, founder's son?" he says eagerly.

"The message from Fireseed is clear," I announce in as forceful a voice as I can muster, while stretching out my arms out like a Stream actor playing Zeus. "It is saying it will never manifest as long as you hold the founder's son, or the son's girlfriend, or anyone the son is connected to. Get it? It's saying that soon you'll have nothing. No god, no food. You'll all die in this forsaken desert waiting for the rapture."

Hollow-Eye looks dubious. Hunchback starts pacing as he strokes his whiskers.

Marisa is yelling something from under the mask. I wish I could hear what she's saying.

Another bolt of lightning blasts the ground near us, sending up a rush of dirt. The storm is directly overhead. We must get off this flimsy porch to safer cover. *Now.*

"Heed my warning, or the rapture will not come," I repeat loudly.

Hollow-Eye and Hunchback march down the porch to continue their argument.

Hollow-Eye glares at Hunchback. "He says Fireseed will never manifest as long as we hold him."

"He is the son, not the founder," Hunchback counters.

Marisa and I exchange worried looks. My lines aren't working.

"But the son is of the founder; he's in the sacred circle," says Hollow-Eye.

Hunchback taps his foot impatiently. "Not necessarily. Your interpretation's too literal."

"And yours is too open-ended." Hollow-Eye starts getting up in Hunchback's space, clearly gaining the upper ground. "We saw them by the Fireseed mimetolith," he adds. "That is a crystal-clear sign. He can tell us the next prophecy. I insist."

I yell at the top of my lungs, "I'll tell you that prophecy right now! You've made Fireseed very angry. If you don't let me go,

Fireseed will kill you as we stand, on this porch!"

At this moment, the sky literally opens up with firepower. I almost believe it's the wrath of the great Fireseed when, with an earsplitting crash, the heat storm's heavy artillery strikes a porch column to the left of us. It severs into pieces, toppling the porch roof with it. The cult leaders flee to the yard, dragging us after them on the rope.

"Get rid of them. Now!" yells Hunchback. "This one is not like the founder. He's a false prophet. Free them before they kill us all!"

As the sky continues to rain down high voltage, Hunchback and Hollow-Eye run us out beyond the compound. Hunchback fishes a circular gadget out of his pocket that unlocks our strange looped hand binding. They frantically gather it up, then scramble back to their yard and disappear behind the walls of their dubious sanctuary.

Marisa and I charge out of there, dodging the arrows of Fireseed, or whatever one nicknames this weather disaster. It's hard to flee with constant strobes in my eyes. Even when I blink shut, I see veins of white heat behind my retinas. As we run, me gasping and choking, we strain to recall which direction will get us safely back to our darter.

24.

After a false start and a hit from a lightning bolt that singes the top of Marisa's backpack, we trace our path back to the point of the mimetoliths. It's intense to see them again. It's like I have a deeper relationship with them now, knowing how sacred they are to the cult, and to my dad. And I already thought they were the new wonders of the world.

Marisa and I clasp each other as we walk from there to find the darter. She still has her mask on, but at least we're free to try sign language. We hold each other even tighter as the wind stirs up stinging sand in my eyes, down our suits, and up my nose. Even though the lightning's eased off, the sandstorm renders the air thick and brownish. It's hard enough to see at night, but near impossible in this brownout. It's as if we're struggling against a semi-solid undertow.

In one of the last bursts of electrical heat, the sky is illumi-nated through the thick wall of sand and we catch a glimpse of my red darter peeking from behind the low butte.

It's never looked so good! I can't wait to grab the backup oxygen and suck in a clean breath, ease the sick ache in my lungs and this weak, dizzy feeling.

In a happy burst of energy, we pick up our pace, ready to unlock the doors.

Something's very wrong. Marisa is pointing with her mitt to the passenger door. The darter's already unlocked. Beyond a doubt, we locked this thing up when we left this morning. We plunge inside and slam the doors shut. Marisa removes her mask and shakes out sand from her hair.

"The video bird's gone from the back porthole," I tell her. "Oh, no. The latchbags with the seed disks are missing! Lots of supplies are missing." I climb in the back hatch and dig through things.

"We've been robbed!" Marisa states the obvious. She's pawing through a supply bag she left on the floor of the front seat. "They took the food packs and our water pellets!" she exclaims. "I only have two thermoses in my backpack. Do you have more in yours?"

I check my pack. "I've got two thermoses, and a water pellet." Enough to live on for a week if we're lucky, but I don't dare say that. Pure animal terror fills my hollow body. The cult terrified me, yet I sensed they wouldn't kill me—the founder's son. I was less sure what they'd do to Marisa. "Now we're on our own," I say. "We need to keep up a fast search for the Fireseed and get out of here before supplies run out. God knows how the agar plants are back home."

Marisa nods slowly as she brushes sand off her lap. "If we're starving, we could sneak back to the cult to steal some food," she says.

"Bad option. Not sure we could find our way back again. It was a fryin' miracle that we navigated here in this storm."

"That lightning was unreal," she agrees. "And this sandstorm's rocking us like we're in a toy boat."

It's true. As I dig around in back, I keep losing my balance and smacking my elbows and my head against the wall. Despite this, I manage to examine the contents of another stash box under the hatch that someone's rifled through. "They left the topical antibiotic, the Skiin injections and some Cipro; a few bandannas, some clothing . . . Burn it, Marisa! They took the extra mask and the oxygen and hydrogen tanks. That means we can't even make water with the pellet we have."

"We're screwed."

"Had to be the cult," I say under my breath.

We gape at each other in horror.

"Who else would be crazy enough to run around here in this, this—" She picks up her oxygen mask and throws it on my lap. "Here, breathe some good air," she shrills. "It's on me."

"Try to calm down. Save your energy."

"For what? Dying?" She grabs the mask, clips it on, and turns the door handle.

"Where are you going?" I take her arm.

She wriggles free. "Don't know. Give me a moment. I'm freaked out."

"But the storm!"

Struggling against the wind, she crawls out and slams the door. I'm left staring at the sand biting pinhole notches in the windshield. Agar's destructible after all, my sluggish mind tells me.

After a minute of this, I tie a bandanna, one of the few things the cult so generously left us, around my face. Then I bungee on my sunglasses, grab my small infrared from my pack, and brace for the sandblast as I venture outside to rescue Marisa from herself.

I manage one tentative step before the wind swoops me off the ground. It's like going up in an elevator way, way too fast. Then it drops me down hard. Picking myself up, I jerk around to see where Marisa has wandered off.

Stumbling through the blast with my arms out in front of me, I march stiffly ahead, one cautious step at a time. The light only helps so much in this sandy onslaught, but in a minute or so I catch a glimpse of her mitt, waving me over.

She's kneeling down, turning something over. I lift my shades for a split second. Sand batters my eyeballs as I glance down to see a beak, a dirty wing bent backwards. She raises her mask just over her mouth and shouts over the high roar of the sand, "It's the video bird! It was lodged in the butte, and—"

"Let's get back inside the darter!" I shout back.

She nods and slips her mask back on. We manage, against the sand torrent, to collect the stash.

Inside, we inspect the objects more closely: video bird, two food packs, and another of our infrared hand-lights, all in a clear bag. Marisa opens one of the food packs and doles out a handful of raisins. We savor them. It's been so long since I've eaten that blood rushes to my gut in a huge mineral rush. I pick up the video bird and roll it around. Before I wedge it back in the rear porthole, I open its head to make sure the parts are intact.

"There's a note in here!" I exclaim.

Marisa tosses her last handful of raisins in her mouth. "Let's see it."

I unfold it and read. *"Sorry,* is all it says. *Sorry."*

"Wow. Someone felt bad about robbing us, I guess." Marisa lets out a derisive snort. "They could've felt sorrier and left us an extra mask. I mean, how will you explore in this weather without your good mask?"

"Not sure." I lean back wearily against my seat.

But sorry is a lot. I have about a minute to contemplate the balance between good and evil, whether the world is more evil than good, or more good than evil. And to realize that maybe it's skewed slightly to the good side, because there was one good Samaritan wandering in the desert and at least we weren't annihilated like my mother was out here. All of this before our darter is whisked up in an epic sand funnel a million times stronger than the one that lifted me off the ground moments ago. Think headrush from the Disphotic to the Euphotic Zone in two seconds. Think instantaneous migraine. My ears pop. I flail for solid footing as I'm suspended over my seat. So, this is why people wear seatbelts! My brain has reverted to stupid time to compensate for its free-floating fright as I review the obvious.

Marisa grabs onto me. I guess she knows this might be the end. "Remember. You're my favorite person in the world."

I fold her in, and start to say, "And you, me." For a split second we're in a terrifying holding pattern in the sky. And then we slam down.

25.

I wake to my head exploding into shards of pain. Fry me, where am I? My mouth tastes like a rotfish swam in there and died. My limbs feel stuck in seabed muck and my ribs are throbbing. The dawn sun is only a rising pink sliver, but already it's hotter than frying hell. I cautiously lift my hand to my cheek. It feels as if it's missing a layer of skin. I brush it lightly, which causes it to sting unbearably. Drawing my hand down to where I can see it, there's blood, blood mixed with sand and oozing liquid. I moan as I try to lift my upper body off of what I realize is my darter seat.

It's all rushing back and filling my head with horrid clarity. We crashed, that's it. We're in the desert and we flew off the ground in a sandstorm and we landed . . .

"Marisa?" I say, casting my right arm onto her seat, in an attempt to reach out to her. She's not there. She was sitting next to me, so where is she now? Was she thrown from the flycar, is she . . . Don't even *think* the D-word. "Marisa?" I yell louder.

Where is my Marisa?

I jerk up in the seat. As I do this, sand that has blown inside cascades off me. I see the windshield is cracked, and the darter front is half-buried in the sand, although it's no longer storming. Marisa's door is bent back, exposing the car interior to the wind, which swirls into the open space. She was thrown from the vehicle, I realize with dread.

"Marisa?!" I yell. Groaning, I shove open my dented door.

The sky is turning back to blood-orange. As I creep out of the flycar, it rocks unsteadily. The front hood is sticking up and the back is sunken in a jumble of rocks that must be loose, judging by the way the vehicle lurched when I climbed out of it. The darter's totaled beyond belief—dented sides and crushed tail. I get down on my stomach and shimmy over to the right front wheel to peer down between the rocks. "Marisa," I call, "are you down there?" I angle my hand-light through the rocks. I can't see much, but it's not all rock. My light bounces off a surface a few meters down. There's some kind of hollow space in there, who knows how deep? This means the rocks could give out any minute. If they caved in, the darter would fall in further.

Wriggling slowly back, I groan in pain. My chest is killing me as I rise to my feet. The sun has seared sand into my raw cheeks. Got to find Marisa. I start to stumble around in the rust-tinged clouds that seem to be eye level. I look off into the distance. Walk to the edge of the crest. Realize that I'm hundreds of meters up when I see more clouds below—and through them, sandy desert.

Sweet burning ice!

I'm way up on a rock formation with a wide flat crest, and the force of the crash has smashed my flycar into the middle of the crest. This space up here is so wide that I can only make sections of the edges. "Marisa?" I call out.

Except for the crash site, which cracked some of the rock, the surface is flat and solid. Nothing's growing up here. I get one of the bandannas from my pocket and inch it over my raw cheeks. If the wind picks up, I can't afford to have more sand lodged in my face. I start charging around, reeling from the pain, desperate to find my girlfriend.

Tears of joy spring to my eyes because I see her near the lip of an edge about fifteen meters from me, and she's moving. She's moaning, and rolling over and . . .

"Don't move, Marisa!" I shout as I limp-run over. "You're right on the edge of a cliff. Stay put." For once will she listen to me without being belligerent and doing the very opposite I ask of her? "Don't move!" I yell again, already kneeling by her side.

She looks up and smiles. The smile shifts into a grimace of pain. She reaches out her hand, which I take and begin to stroke. I notice she's bleeding through the arm of her suit.

"Are you okay?" I ask softly.

"Mnnn. Wha? I uh . . ."

She's slurring her words. Oh, man. Did she hit her head, too? Does she have a concussion? "Do you remember what happened?" I ask nervously.

"Um, uh, yeah . . . a sandstorm," she answers. "It was . . . bad, wasn't it?"

What a huge relief that she's talking, thinking straight. "Bad beyond belief," I answer, as I gently brush sand off of her. "The wind lifted the flycar right off the ground. Blew it all the way up here. We crashed on a butte or something." The muscles in her hand tighten. "We didn't lose everything," I say. "We have those supplies you found." I don't let on that I'm crazy worried or that I have no idea yet how to get off this rock if we can't start my darter. And the likelihood of starting it is remote.

"Can you walk?" I ask her.

"I think so." After a few tries she gets to her feet, then she loses her balance. The second time she stays up. We help each other over to the darter. It creaks and sways as we climb inside it. I tear off more of the insulation to use as bandages. Thankfully the cult members spared our topical antibiotic.

I try to start the flycar. Nothing doing, just as I suspected. The thing is dead, dinged up beyond belief. Audun would shit a king crab if he saw his amazing custom job in this condition. At least we can use it for shelter until we figure out a way off this behemoth.

Because up here, this high in the sky, the sun will kill us otherwise.

That reminds me. The Skiin sharps! I hid them under the floor mat on the driver's side to keep them as cool as possible.

They're still there. I get them out. It's time. Going outside again without protection isn't an option. I offer to inject her.

"You first," she insists.

The stuff in the vial is years old. It was refrigerated, sure, but it's an unsettling pink color, and I remember it as clear. Enough dithering. Time to take a deep breath and inject myself. I lurch forward from the mighty pinch and sting that jets up my backbone, branches out into my nerves. It's like being attacked from the inside by an entire hive. I shout in pain and hug my ribs.

From the force of my sudden movement, the back of the darter squeals and shifts.

"Whoa. Are you okay?" Marisa looks over worriedly and wipes beads of sweat from my forehead. I shuffle my head up and down in a stunned nod. If I reveal how badly the injection hurt she won't do it, and she must. Marisa rests her good arm on my knee and pulls up her sleeve. "Do you really think this will help?"

"Growing a layer of leather is the only way we'll survive another day here." The sting of my shot is now a distracting throat-to-gut itch that has me wanting to tear at my skin with my claws. I give her a smaller dose. God knows what this stuff might do. She flinches, but tries not to make any fast moves. I'm impressed.

Climbing out of the darter is precarious as it moves under our feet, and more stones below the darter crash down inside the hollow. We'd best use the vehicle only for the worst heat of day.

Marisa seems to have a broken arm and a few alarming head cuts on her scalp. Besides my burnt face and numerous gashes on my legs, I'm pretty sure my ribs are broken. Either that or the CO_2 has damaged my lungs so badly they feel as if they're being ripped out with a wrench whenever I take a deep breath. I make Marisa a sling for her arm out of the insulation. We share the oxygen. It won't last much longer anyway.

Back outside, we hobble as close to the edge of the cliff as we dare, and then shimmy the rest of the way on our bellies. Marisa's scared of heights, and both of us are unsteady on our feet.

Sweet ice! Looking down and across from this dizzying bird's eye view, I see the spikes of the stone flower pointing up at us. I turn. The other stone spectacles are lined up beyond.

"We're on top of the cup mimetolith!" we shout in unison.

The sandstorm might have been a blessing after all. An opportunity to search the crest! I'd thought of trying to scale the walls, but not this crest. Pretty sure my ropes aren't long enough to get us off of this thing, but one step at a time. This is the cup mimetolith that my father grew those ten plants up by.

26.

Dumbfounded at the view, I see the rust-tinged clouds have shifted away, revealing a rolling blanket of new sand dunes over the patchy, crackled land. It resembles the snowy fields in my granddad's old digital photos. I remember imagining what it must have been like to go cross-country skiing like my grandfather could. Now I wonder how we'll ever get off this towering rock, and if we do, how in hell we'll trek across these dunes to safety.

"Shit," I mutter under my breath.

Marisa points to a spot due south. "There's the cult compound." A glaring red rectangle shimmers in the distance. They've already cleared off the mountains of sand from their walls and roofs.

"We must've hiked at least two kilometers through that storm," I say. "There's the ceremonial grounds with the statues, see it? Between the mimetoliths and their compound."

"Oh. Yuck." Marisa skitters back on all fours from the ledge as if she can't get far enough away from that branding scene. "No ritual flesh-burning today," she remarks dryly.

I snake back too and groan as I struggle to my feet. "You could sauté a fryin' whale out here."

The sun is fast becoming oppressive. We cover up with everything we can—the darter's floor mat, a towel, and a pair of long pants. I look at my arms. No thicker skin on them yet. Before long we're forced to crawl back inside the darter, which keels and bows in a terrifying manner over the jumble of loose rocks. With so much of the insulation stripped, the flycar doesn't offer much protection from the sun, but any heat shield is better than none. We manage to bend Marisa's door back in place, leaving only a gap the size of a hand held sideways. Once we're inside the darter, it's easy to keep still. With our injuries and third-degree burns, mostly what we long for is sleep. We nibble the rest of the raisin pack and doze until nightfall.

In the moonlight, we gather up strength to inspect the entire crest of the cup. I search and search for any sign of charred stubs. Or larger red stalks. If Fireseed grew up here, on this mimetolith, it could hide itself from all of the cult members below. But all I see is flat, dull rock, with no trace of Fireseed or any other hint of burnt-up plant. We also inspect the smashed-in area under the darter, by shining my infrared and Marisa's smaller pocket light down through the larger gaps near the back wheel. It must be a deeper hollow than what I can see, because the light won't reach all the way down. It occurs to me that I could climb inside to explore, but moving any rocks could unhinge the darter, plus I doubt the occasional cracks in the interior walls would hold my weight. I might do it, though, leave nothing to fate. In the process of inching back up to a standing position, my eye catches on the video bird, propped up again in the back porthole. His head's cocked at a crazy angle, and he's glaring at me as if to say, "What now, buddy?"

With this, another idea occurs to me. I creep into the darter as my ribs and lungs screech in silent pain, and collect the old bird. Bringing it back to where we're sitting, I say to Marisa, "What if we send Victor Vidbird here to your activist friend, Nevada Pilgrim, with an SOS? She might be batting for the other team, but I can't think of anyone else who would venture down here."

"It's a long shot, Varik. Nevada might seem approachable, but she's part of the ZWC. Second, what's to say Bryan doesn't intercept it?" Horrible thought. Can't even go there. Seeing my apparently downtrodden expression, Marisa takes a more gamely approach. "We should try it, though. I mean, finding our way back here in that storm was also a complete long shot."

"Or even surviving this crash," I remind her.

We set up the hand-lights so they're shining on our faces. We make it short and sweet.

Marisa starts. "We crashed in the desert, Nevada," she says into the camera. "No matter what you think of Varik or his politics, we're desperate. We need help."

I take my turn. "Nevada, whatever you thought of my father, I sense you're a good person. Our darter crashed on the cup mimetolith in the Chihuahua Desert. You must know of that in your travels. We're burning alive. Help if you can. I'll owe you. Big time." I announce our coordinates and click off.

We program in Nevada's pager number and seal the bird's head with one of the last viable strips of heat insulation. With her good arm, Marisa paints a sloppy 'NEVADA' on the bird's wing in purple nail polish she had in her pack. I never imagined I'd be grateful for a girl's endless stash of "necessary" trinkets.

Then we activate the send trigger. The bird is corroded, and sand is streaming from it. For a while all it does is spazz out with its wings whirring but not flapping. Just when I've given up on it, its wings come unstuck and it lurches up. We chant Rain's prayer as we watch it falter northwards.

After that, we crawl back into the flycar and collapse in each other's arms.

Day Two: Marisa's burning up with fever. Even though we're both dehydrated and fighting infections, hers seems worse, so I give her the last Cipro tablet. Her eyelids and cheeks are swollen and her hair's in a sodden, red tousle. She must be fifteen pounds lighter than when we started this trip. No doubt my face must look like fish guts, while my body is mummified in gluey, filthy insulation that keeps sticking to my seat. We're the breathing pre-dead.

I do see, with a spark of hope, that our skin is thicker, tougher. The Skiin formula is making some difference after all! It may buy us some time. Marisa sleeps most of the day in the flycar, while I wait out the sun next to her, drumming my fists on the steering wheel as I think up strategies. We have rope. I could shimmy down the outside of the stone cup and try to get help; but from where, the cult? Certainly not from Hunchback or Hollow-Eye! Come to think of it, the outside walls may house some Fireseed nubs. It's worth a try to rappel down.

At dusk, I unearth our three ropes—another thing the cult missed because they were in a hatch under my floor mat. I tie them to each other, moving very slowly, as my ribs are killing me with each reach and step. There's no good choice of anchor to secure the rope to if we were crazy enough to go down it. For now, I tie one end to the darter's back fender, rest the bulk of the rope on top of the vehicle, and stick the other end in the side door handle.

Again, I shine my light into the hollow, reaching deeper this time. The interior surfaces of the walls are curious. They're studded with about a dozen knob-like protrusions. Nubs! My mind starts jumping all over the place. A long shot, but could these be petrified remnants of Fireseed? I try to touch one to see if it has a charred surface, but I can't reach it. I rig up a bandanna on a pole and rub some of the nubs. Pulling them up, I'm disappointed. No trace of charcoal. But what's further down in that hollow? I need to explore every possibility.

When Marisa finally wakes up, we share half of a water thermos and I dribble some on her forehead.

"I'm considering exploring the hollow," I tell her. "Or I could rappel down for help."

And to look for any charred remains of the flower plant.

"Either way it's so dangerous, Varik. Either way it could mean death. Can't we wait for a flyover?"

I stroke her forehead surreptitiously, guessing that her fever's even higher. "We need better shelter," I tell her. "Even with our tougher skin, we're getting sun poisoning."

"Don't leave me here. I'm too weak to climb down that rope," she says in a barely audible voice. Marisa's always game for anything. This new faintness of heart upsets me more than her fever. As we search the orange sky for flycars, I cradle her in my arms. "We'll be found," she says. "Someone's bound to fly through here on his way east."

"Maybe," I say. "Or the Samaritan from the cult who left us our supplies may come back around and we can call down an SOS." Truth is I wouldn't know that guy from anyone. Very soon I'll have to defy Marisa and use that rope. I need to explore that hollow.

I break open the last Restavik-boar food pack, hoping it will bring back Marisa's strength and remind her of home, which will hopefully lift her spirits. She rallies enough to suggest we tie her red bandanna up on the side trim we wrenched off the darter, in case any sympathetic flycars are passing over.

We wedge the trim rod into a tiny fissure about ten meters from the darter and attach a bandanna to the top. It provides a speck of hope, flapping under the stars.

Day Three: Even in the darter, we're broiling alive. Through the cracked agar pane, the heat creates globular mirages that turn into leaping speckles. Not trusting my eyes, I turn away from the sight. I funnel part of the last water thermos to Marisa, and then get the second set of Skiin sharps out. I've noticed lengthwise cracks in our skin opening up—a result of rancid formula? Fissures are better than the flesh burning clear off. After I inject myself, I'll shimmy down the rope into the hollow. Inspect the place for nubs. Check out every angle. After all, this is the cup.

The needle goes in and I press the dispenser. The pain is merciless. Like nettles pressing through my flesh into my veins. I can't help but violently jerk. Marisa comes out of her stupor to hold me. The darter shudders, nose up. We're tilting wildly upwards now as if we're about to blast off from an almost vertical trajectory. We stay absolutely still, ready to scramble back onto the crest if need be. But the darter miraculously stabilizes itself.

I start to say, "Let's get out of this darter before I—" when more rocks drop away and we're catapulted backwards. I clutch the door handle to keep from falling upside down. As I do, the Skiin sharp slips from my hand. With a tinny echo, it clatters to some unknown location along with the medical kit.

"Hold on!" I yell as Marisa slides backwards, over her seat.

In a burst of energy, I open my door and take hold of the rope that I hung from the outside handle. "Grab on with your good arm!" I yell, offering Marisa a section. I reach for her and clasp her around her waist. With all my might I shift us both out my side door and try desperately to gain footing on the rocks around the crash site. As fast as I step onto what appears to be stable rock, it drops away underfoot. The weight of our falling bodies jerks the rope taut and leaves us dangling in the ever-widening hole under the back wheel of the darter. Judging by the way the darter lurches and squeals, it will soon crash down, too. I curse the fact that there was nothing else to tie the rope to.

Marisa screams as we swing wildly in the blind murk of the cavern. For an undetermined amount of time we manage to keep our clutch on the rope. Terror buzzes in my limbs, and fever, and the weighted, grim sense that this might be our last resting place. Further down, our feverish limbs give out about the same time, and we fall in tandem, with Marisa and I reaching for each other in the absolute dark as we hear the darter crash below us.

27.

I manage to move my head, and open my eyes to impenetrable gloom. The flashlight. My pack. An experimental roll onto my stomach feels like a brutish fist pounding on my massive chest injury. Groaning, I roll back and test each rib lightly with my thumbs, recalling dimly that they were already broken, or at least badly bruised. Why am I always forgetting? I strain in the dark to think.

A streaming visual floods my head; of the rocks giving way, the darter slipping down, and of the petrifying freefall. I twist to one side, inch my pack off my shoulders and fumble inside it for the flashlight.

With every limb aflame, I struggle to my feet and aim the light ahead of me. When I happen to glance down at my arms, I recoil. They are hardened toad flesh from the Skiin injection, and the fissures have widened to oozing slits.

Wheeling around, I search in different directions for Marisa as I shout her name. My insides turn to black ice when she doesn't answer, and walking further, I see her body, unmoving. I race over, every step pinching the air out of my lungs. "Marisa!" I kneel, and turn her gently so she's facing me. Her mouth is slightly open, tongue lolling to one side. I check to see if she's breathing. Yes! My eyes fill with grateful tears as I hug her.

She moans. Her puffy eyelids stay closed. "Where . . . are we?"

"Shhh. Just rest." I'm almost afraid to tell her. The stale air is warm, and slightly acrid.

She whispers weakly, "Sweet. Varik. If I . . . don't make it back, tell my father I'm thinking of him?"

"Of course." I stroke her blood-streaked hair. From the light of my flashlight beam I see that the impact has reopened her head wounds. "But you'll get back home. Don't talk nonsense."

"I'm . . . just saying. Yeah, we'll . . ." she whispers. With her eyes half open she reaches for me. "Varik, your . . . arm, your face, they've got open sores."

"The second Skiin injection," I remind her.

"Oh, my God. Does it hurt?"

"Like being burning alive," I admit.

She tries to hug me but she can't quite sit up. "I'm sorry you're in pain."

"Me, too."

She whispers, "Tell me where we are?"

I gather up the nerve. "Marisa, you won't believe this but . . . we're inside the cup mimetolith, on the floor of it." Every bone on my broken body is aching to explore.

"Oh!" she says, and then louder, "No." She opens her eyes wide and tries again to sit up. Slumps back down.

We look up together. Crane our necks to see the equivalent of hundreds of stories above us, the faint light shining through the hole in the crest that we've fallen through, with its occasional pinholes of light in the sidewalls. The seriousness of our plight hangs over us like the weight of mountains.

"I want to explore this place, but not without you," I say, stroking her good arm. "I'll wait until you can walk."

She slowly props herself up on her good elbow. "Don't wait for me. I may not be able to—"

"Don't say it. Don't think it. I regret getting you messed up in this."

"Look, it was my choice," she catches my gaze with her pained eyes. "Don't ever regret it."

"Marisa? There's something I didn't tell you."

"Huh?"

"Right before we left, I found another cert. Fireseed was more than just a drawing on paper. My father grew up ten plants next to this cup mimetolith. And they burned up. Sorry I never told you. But I need to see what's in here. I need to explore."

Her eyes become dull with sadness—I know she's thinking that I never really trusted her. Because it makes sense that I wouldn't. But it wasn't even that, really. More like I needed to keep a piece of my dad to myself—*a piece of hope to myself.*

She pipes up in a weak but determined voice. "Of course you need to go without me, silly. I'll be here." She laughs breathlessly. "It's not like I'm going anywhere." She's inching back down, when she sees me hesitating. "Go. Please! Just hurry back and give me a full report."

I make sure she has a decent flashlight, and I have the infrared light. We touch lips—in a worried and reluctantly parting kiss. "Must feel like you're kissing the frog prince," I say.

"A little," she whispers.

Stumbling to my feet, I shine my light ahead. The floor of the cup mimetolith is colossal, four times as big as the new hockey stadium in Tundra. Walking in the dim light, I can't quite see to the other end. I aim my light down. The same type of knobs that coated the inside walls pepper the floor.

I touch one. It's not stone. It could be old sediment ridge that didn't quite petrify, or something man-made . . . or . . . It's cool to the touch, which is odd after being exposed to so much grueling heat. Some of the nubs appear charred. In fact, my hand comes away with a trace of blackish powder on it. Oh, Great Ice! Dare I hope? Was there some secret access to the interior that Marisa and I didn't see? The pinholes . . . Could tiny seeds have drifted in through those pinholes, or from underground?

Or did the cult have fire rituals in here, too? These protrusions could simply be totems that the cult carved and then attached to the walls. Unlikely, I decide as I hike further. In our earlier trek around the cup, we meticulously inspected and saw no sign of an entryway.

Play the game.

Rack up the abalone chips.

They'll fry your brain and dole it out, thinking they're eating the founder's DNA.

If there ever was life out in this desert, I can't imagine what it fed on. It couldn't exactly suck minerals from dry stone. At least in the Black Hills Sector where Rain and Armonk live the rocks have gaps and crevices that accommodate beetles. At least underwater in Ocean Dominion, way down in the oxygen-free Aphotic Zone, extremophiles dine on acids and chemicals seeping from melted peat. And my father wrote in that cert that Fireseed was bred to live without water. But how is that even possible?

I've stumbled on for about fifteen minutes, studying every fraction of floor. No more nubs in this section. I shouldn't hike much longer because I'm worried about Marisa. *I could always come right back after I check on her,* I'm thinking, when I notice that in this section of floor, the nubs are more frequent, and taller. A few of them reach to my knee. They're hard, but no longer black. They're rather stringy, with vertical ridges. I feel a firm flip of hope in my gut.

Change. This must be an overeager delusion conjured by my high fever. I rub my tired eyes. I'm still itching from the injection. *How long it will take for the symptoms to fade?* I wonder, hoping my skin won't be toady forever. Does it really matter? Because we're not getting out of here, even if I do discover Fireseed.

I scold myself for my cynicism. My dad wouldn't approve. I charge on, ribs burning with my every step.

Little Hunter, don't get discouraged.

Let's find some exquisite pirate treasure.

—hidden in every leaf and tree . . .

Fix Juko, fix Audun's pet bird, but . . .

I trip over a nub that's tipped sideways. Catching my fall, I happen to glance again at my arms. Between the open lesions the skin has developed a scaly pattern like Rain's photonic fabric. Has the toady flesh become so stiff that it has split in places? Lifting my burn-suit pants, I see the same, oozing lesions on my legs. Ironically, we don't need solar protection inside this strange stone heat shield. My old skin—well, I suppose it's my new Skiin—crawls in horror at the sight.

Don't fold your cards yet; collect more abalone, son.

Want a steamy bowl of chowder at Tundra Squidhouse tonight?

Play the game, Space Strawberry.

I want to push on further before I check on Marisa. I'm weak, so weak. The need for rest consumes me. Shining my light beam ahead, I trudge on. Curiously, the next batch of spiky nubs is red—unlike the earlier ones. These are like the fibrous spikes of dead coral beds, or year-old vegetables. And they're even taller up ahead.

I'm running now, leaping over the old stems, ignoring the fatigue and ripping pain in my ribs. I'm so terrifically excited that I'm hyperventilating. I see them! Up ahead, and it's not my sun-poisoned hallucination.

"Fireseed!"

A flank of proud star flowers bow towards me. As if they've known all along I would come for them. They're almost my height; bright-red soldiers at attention. I feel a funny sense of pride for them. They've battled sandstorms and wind and blistering heat. They've found a perfect hideaway from all that to propagate, safe from the meddling ways of the Fireseed cult. From the speculators out for new gold. My father was the cleverest man of all, for having invented them. His second favorite koan sneaks into my head:

The Giver Should be Thankful

He was a giver once. Is he thankful that I found all this; thankful I want to give it to the world—to the refugees, too? I want him to be. I so, so want him to be.

Behind the first flank stands an entire troop of the plants. Vibrant, beady pistil-eyes look my way. They appear ready for an order.

"Father!" I shout. "It wasn't in vain! They fought back from that burn. The seeds blew in here and took. Dad! Can you hear me?"

Touching one of the Fireseed leaves, this time I feel it—my dad's spirit in the vibrant brushy leaf that bristles in my palm. His energy rushes in from everywhere, filling the cavern; his beard shakes as he chuckles, his voice booms in my ears.

"I'll be a sotted sailor if you didn't do it, son. I would've never imagined my good plants in here, after they cooked themselves. To think, ten or fifteen years later my own experiment would outwit me." In my higher brain, he launches into another round of chuckles, this time edged with darkness. *"Varik, I hope you're right about those refs. Good folk, huh? I'll try to take your word for it. Share it, son. You've earned your abalone chips, earned 'em fair and square."* And then my father's energy fades, as swiftly as it swooped in.

"Thanks, Dad," I mumble to myself. "Great to hear your voice. Need to tell Marisa."

But before I go find her, I have to touch the Fireseed one more time. Clasping a thick stalk in a longing hug, and half-thinking it's my own father, with my arms leaking gore, I sink down to the cavern floor.

28.

Somehow, everyone's found out that there's food in the mythic south. Now that all agar's extinct, entire populations of the northern Dominions are rampaging across the border to the Hotzone. I'm dreaming, right? Time can't just skip like that. It doesn't work that way.

"New crops in the Texas desert," they say; *"Plenty of water pellets in all sectors, and there's newfangled irrigation from Geo Man's cavernous drilling to a bunch of magical underground lakes,"* they report to me, as if I'm the last haggard skeptic. Who are *they?*

So many desperate northerners from Ocean and Land D have hacked past the BotGuards that there are permanently open passageways in the border through which one can pass. Live guards defecting as well. I watch, as if through a transparent screen, as many civilians are shot. Even though I'm screaming, I'm unable to stop people from stomping over their bodies in their haste to migrate south. They can't hear me.

That's it. This is only a dream. More like a nightmare. The

Stream blares in my head. It's all wrong! I shouldn't be able to hear the Stream down here in the Zone.

Eruptions from the Hotzone! The Fireseed cult is hosting a massive feast of beetle loaf at their compound. New recruits eat free, with required Fireseed arm-branding and surrender of all Dominion credit cards to guru Bryan. First recruit, Audun Fleury, formerly of Tundra Island, Ocean Dominion, fled south after the death of his friends and family in the agar famine.

Holy freaking ice. Behind my eyelids Audun is decked out in a red burn suit, with a fashionable triangular face mask of photonic-lined Black Hills hammered iron. I call out to him but he can't hear me. He sits next to Bryan on a matching red throne at the ceremonial grounds in the Texas desert, drinking Wolf Spider rum while watching children from the North be initiated by branding. The Chihuahua Ocean laps at their feet.

In the red sky just above them, the video bird is flapping its crude wings. "Varik!" It squawks, "Where are you? Marisa, are you there?"

Something is very wrong with this picture. Video birds can't talk, and they certainly don't sound like girls. Plus, since when would Audun be cooling his heels with a notorious criminal?

Where am I in this?

"Varik!" the video bird swoops dangerously close to my head. "Marisa!"

With eyes closed, I shift my broken ribs in a cautious, experimental stretch, and brush my swollen tongue against the sour coating in my mouth. Drifting off into delirium again, and leaning forward on something solid yet pliable, I strain to revisit that confused dream world in order to make sense of it.

"Varik!" calls a woman, not Marisa. This voice is higher-pitched, louder than Marisa could ever muster in her precarious condition. Straightening from my leaning post, I startle awake, blink my eyes in the sudden glare.

I'm hugging a Fireseed plant! Its stem is as wide as my upper arm. Looking up, I see its plush leaves sheltering me. My legs are prickling. My rump is numb. I've been sitting here with my legs splayed on either side of the plant stem for shit knows how long.

"Varik. Up here!"

Straining to raise my head, I'm blinded for a moment by the beams shining down. Then I see. It's Nevada Pilgrim! She's waving at me through her crazy bubble-shaped copter windshield.

"You came, thank God!" I yell. "Marisa's back there." I point to the stone floor that stretches on behind me. "Did you see her? Is she okay?" Hoisting myself up by the stem of the Fireseed plant, I inch my way to standing position. Its flower head bends over me, like a living umbrella.

Nevada lands about twenty paces to the side of me, in a field of Fireseed. Snaking through the crimson plants, I stumble over to her flycar. To my great relief, Marisa's already inside, reclining on the passenger seat. She waves weakly. I'm happy to see that Nevada's already put a flask of Rain's green mineral drink in her hand.

Nevada jumps out and stares at the giant red plants. "Are these what I think they are?"

"Yes! Yes! It's hard to believe." I give Nevada a tentative hug and thank her profusely. In my hands she's as wispy as the leaf designs on her cheeks. She smells of years of dust and minerals, as if she's been rooting around in this desert under rocks and sand dunes her entire life.

"You found it!" she exclaims, gaping past her thigh-high dinged-up boots to a young plant. She has on one of Rain's green burn suits and a hip pack full of tools. She sneaks a look at me. "Varik, you're awfully burned. You need to find a doctor."

I lift my hand and brush my face. Understatement. It's tougher than alligator skin, and although some of the original fissures have started to close, new ones have formed. I'm too embarrassed to tell her my own Skiin formula is mostly to blame. It's touching that my dad saved it as a memento to my childhood, but in the future I'd better stick to making prosthetics.

"We were stuck on that mimetolith crest," I tell Nevada. "It was brutal. And then we crashed through the crest. Hey, I need to dig up a few of these plants," I add, "and then we can get on our way."

"Plants?" Marisa sticks her head out of the window. "Tell me, what plants?"

"I found them, Marisa! I found Fireseed!"

"No! Omigod! Really?" Marisa tries to get out of the copter, but I stop her.

"I'll show you. I'll bring them over. Don't hurt yourself."

Marisa complies, cheering and squealing. "Hurry! Dig them up! I want to see them."

Nevada rummages in the compartment next to her seat and holds out a rusty camp spoon. "Amazing! So amazing. Will this help?" she asks.

"Sure. Do you have any kind of container?"

She flips up the rear hatch of her flycar—a patchwork affair of agar and metal and hammered leaf appliqués—and digs inside it. Returns with an antique plastic cooler that's missing its lid. "Will this do?"

"Perfect! Thanks again, really." I'm dismayed. It will barely hold two plants, but we'll make it work.

Whirling around to the plants, I cringe from the sharp, stabbing pain in my ribs. How to decide which ones to take? They're all waving at me, each trying to get my attention. How is that possible? There's no wind down here. It's unsettling how close to human they seem. As if it's an honor to be picked—each bright student with his hand flying. As if they could separate from their roots with a quick twist and walk right over to me. If I pack them in, I can squeeze three in the cooler. Even with that, I'll have to bow their stems to fit them in the back hatch. They're pliable enough, but I worry that wildflowers often wilt after uprooting them.

These are wild, for sure.

I pick the one that's brightest red, a second one with a broad flower head, and a third that almost seems to be pointing to me with its velvety leaf fingers.

The roots. Problematic. When I kneel down to examine, it's clear that they're not lodged under the rock crevices, but thoroughly stuck on the rock surface by some unseen dry glue. I end up wedging my fish knife under their starfish-like suckers and prying them loose. Pieces of precious root fly off in the process. As I place three in the cooler and prop them up against each other, I fret they'll wither without their rock bed—or without the dark, or whatever mystery element nourishes them here that I might lack up in Ocean D.

I take a last look at the remaining Fireseed plants. I hate to leave them here. I want them all! As an afterthought, I extract one more and stuff it into the cooler. I carry the chosen ones to the flycar and present them to Marisa.

"They're spectacular, Varik. They look just like Nevada's picture. Omigod!"

"You're the first two to see this," I say, and kiss Marisa gently. "I wouldn't have known about them if it wasn't for you."

"You found them. You did it," Marisa says. "I'm so, so proud of you, Varik. Your dad would be too." She plants a soft kiss on my toady cheek.

Nevada helps me secure them in the hatch, gently bending their stalks downwards.

Opening the side door, in my joy and relief I almost forget my excruciating pain that now chokes the air out of me when I crawl into the cargo hold behind her.

"We got them," says Marisa, reaching her hand back to hold mine.

"We got them," I gasp, taking her hand and squeezing it.

Nevada pilots us up inside the cup mimetolith, her flycar beams crafting shadows on the undersides of the root nubs that pepper the walls. We blast through the gaping hole in the crest and steer north over the desert.

29.

"Tornado's in jail," Nevada announces after we reach cruising altitude.

"What's the charge?" Marisa's voice is livelier since the infusion of Rain's special drink.

"He was Bryan's fall guy," says Nevada matter-of-factly.

"Where's Bryan?" Marisa asks, not a smidgen of longing in her tone.

"Gone," Nevada answers.

"Where to?" I ask, not sure I want to know. It better be far away from Marisa's world. Marisa and I are holding hands in the back, and even his name is an intrusion.

"He's in the Zone, in a far-off pioneer town," answers Nevada. "Not sure which one. Heard it through the runners." She turns around momentarily to Marisa and smiles. "I left the ZWC."

"Yeah?" Marisa raises her head in surprise. The ends of her choppy red hair are knotted with dried blood.

"Yeah. Bryan took out his anger about you on me." Nevada

flicks back her dirty braids. "He beat the tar out of me." She rolls up her sleeves and shows Marisa bruises on her arms.

"That's terrible," says Marisa.

"It wasn't just that. I couldn't stand his politics anymore," Nevada rolls her sleeves back down. "I hated him when . . . he admitted he'd killed Varik's dad."

Cold runs up my windpipe.

"So what now, Nevada?" Marisa says after a long silence. "Where will you live?"

Nevada flicks on the auxiliary air vents as we ascend closer to the sun. "Oh, around. Pretty much the way I was before. Sometimes at Rain's, sometimes in my yurt." She erupts into a giggle fringed with pain. I find myself hoping she had at least a few carefree childhood years, coloring and playing hopscotch.

"Do you prefer the nomadic life?" I ask her.

"Well, it's hard to find shelter. I do find it—in old swimming pools, cellars, caves." She pauses. "But, I'm a runner." She says this like she's saying she's blonde, or she's petite—as if it's inherited. "I meet lots of people," she adds. "They *need* to be my friend. So, I'm never lonely."

I wonder about that. It's a long, desolate haul from one community to another down here. We're passing over the Black Hill Sector. From up here, the rock caves are striking against the stark flat plain.

Nevada suggests that we stop in at Rain's for the night. It's tempting. I'd love to see Rain and her boy, sit with them on the rocks at night and watch Armonk shoot his arrows. Or have a beetle-collecting marathon. The boy touched me. He made me think about what it would be like to endure life in the Zone. I guess I saw myself in him.

But I need to get these plants back.

Nevada and Marisa and I are silent for a good long time, staring out at the ruined cities, the sand dunes, and waving at the very occasional flycar.

"The agar situation," I ask Nevada finally. "What's it like? We've been, you know, cut off from things." We've already told her about the saga at the weird cult headquarters, and the attack on Marisa in Vegas-by-the Sea.

"I heard about the agar crisis on the altStream just south of the border. It's bad." Nevada glances at me in the rear view. "I hate to tell you this, but people rampaged through your skyfarms. They trashed the warehouses and stole lots of the kelp." She looks philosophically down at an old highway littered with shells of cars. "I hate to say it, but your food crisis and all, well that's the same thing that happened down here way back, when the farms dried up. In no way am I defending *him*, but, um . . . maybe you'll understand how a guy like Bryan could have developed."

"Hmm." I imagine the galley at Agar 6 trashed, the feeder tubes slashed, the Finnish kelp and Flyfish ferreted away in boxes, Serge overpowered by the mobs. A huge part of me dreads going back. My place could be ransacked as well. Will they have destroyed the two frail agar plants? Audun could be tied up and gagged somewhere. I can't dwell on that.

I recoil in surprise, when, for the first time in days, the Stream blasts in my head. We look at each other with the silent affirmation that we're all hearing it, which means that we're all attuned, and we're almost to the border.

It's the "Snorkling for Gems" show" with me, Au—uu—dun Fleury! I'm here with Cherry Froth. Hey, just because we have a serious agar famine on our shores doesn't mean we have to go all grim and goth, does it? Cherry, before I ask you about your upcoming role, I have to say you totally rock ice in that striped-bass-inspired gown. And, if I'm not mistaken, those are SnowAngel's new Bering Booty boots.

Like them? I adore the blue boots with the dress's teal stripes.

Absolutely, so, um, in your futuristic feature video you play a petulant yet fearless Cloudland empress who rescues her empire from a six-headed sea dragon.

Right. I did all of my own stunts: I took lessons at the Whale Academy
and learned to ride bareback. Of course they had a cheat harness on me.
(giggle giggle). I'm no ace swimmer.

Ha! You can doggie paddle on over to my place any time. We'll have lots
more gems from Cherry after these words from our sponsor.

Brought to you by Anchor credit cards. When times get tough, sink
anchor with us, and take out a zero-interest loan to pay for that pricy hijiki
stash you'll need to soldier through the food crisis.

Audun's okay! "The shark. So that's what he was working on.
He did it! It's not exactly hard news, but he got his own show," I
exclaim. I'm not sure whether I'm more amazed, or irritated that
Audun can seem so carefree during a crisis. He'd better have
allowed time to care for that secret agar plant. And keep it hidden from the crazed, starving throngs.

"Dominions could crash and burn, but some people will
never change," Marisa remarks dryly.

"But he *has* changed," I tell her. "You have no idea how hard
Audun had to struggle past his father's low opinion of him to get
his own show."

"That's sad." Marisa sounds willing to rethink the airhead she
thought Audun was.

"We're approaching Baronland," Nevada announces in her
professional runner voice. I can picture her gliding into a sector and handing out parcels to the hideaways in cellars and old
water mains, then gliding out to another isolated sanctum.

"What's the plan for crossing the border?" I ask her, my pulse
quickening as I see the border wall strobing blue and red in the
distance.

"I was going to ask you guys that," Nevada says.

"Can't you hack it?" I ask. "Aren't you an expert?" Marisa's
noticeably silent.

Nevada shrugs her narrow shoulders. "I quit the ZWC. I no

longer have access."

Another Stream blasts in our heads and on Nevada's radio as we fly over an encampment of hastily built agar huts west of Baronland South. According to Marisa, those huts are for the refs working construction.

Land Dominion Uplink: Last night, a splinter ZWC Hotzone terrorist group sent Melvyn Baron a lock of his daughter's hair, demanding ten million Dominions for her safe return. DNA is a match. Mr. Baron, who has been in frail health, is conferring with close personal advisors as to his next step.

Brought to you by the Kaffe Samovar, a Siberian-strength espresso bar, with convenient branches in Baronland Emporium, Restavik, and Landlock.

"So, *that's* what happened to my hair," Marisa says in a steely voice. "We'll go through the Baronland South border." She brushes a hand through her tangles. "Let me off there."

Nevada looks over at Marisa. "Are you sure? You need to see a doctor; your head's all cut up. And that arm."

The determination in Marisa's voice is unequivocal. Perhaps putting on a cool, businesslike air is the only way she can deal with us parting. I sensed this might be the way we would end—at least for now. Still, it smarts. I'm already missing her.

"It's the least I can do to get you through," Marisa says, squeezing my hand and touching me with a passionate gaze that reassures me of her real feelings. "I need to see my father. I'll get medical care, Nevada, but thanks for your concern. And all you've done for us."

We reach the condoplex construction area and hover in place as Marisa clicks open her HipPod. "Melvyn Baron, please," she says. "Tell him it's his daughter."

During the weighted pause, the frenzied chain of communication from one end of Land D to the other is almost palpable, and like desert lightning through the monolith offices of Baron

Enterprises, as they're surely ferrying through the good news that the heiress is alive.

"Daddy? I'm here," says Marisa. "We're um, in Baronland South. . . . Yes, alive, yes, okay—well, a little under the weather. . . . I do want to talk. . . . They cut my hair. . . . No, nothing else. We got away. . . . I heard about your heart attack. So sorry to hear you're under the weather, too. . . . I'm glad you feel better. Listen, I need to ask a favor. My friends are with me. . . . Whatever you've heard on the Stream about Nevada Pilgrim, she's not a terrorist. . . . Now wait a minute, I know what I'm talking about. . . . And Varik Teitur. . . . Yes. . . . Uh-huh. . . . Please, let me speak. They need immunity and safe passage north. . . . I know you had a conflict with his father. Does that really matter now? . . . Well, it seems petty; sorry, but that's the way I see it. . . . Yeah, okay, I see how that might have bothered you, but—" Marisa gets my attention and scrunches her face in good-natured annoyance. "Uh-huh," she continues, "I disagree. . . . Immunity. Free passage. That's my bottom line, Dad. . . . See you."

She snaps her HipPod closed. It occurs to me that we're finally in range, and that I could call Audun. Find out about the agar. Feeling for my HipPod in my pocket, I close my hand around it. I'm afraid it'll jinx things if I say the word *agar*. Or hope too much. He can't tell me it's already dead. Cannot. I'll just fly there. I release my grip on the HipPod.

"So, is it a go?" asks Nevada.

"It's a go," says Marisa.

"And I'll get safe passage back?" Nevada asks.

"Are you sure you even want to go back?" The two girls exchange a long look, as if to seal their friendship and service, their activist past, and to negotiate how they'll stay connected. "You can stay with me for a while in Land D," Marisa adds. "I could easily get you a job at the Emporium. The camp store could be fun, since you like the outdoors, or—"

Staring straight ahead, Nevada slowly shakes her head. "Thanks, but my home's the Zone. I'm a runner."

Marisa sighs through her words: "And I've got to negotiate with my father over his relationship with me, and the refugee workers, and the entire corporation, so I'd better get started."

I think of my farm, and my own onerous responsibility. I'm oddly eager to get back and deal with it . . . however horrific the circumstances.

Baronland South construction has progressed since we flew over it a couple of weeks ago. Another building's roof is on, and a skyway from one condoplex to another has a new railing.

Even after two passages through it, I'm still intimidated by the border wall, with its sectors of uniformed holo guards. My pulse races at the possibility that Melvyn, defying his daughter's wishes, has instructed guards to frisk us, and check the cargo. I'm most concerned about the hidden red flora in the hatch.

But there's none of that. The border gate's wide open, the guards, throwing us curious stares, wave cordially to us as we pass. No BotLink alarms sound. Blessedly, there's no Fleet, and no swarm of rabid Streamerazzi.

No Stream, ha! That won't be the case for long, especially with Audun, the new host of "Snorkling for Gems," twisting my arm for an exclusive.

Nevada glides into a handicap slot in the vast Baron Inc. lot. She stays inside the vehicle while I help Marisa climb out.

As Marisa looks up at me, traces of regret at leaving work the corners of her mouth. Even burned and emaciated, she radiates beauty. The Hotzone has grown her up, replaced her tough bravado with a new womanly softness and determination. It's hard to gaze into her sapphire eyes without wanting to whisk her away with me forever—to be my companion up in my lonely world.

"I'd love to go up with you," Marisa says. "You must know that."

"Why don't you, then?"

"I need to face my life."

"But you hate that greedy world." I pull her close. "Talk to your father, and go see a doctor for your head wounds. Work it all out and then fly up to Vostok."

"It's not that easy," she says. "Could you just leave your world and move down to Baronland?" She brushes a stray hair from my forehead and runs a gentle finger down the slope of my nose. "At least I can make Baronland South a more humane place."

She's so close, so present, and so much a part of me that separating from her will be like tearing off my own limb.

"I won't forget a moment of it," she whispers.

"Me either." We kiss, openmouthed, with all of our heart and passion.

I press into her warmth, feel her feisty strength, and memories of the hard times that cemented our friendship. "I'll remember you dancing," I murmur in her ear, "and making me a burn suit from flycar insulation." We laugh.

"I'll remember how we were tied together at the cult headquarters," she says. "And how you saved me from those creeps at the Shark Bar." She kisses the swollen, knotted scar on my arm.

I kiss her cut forehead.

Nevada gets out, and the girls exchange hugs. They ramble on about some private things, while I try not to listen.

When Marisa comes back over, I ask if she wants me to walk her over to her father's office. I have a mind to give him a stern lecture about the nature of greed, or to ask for her hand in marriage.

Marisa smiles at me. "That's really sweet, but. . . I have to do this alone."

Nevada and I watch her walk across the wide agar-blue skyway, over the refs below, noisily securing the next section of condoplex.

Halfway over the skyway, Marisa spins around, the sun framing her in shimmering gold leaf. "Good luck," she calls. "Let me know what happens." Then she disappears over the downward arch of the bridge.

For a moment, I feel that boyhood terror of seeing land evaporate in the suction of the endless tides. Then it passes.

30.

I see it!

My island: a star in an early-nighttime sky of water. The sight of the ocean all around it brings tears to my eyes—its iridescent waves, the gentle sway of the old Tern boats, even the obnoxious orange buoy adverts flashing their buy-lines. Like a fish leaping full circle from water to sun, sun to water, I'm relieved to re-submerge myself in marine life. It's so much of who I am.

It's sad that most people in the Zone live without ocean, or even a trickling stream. But they have beauty there, too: in the mimetoliths, the red desert sky, and the lonely plains of the Black Hills.

If only they had farms or wells.

I remember how even weeks ago I despised the refugees. I thought they were all criminals. Certainly some, like Bryan, are incorrigible. Extreme dehydration and starvation make some people crazy and dangerous. But many, like Rain and Geo Man, and even that guy from the cult who left us a few of our supplies, are decent folk.

I think of my parents, who left their comfortable world up here to help them. Despite how hard it was for my father after what happened to Mom, it was wrong of him to turn against those brave people. Only one person should've paid the price for her death, not an entire Dominion. Even the children of the cult deserve to have healthy bodies, without limbs that are burned—or branded. But I don't hate my dad for his bitterness. If I did, I'd have to hate myself for my own old prejudices—a waste of precious energy. Besides, I think he saw it all through me.

I think he changed his mind. I'm convinced. The secret about the Zone is that it was normal folks, all that time. We were the ones making up myths, trying to make ourselves feel better about keeping them out. If the Fireseed takes, I'll rethink the food shipments—try to open up the distribution over the border. If . . . I'm way ahead of myself, as usual.

"What?" says Nevada, who's been trying to give me my space, but is clearly too curious.

"Oh, I was thinking about the world, how screwed up yet how amazing it is."

"Yeah."

We're homing in over my island house. The scrub bushes bow from the force of Nevada's vehicle. The brackish surf laps against the dock like nothing ever changed. Except Juko's not here, I see with sadness. I wonder if he's dead, or lost, or there's some other explanation I haven't thought of. I'll go looking again as soon as I can. My front door's closed. No one's broken in or burned the place down.

"I'm going to go now," Nevada says as I climb out, with my ribs aching. "Will you be okay?"

"I'll be good. I can't thank you enough."

"Keep me posted. You have my pager. Mostly it times out unless I'm in the northern part of the Zone, but I'll get it sooner or later." Nevada leans toward the opened passenger door. For the first time, she looks frankly at me. Her doe eyes and delicate bones, her luminescence despite her ravaged skin, are beautiful. So is her pioneer spirit, her willingness to endure dust and heat and the endless road.

I admire her complete discounting of society's niceties. In another time, another place, I could see getting together with her.

But in this universe I'm way too in love with Marisa.

Hauling my valuable cargo along the dock path, I note the Fireseed plants are all slightly wilted, and one's actually crumbled into a heap. I've worried so much about whether the agar will be alive I forgot to worry about the Fireseed. As I hurry into the house, the still-healthy flower heads tilt up at me, bumping along with my steps.

I open the door to a mess. Already three pm and Audun is still snoring on the sofa. Brandy flasks and soiled plates clutter the counter, and the kitchen bot is broken, with one grabber claw bent backwards. Wrinkled pants and fancy boots are sprawled over the living room like shells after a clambake. For a fastidious fashionisto, Audun sure is a slob!

With the container of Fireseed plants in hand, I bomb past him up to tier three. It's infuriating that Audun carelessly left my father's office door ajar, and the agar vulnerable to draft. Primitive terror of what I might encounter churns my gut as I storm in.

I place the plant cooler on my father's desk, and then wheel around to the agar incubator. Holding my breath, I open the top.

One spindly agar stem remains. A lone, blackening leaf dangles from its stem, ready to drop at any moment.

Great Ice, save us. The last of the world's food source is a frail stem.

With deep sadness, I turn around to the desk, remove the

dead Fireseed plant from the makeshift planter, and place it gently on the porthole sill for later study. So hard to lose even one. Then I push aside Audun's HipPod and coffee cup to one side of the desk, and sit down to study the three living Fireseed plants. It's a quandary as to how to nourish them. Serge isn't here, and anyway, neither Serge nor Pyotor would know about such an odd desert growth. Fireseed needed no water inside the mimetolith. It had no sunlight, either, and I wonder if sunlight will kill them. Odd, considering they were bred to withstand killing amounts of UV. Hurrying over to the picture window, I snap the curtains closed. Then I worry that the agar won't get enough light. So, I open the curtains a crack.

Next I place the Fireseed container next to the agar incubator on the table behind the desk. I do my best to straighten their curled stems by taping them loosely on the wall to support the stalks. This means standing on a chair, because the star-headed plants almost reach the ceiling. They are the freak giant trio next to the midget agar stem. To breed they would normally be in the same container. But what if I put the Fireseed plants in with the agar and the soil's moisture mildews the Fireseed? Even if Serge was clueless about Fireseed, I wish he were here to walk me through this. From the years of listening to my dad, I know that normally you transfer the pollen from the stamen of one plant to the carpel of the other, carefully collect the pollen, and brush it onto the carpel of the other plant. But this is no normal plant. My father's cert said that Fireseed had amazing powers of fertility, and only needed to be placed close to another pollinating plant for the crossbreed.

My ribs throb with tension as I gently slide the containers closer with their tops open until they're touching. I see the pollen—red, dusty stuff on the Fireseed stamens. The agar seems to have grown just enough to have mature carpels, though I can't be positive.

There's a loud clomping on the stairs, and then Audun bursts in.

"Drifter!" His hair's bundled in a messy ponytail and he's wearing silly kid pajamas with stingrays on them. "Thanks for all the notice," he adds when I don't look up or answer him. Grabbing his HipPod, he looks closer at me, and freezes. "Lord, Drifter, your face! Are you okay?"

"Why'd you leave the office door open?" I snap. "I told you plants are subject to draft."

His black eyes gleam. "Why didn't you call me so I could clean the place up?"

"Why'd you let the place get so messy?" I shout.

"This is the thanks I get for babysitting a colicky plant since. . . Serge. . .?" he yells back. "Look, I'm not as much of a clean freak as you, but I watched that agar very, very carefully."

I lower my voice to a whisper. "Okay, okay. Let's go downstairs. Plants react badly to anger."

"You're one ungrateful jerk, you know that?" Audun shakes his head in disgust, but clomps downstairs ahead of me.

He brews up espresso with slivers of dried sea apple to sweeten it. Then we sit down across from each other. The caffeine bombs through my system at warp speed, and the flavor of his homemade grape scone bursts like a laser show in my mouth.

"I held out on the scone mix for a long time, dude. I was aiming to save it for your return," he says with more than a hint of spite. "I've been rationing food, choking down soggy crackers and cans of minced rotfish." That's the rancid slop that the poorest of ocean nomads buy whenever they can make it to a grocery.

"I feel for you," I say, meaning it, but also conveying a flicker of my own spite. "Thanks for the scone. It's delicious, really."

With the cup balanced on his knee, Audun leans forward. "You look like a deep-fried iguana," he says, "with, like, a really pathological cutting disorder."

"Gee, thanks. I also have severely bruised ribs and a fever. And, oh yeah, I got stabbed."

"No fun at all." Audun stares at the knotted scar on my arm, and then back at me. "It's so great you got the Fireseed plants, huh? What was it like down in the Zone?"

I tell him we got captured by a deranged cult and about the Shark Bar incident. I tell him about hanging out with terrorists and being chased by Freddie Vane, the most infamous, hooked-up Land D publicist that ever walked the planet. Stuff that Audun lives for. His expression gets all wonky, as if I'm a Stream Star. I admit, I'm lapping up the attention.

"Where's, um, Marisa?" he asks.

"She needed to speak with her father."

He leans forward in his seat. "Did you, you know . . . get together with her?"

"It's private."

"You're so girl-whupped." He snaps an invisible whip.

"Whatever," I say, and shrug.

I ask him about the new "Snorkling for Gems" job.

"I got it by charming Cherry Froth when I was freelancing at the station as assistant producer. She put in a good word." He nudges me, which sends fire through my bruised body. "Dude, it's rumored that Cherry's overrated as a kisser."

"Says who?"

"My sources shall remain anonymous. I can introduce you, though."

"I'd be up for that." I wonder if Marisa would be jealous. "Audun," I say, "I'm proud of you for landing that show."

"Thanks, man."

"What'd your father say?"

"Hated it at first. He was losing his day laborer at the store. It's weird, but I think he was almost jealous. He said he was proud of me, too. That was the best. He loved it when I said I could get him darter adverts at a discount."

Same old Audun, same old me, not counting my injured ribs and toady skin. Let's hope there's not another layer of it underneath.

I excuse myself to go up and reexamine the plants. In the office, I try talking to them, and chanting Rain's Lakota prayer, and playing some of my dad's soothing classical music. They still look the same. My dad wrote that they grew five feet tall in, like, one day; that crossbreeding was simply a matter of pressing them together. Is there something wrong with this batch? Are they infertile?

It's dusk when Audun and I suit up and take out my darter to visit the boarded-up farms. When we near Agar 6 and I see the Fleet's yellow crime tape around the perimeter, my mood sinks.

The Fleet's ready to put me through a full interrogation until they recognize me. They ferry us through, and we sink anchor. A lot of good they were when my father died, or at saving Serge, or stopping the rampage on the farms. "Too little too late," I complain to Audun as I hobble next to him, along the cut feed lines and, after shooting up the lift, along the emptied tiers. It's a shock to see the beds devoid of even their brown soil. I guess they're being thoroughly disinfected.

We meet Pyotor at the blue-kelp prairie building, where security's even tighter. The Fleet's armed with photon guns, stunners, and tube-like weaponry I don't even recognize. No one's pinching any more free produce.

I swear, Pyotor has aged a good five years. His fluffy white hair has receded, and worry lines etch his ruddy forehead. He's shocked by my appearance, too, and I have to reassure him that I'm not going to keel over dead on the dock. He explains the looting came in three waves: a small break-in after the first rumor of blight; a second, larger raid after the rumor was confirmed; the violent stampede that killed Serge when people got hysterical over the idea they could starve before the year was out.

Pyotor says he's trying to speed up the growth of the kelp, but there's no changing the fact that it's a slow-growing, touchy plant. He asks me what I found down in the Hotzone. I describe the Fireseed.

His jaw drops. He also drops the set of feeder hoses he's repairing.

"There's no way to tell if it will crossbreed with the agar plant," I caution, so he won't get too excited. "Let's just keep on nudging the kelp, in case . . ."

"I'll keep my fingers crossed," Pyotor remarks.

"Me, too," says Audun.

This worried talk fills me with an unstoppable urge to head back and check the plants.

By the time we raise anchor, the sun has set and the air is misty. I'm so used to the raging heat that Ocean D, at one hundred ten degrees, feels positively subzero.

Halfway back, the orange flash of a buoy advert catches my eye. It's blinking off and on as if it's stuck in a crash mode. "Look," I say to Audun. "It's supposed to say 'Put Hijiki Steaks on the Grill,' but it says 'Hijiki steaks ill.'"

"Their high price is certainly sickening," Audun says, fanning his eyes with his hand.

As I start to turn away, something else about the advert catches my eye. Its buoy is keeling in the wind, except it's not windy. "Whoa."

Audun's busy with trying to open one of the last of my sea-grape sodas.

I steer the darter closer, spot a curve of ivory-colored agar breaking the water. *Don't get too excited*, I tell myself. "Hey, boy!" I shout.

"Huh?" Audun turns to look again at the buoy.

In a frothy fanfare of foam, a dolphin with cream-colored agar flippers breaches joyously toward us.

"Juko!" I cry when he reaches the starboard side and raises his bottlenose to nudge my hand. "Juko! We found you."

"I feel for the little guy. Must've been scared off by all the chaos." Audun hurries over to greet Juko.

"No more Streamerazzi anywhere near my place," I say firmly.

"Okay, okay." Audun pops Juko a soggy Sardino that was sitting in the hull. "We'll interview you on neutral territory," Audun promises. "Hey, maybe at L'Ongitude."

"Anywhere but my island."

"Deal."

Juko swims next to the darter all the way to the dock. I tell him that he'll never again have to be upstaged by Stream ships, and that I missed him and worried about him constantly. In response, he zips back and forth, parallel to the shore, the way he used to when he was happy. Then he settles near the dock, with his nose peeking up like a periscope. Who knows if he gets my message? I'd like to think he understands English, on some deep level of human-to-dolphin audio modulation.

Back at the island house, Audun cooks the last of the braised skyfish that I froze last winter. We share a bottle of wine, while I neurotically limp up and down the tiers to check and recheck and recheck the plants.

There's been no movement or growth, nor further disintegration of any of the plants. They're in some kind of weird stasis.

"I forgot to really thank you," I say to Audun as we down the last of the wine in the den.

"I noticed," Audun grumbles sarcastically.

"I was just in shock that the agar was only one shaky stem."

"Yeah." He props his head in his hands. "I was ready to consult a witch doctor or something. Without Serge, I was totally and completely freaking out. That's why the place was such a mess."

"Pretty lame rationale." We share a chuckle. Audun's room was always a train wreck.

"Drifter, it's good to have you back." Audun gives me an unexpected hug as he gets up to head back to Tundra Island for the night. He needs to check in with his father and grab some clean clothes. He's still in his kid pajamas, with only his spray jacket to hide the shirt part.

I hug him back, and walk him out to the dock. "You're a true friend," I tell him as he lifts anchor.

After he leaves, I shuffle upstairs in my father's office and slump in my father's desk chair, promising myself to get medical help for my ribs. Breathing is painful. My ribs feel as if they've separated from my breastbone and are poking around like loose fishbones inside my chest cavity. Before resting my head in my hands, I turn and check the plants yet again. No movement, no growth.

31.

Something tickles my shoulder, then my bare feet.

I shift position, try to remember whether I'm in the Black Hills or wrapped in Marisa's arms in Rain's cave. I feel the tickle again, this time on my face. Marisa must be stroking my temple.

"Marisa, stop," I giggle, before my consciousness shifts upwards to light, to the memory of days. In an excruciating flame of pain, I bolt upright, bump my oozing lesion-filled arms against my chair. My eyes open to what must be paradise.

I've died, that's it.

Morning light filters through the crack in the curtain on a dense jungle of green plants with shiny oval leaves edged with red. I'm surrounded! One has wound up my armrest and is touching my cheek. Another has grown up the back of my chair and is curling over my shoulder. They resemble agar plants, but are four times as large. As the Fireseed plants did, these plants sway in a bizarre, slow dance. What did my father put in the original gene-splice glyph code to make them move in such a way, essence of frying belly dancer? I struggle to my feet, gape at the vegetation growing on the carpet, up the walls, even on the curtains over the picture window.

Great, sullied ice! The crossbreed took. It was such a long shot that I can't believe it. Food, we'll have food; plenty for the refugees, too.

Shall I call it Fireagar? Agarseed? What?

There's a delicate scraping like a paintbrush being pulled across rough paper. Burn me if it's not the sound of the plants stretching upwards, the whoosh of their leaves unfurling. The things are growing so fast that when I fix my gaze on one, I see pink leaf buds form on its young stalk. From nothing to this—it's, well . . . unnerving. I straighten in my chair and gulp down an irrational roll of panic. The room is popping, whooshing—*alive.*

Jubilant, floating, hypnotized by my incredibly good fortune, I reach for my HipPod to call Pyotor.

32.

The next afternoon, I spend some time lying in my bedroom on tier two before my doctor's appointment. I've had to come down here because the bushy hybrids in my father's office have crowded out the desk, the floor, the entire room. Also, I'm beyond exhausted. It's a good kind of exhausted, although, with my ailments, I feel like a scalded cadaver. All day yesterday, and into the night, Pyotor and I wedged up plant roots and transported the Fireagar to the skyfarms. As fast as we cleared out a space in my dad's solarium, new hybrids took hold. It was hard to suppress my uneasy wonder at how the stalks wound around my injured arms as I carried out each box of plants. With the way they grow, we'll be doing this for weeks.

Early today, we fully briefed the Stream. Endless new food source, I told them, an embarrassment of riches for everyone. After that, Audun interviewed me for his show, and just about every Streamerazzi poured in for a press conference, which we held on the docks of Agar 6. Some mega-rich sim-game tycoon from Tundra Island promised us emergency funding for reconstruction of the ruined farms.

I have a free moment to call Marisa before my doctor's appointment. They'll do reorg on my ribs and on my ugly knife scar. Who knows how they'll deal with my lizard skin and festering cuts.

As I grab my HipPod to call Marisa, I spot a threadlike thing emerging from a lesion on my left inside forearm, just under my elbow. A ruddy thing, shaped like a doll-sized Indian-Pipe plant. It must be something that fell off the Fireagar, like a pistil or a leaf worm. I brush at it, but it's attached, and the action stings my arm. The raw flesh below the growth crawls.

This time, I try to pick it off more gently. Nothing doing. Burn me! Whatever this thing is, it's sprouting from a Skiin lesion. I seize up in fear. Why did I shoot myself up with my rancid old formula? These open lesions made me vulnerable to all kinds of horrible microorganisms. And what was my father's reason to keep my formula for so long? Did he actually believe it might work? Or was it some kind of satisfying voucher that proved his son would never make as good a biologist as he? Could this actually be a . . . seedling?

I had my oozing arms around that Fireseed in the hollow for hours!

I should've realized that Fireseed's nymphomaniac hybrid abilities could somehow infect me. I should've always used gloves, covered every inch of my flesh at all times. Now I'm literally part of my father's cursed experiment. What does this mean? That I'm a freaking crossbreed? Impossible.

Anyway, I'm not cursed. There is good that comes out of this! Fireseed's children will feed the world. This alone is miraculous.

"Hello?"

Marisa! I almost forgot that I punched in her number. My whole body's shivering, so violently that my shirt fabric's shuddering. It takes real effort to unclench my jaw.

"Who's this?" Marisa asks, confused, and with suspicion. I can only imagine what kind of pressure she's gotten to give interviews.

"Oh. Oh, hello," I manage to blurt out finally. "How are you? It's Varik."

"Varik! I'm great. I miss you so much. I heard about the hybrids!"

"Hard to believe, isn't it?" I say. "It happened so fast." The alien growth on my arm happened fast, too. Or was it my imagination? I hope and pray it was. Glancing down, I see it's still there. But it can't be. I won't accept it. "I miss you, too, Marisa. A lot." If she were here she could help calm me down. She could throw her arms around me and insist it'll be okay. But I can't tell her, not yet. Maybe this . . . thread on my arm will go away. Shrivel up and disappear. Leave no trace of evidence.

"What're you up to?" I ask her. "Tell me everything."

"I'm working out some issues with my father," she answers. "And I just signed a deed to a condoplex in Baronland South. I'll live down there, on the south side of the border. Kind of exciting, yeah, living amongst the refs! I'm concentrating on getting them better living conditions, and employment. My Zone liaison is Rain. We've already begun to strategize." She pauses. "Not so different from what your mom was trying to do."

"That's great, Marisa! I'm happy for you. You always wanted to do something for them."

She pauses. I hear her heavy breaths. "Varik?"

"Yeah?"

"Will you come see me?"

"Um . . . sure. Definitely! I'd like that." I glance down at my arm. The tiny stem is sprouting tiny leaves. My gorge rises. Marisa will be scared of me now. How will I begin to explain this to her? She'll stop loving me. What would my father have thought of this thing growing on my arm? Did it ever happen to him when he was experimenting with the stuff in the lab?

Come to think of it, he always wore long sleeves. Did he . . . ? Was that why he kept my formula? On purpose? To crossbreed? No!

No, no no. I wonder if he'd consider this a horror, or some unexpected breakthrough. He'd probably consider me damaged goods; the same way he'd view those burned refs with their dimers. Or how he'd see Armonk with his peg leg. "Give me a few days to clear out my schedule," I tell Marisa. "It's crazy right now."

"Yeah, well, I figured." Marisa sounds disappointed, but perks back up. "Oh, by the way, I got arm and scalp reorg. They did a pretty good job. Have you seen a doctor for those ribs?"

"I'm going today." I stare at my forearm as if it belongs to one of those cult members, or Geo Man—anyone but me.

"Good boy," Marisa says, like a mom checking on her son. "Varik," she warbles after a moment. "You saved the world! You're my hero. Do you hear me?"

"Thanks. You were a huge part of it. Don't forget that. For sure, it's incredible; hard to believe. I wish my dad was here to see it." I struggle to control the tremor in my voice. "Pyotor's already shipped out the first Fireagar orders. You should get yours in Land Dominion tomorrow."

"Gee, I wish I could have seen the first plants grow. Was it the most incredible thing you ever saw, baby?"

"Incredible! I woke up and they were all around me. And they were springing up so fast I could *see* them growing." I fumble for a scissors in my desk drawer. After a moment's hesitation, I clip off the miniature flower from my arm. Feel a sharp twinge of pain, as I watch it fall like a meaty parachute into my wastebasket. In its place, a speck of watery blood leaks out.

"Wow. Maybe I'll fly up to you, see the plants growing. I'll kiss you all over," Marisa coos. "How about this coming week?"

"Sure! I'd love it. Can't wait to kiss you, too." I imagine myself covered in Fireseed threads like an infected alien on the Stream's "Deep Planet Pathology" show. Recoiling from my own body,

I picture Marisa making a valiant effort to kiss my sprouting flesh.

We make plans; all the while I torture over how to break this latest news.

After I hang up, I set the island on a higher speed. I want to shove off all creepy invasives. Shove off my own damage. No, that's stupid. Speeding up the island orbit will shake off invasive vines, but it won't help me.

I think again of Armonk. He's damaged, too, with one leg lopped off. He's fatherless, isolated, broiling in the sun. But Armonk's also a unique hothouse cactus. Any life is a wonder in this chaotic pulse of life. I think of my father, whose final view of himself was probably as a failure, as bitter traitor to the cause, as deserter. But he sowed life in the desert.

Life. I glance down at a new thread, unfurling, on my wrist this time. Any life, even *this* strange new life, is a decided miracle. What will it do to me? How will I change?

A clarifying feeling pours out of me like a rush of water, out over my broken father, over Audun, and Marisa, who's trying to carry the weight of Baronland's people and politics. It pours out of me onto Nevada and Rain, and especially her boy.

Armonk.

I resolve then and there to face every question about my future with dignity. No, more than dignity—face the future with the mastery of a healer, and the joy of a small boy running out into the Hotzone on one rickety leg to catch a sunbeam.

Pulling open my desk drawer, I paw inside for paper and pen. In a torrent of notes and sketches, I design little Armonk a super-agar prosthetic with plenty of sensors for running, and the finest bow and arrow I can muster up.

The adventure will continue in *Children of Fireseed*,
the second of the Fireseed novels

Acknowledgements

I'd like to warmly thank my editors, Tamson Weston, Sarah Cloots and Rekha Radhakrishnan; my writing group who read many drafts over coffee, chai and cookies: Susan Amesse, Kekla Magoon and Holly Kowitt; to my additional readers and mentors: Nancy Rawlinson, Kanta Bosniak, Amy Kathleen Ryan, Katia Lief, Sally Donaldson, Vicki Wittenstein and Diana Childress; to the Cape Writers: Helen Mallon, Maggie Powers, Shawne Steiger, Lisa Rubilar, Margarita Cárdenas, Andrew White and Eric Edwards, who all heard drafts after dinner; to Joy and Lila at Paragraph Writing Space in NYC, where much of this was written. Thanks to my family for their support and astute comments: Norris Chumley Ph.D., Jack Chumley, Nate Chumley, Dr. Ellen Chumley, brother John and the extended Stine family; and to my wise and patient agent, Ethan Ellenberg, who gave his blessings to me going indie on this project; to Elizabeth Ennis, my talented book designer, and Jay Montgomery, my crackerjack cover artist; to Taili Wu, my map designer; to my students—all—you make me proud and I hope I do, you; to ABNA for reigniting me after *Fireseed One* burned through to the quarterfinals; to my old pal Tate, a visionary soundboard and to the memory of my even older friend Shelley Tyre, a central inspiration in writing this novel.

About The Author

Catherine Stine's first novel, *Refugees*, earned a New York Public Library Best Book and a featured review and interview in *Booklist*. Middle grade novels include *The End of the Race* in the Wild at Heart series and *A Girl's Best Friend* in the Innerstar University series. She is also an illustrator and painter, whose work has been exhibited in New York, Philadelphia and Miami. Stine hails from Philadelphia, and lives in New York City.

Learn more at www.catherinestine.blogspot.com and www.catherinestine.com.